RAISI
ANTI

The Weedless Widow

"Deborah Morgan, an award-winning author of mystery and historical Western short stories, should give lessons on the correct way to write an amateur sleuth mystery. While other authors in this sub-genre stoop to gimmicks and clichés, Morgan continues to show her flair for keeping a character's unusual occupation not only relevant to the mystery, but also central to the twists that logically move ahead the story . . . Morgan's series is a real find for mystery fiction fans and antiques buffs alike."

—*South Florida Sun-Sentinel*

"There is a lot of fishing lore and antique information deftly woven into the plot and those looking for a light mystery with an interesting context will be pleased . . . A fast, enjoyable cozy." —*The Mystery Reader*

"Any woman who wants a man should pick one exactly like the hero of *The Weedless Widow.* He is sensitive, caring, earthy, and strong-willed, so anyone he cares about will know he's there for them. The mystery is enthralling, almost as much as the insider's look at a picker and an antique collector." —*BookBrowser.com*

"Well written and a really fast read . . . Lots of interesting information about antiques and fishing."

—*I Love a Mystery*

continued . . .

Death Is a Cabaret

"*Death Is a Cabaret* introduces an engaging new hero in an unusual and convincing setting—the world of collectors and the extremes to which they'll go to get what they want . . . I enjoyed meeting Jeff Talbot and his unusual domestic ménage. I hope we'll see them all again soon."

—Sara Paretsky

"Deborah Morgan's witty debut is a deft blend of mystery, mayhem, and most terrifying of all, the antics of the antique world. I look forward to sleuthing and antiquing with Jeffrey Talbot again soon." —Harlan Coben

"Lively, well-plotted . . . Deborah Morgan, an award-winning author of mystery and historical Western short stories, delivers an outstanding traditional mystery in her first novel . . . Full of twists and turns . . . Collectors and antiques buffs will be thrilled with *Death Is a Cabaret*. Mystery fiction fans will find a new treasure."

—*South Florida Sun-Sentinel*

"A fascinating mystery that enables the audience to become an intricate part of the plot and will surely bring acclaim to Deborah Morgan." —*Midwest Book Review*

"On the heels of the *Antiques Roadshow*'s popularity comes an exceptional mystery series that's sure to please and tease the treasure hunter in every reader."

—*Publishers Weekly*

"*Death Is a Cabaret* marks the beginning of a new series that will endear itself to antique-loving mystery fans—it's more exciting than *Antiques Roadshow*!"

—*Romantic Times*

DEBORAH MORGAN

BERKLEY PRIME CRIME, NEW YORK

This is a work of fiction. Names, characters, places, and incidents either are the product of the author's imagination or are used fictitiously, and any resemblance to actual persons, living or dead, business establishments, events, or locales is entirely coincidental.

THE MARRIAGE CASKET

A Berkley Prime Crime Book / published by arrangement with the author

PRINTING HISTORY
Berkley Prime Crime mass-market edition / October 2003

Cover art by Maureen Meehan.
Cover design by Erika Fusari.

For information address: The Berkley Publishing Group, a division of Penguin Group (USA) Inc., 375 Hudson Street, New York, New York 10014.

ISBN: 0-425-19283-0

Berkley Prime Crime Books are published by The Berkley Publishing Group, a division of Penguin Group (USA) Inc., 375 Hudson Street, New York, New York 10014.
The name BERKLEY PRIME CRIME and the BERKLEY PRIME CRIME design are trademarks belonging to Penguin Group (USA) Inc.

PRINTED IN THE UNITED STATES OF AMERICA

10 9 8 7 6 5 4 3 2 1

Dedicated to the women who have gone on before.
For what you were, and for what you were to me:

Retha Dade
1935–1998

Liza Drew
1886–1967

Irene Estleman
1908–2002

Louise Estleman
1918–2002

Oris Proffitt
1927–2000

Maurine Stevenson
1905–1991

Alice Whitaker
1908–1992

Acknowledgments

The author wishes to thank the following people for contributing their expertise and support to the writing of this book:

Kym Williams, for helping with a crucial key pertaining to the murder weapon;

Kevin Williams, this time for sharing his knowledge about old pickup trucks;

Dennis and Anita Eros, antiques show promoters, for their continued support and hospitality;

Vicky Terry, for tracking down reference books and answers to research questions;

Gail Henry, for trying to acquire any and all reference book requests, no matter how obscure those requests might have been;

Bret Green, for details about the equipment used by electric linemen;

and Myra Karp, for the Wedgwood lesson, and the cook's tour of her extensive collection.

Excerpt, *Transportation Magazine,* 1943

TIPS ON GETTING MORE EFFICIENCY OUT OF WOMEN EMPLOYEES:

There is no longer any question whether transit companies should hire women for jobs formerly held by men. The draft and manpower shortage has settled that point. The important things now are to select the most efficient women available and how to use them to the best advantage.

Helpful tips on the subject:

1. Pick young married women. They usually have more of a sense of responsibility than their unmarried sisters do. They are less likely to be flirtatious. They need the work, or they would not be doing it. They still have the pep and interest to work hard and to deal with the public efficiently.

2. When you have to use older women, try to get ones that have worked outside the home at some time in their lives. Older women who have never contacted the public have a hard time adapting themselves and are inclined to be cantankerous and fussy. It is always well to impress upon older women the importance of friendliness and courtesy.

3. Give the female employees a definite daylong schedule of duties so that they will keep busy without bothering the management for instructions

every few minutes. Numerous properties say that women make excellent workers when they have their jobs cut out for them, but that they lack initiative in finding work themselves.

4. Give every girl an adequate number of rest periods during the day. You have to make some allowances for feminine psychology. A girl has more confidence and is more efficient if she can keep her hair tidied, apply fresh lipstick, and wash her hands several times a day.

5. Be tactful when issuing instructions or in making criticisms. Women are often sensitive; they cannot shrug off harsh words the way men do. Never ridicule a woman; it breaks her spirit and cuts off her efficiency.

6. Get enough size variety in operator's uniforms so that each girl can have a proper fit. This point cannot be stressed too much in keeping women happy.

Chapter One

JEFF TALBOT SWUNG open the front door and twelve thousand dollars flew out.

He stared at the C.O.D. slip while he kneaded the tense muscles in the back of his neck. He'd known the parcel was on its way, so that wasn't the problem. His wife, Sheila, had told him about her on-line purchase of the antique sketch from a dealer in Philadelphia a month earlier.

The money wasn't a problem either—Sheila had invested her inheritance wisely, and, just as wisely, had put Jeff's name on her checking account. That was a bonus, since she was momentarily in no shape to conduct business.

It was the timing. Timing was everything, he'd recently concluded, and the courier delivering the package couldn't have arrived at a worse time.

Jeff looked past the uniformed young man at nothing in particular, and listened to the distant, tinkly notes of "Santa

Claus Is Coming to Town" drifting from one of the shops a few blocks over.

"Greedy vultures," he muttered.

"Sir?"

Jeff shook his head, stepped aside for the courier to enter, then added, "I just wish the merchants would wait till *after* Thanksgiving to start playing Christmas music."

"I'm with you there. It's gone too commercial." He removed his cap and tucked it under one arm. "I wonder what it would be like if everyone boycotted giving gifts?"

"You'd probably be without a job," Jeff said, and the courier's brows lifted as if that possibility had never crossed his mind.

Jeff led the way to the library. Recent paranoia prevented his leaving the stranger alone in the foyer. He kept an eye on the guy, positioning himself so that he might quickly retrieve his old service revolver from the desk drawer if necessary. When he was an agent, he'd prided himself on his impeccable gut instinct for danger. Recently, however, his confidence had been shaken, and he wondered whether he'd ever again know who was trustworthy. Or, more importantly, who was not.

He scratched out a check, ripped it from the pad, and handed it to the courier. After an uneventful exchange, he escorted the guy back to the front door and sent him out into the rain.

Greer, the Talbots' butler, normally would have answered the door—while keeping everything else in the household running smoothly—but nothing was normal anymore. The butler who hadn't even broken a sweat in the half-dozen years with the couple now appeared wilted. Jeff didn't doubt that everything would get done, but it wasn't going to be easy. He and Greer were still ironing out the wrinkles in a new and stubborn bolt of cloth.

He had practically collided with Greer moments earlier on the service stairs as the butler paused at the sound of the doorbell. He was hefting a crowded luncheon tray for Sheila, so Jeff told him to take it on up to the couple's bedroom and that he would answer the door.

For the time being, they had to operate as a team. It had

obviously been difficult for Greer to throw over his strict training, but he had finally acquiesced.

Greer was not given over to hysterics. The most one might notice was a rare state of flightiness when the young man was faced with a heavy workload. On days when that workload demanded the services of three employees, he busily flitted from room to room, tackling the chores alone. Not only did he complete all tasks, but it even seemed as if bright spurts of surplus energy shot from his body like the sparks of an electrical storm.

But those almost imperceptible moments of excess adrenaline were altogether different from real stress. True stress burned up the energy, burned it from the inside out. Most people would not be able to detect the signs in Greer's well-trained demeanor. But Jeff recognized them. Hell, who was he kidding? He was now *living* them. They matched his own, those he saw reflected back at him every morning as he shaved: The nervous tremors, which resulted in razor nicks as he hastily scraped away stubble, the vertical lines between the eyebrows, the bloodshot eyes.

Jeff now rubbed his eyes, flinched as if all the sands of Alki Beach were in them, then retraced his steps to the library.

His own routine, which had been altered as well after the recent trauma that had been visited upon their serene lives, wasn't much better. He had a list of things that needed his attention—a *written* list, no less, something he'd never before stooped to making.

He retrieved the package and started toward the stairs by way of the breakfast nook so that he might check on the work being done there. Although Greer had been keeping a keen eye on the decorator, it had become a habit of Jeff's to watch over everything more closely.

A few weeks earlier, Sheila had gone through the alcove in a panic-fed rage, ripping the pastel paper and sheer curtains from the walls and insisting that they be replaced with layers of dark velvet. It had taken an inordinate amount of time and energy on both his and Greer's parts to find a decorator who could fill their unusual need; someone who would haul fabric and wallpaper samples back and forth, who could then hang the wallpaper and stitch the draperies from Sheila's choices, and whom Sheila felt would not only be trustworthy but also discreet about her unusual illness and about their personal lives.

They had settled upon an older woman named Dolores, who Sheila said reminded her of Andy Taylor's Aunt Bee, and who seemed equally comfortable in either business suit or painter's coveralls.

After Sheila, who had been so well adjusted to her secluded life as an agoraphobic, was kidnapped by a so-called friend of Jeff's, life as they knew it had gone to hell.

It had happened a month earlier. Jeff had found her intact, with no physical injury, and had returned her to their home with what he hoped was a minimum of trauma.

Ever since then, though, he had beaten himself up over what had happened. If he had stuck to antiques instead of reverting to his FBI training and dabbling in a murder investigation, his wife's emotional well-being might have been spared. She would have disagreed, he knew, had he voiced this belief. Five years earlier, when he had announced his resignation from the bureau's special unit that investigated museum thefts, she had seemed to understand even more than he did that the work was in his blood, that the transition might never be fully complete.

But he couldn't burden her with his nagging thoughts now, so he kept them to himself.

Or, at least, he thought he was keeping them to himself, until the counselors and doctors who had been called in to treat Sheila suggested that a few sessions might do him some good as well. He'd waved them off with neither consideration for their suggestions nor comment on their reasons, and had managed the last few weeks on adrenaline and caffeine.

Following the abduction, Jeff had brought in four psychiatrists with varying specialties, three herbalists and alternative-medicine experts, and two general practitioners. He wouldn't have objected to a partridge in a pear tree if he had thought it would help restore his wife's health—or what was her personally accepted level of health.

Time, that's what it boiled down to. She would need time to adjust to exchanging a once-quiet existence for the parade of medical professionals that tramped through the big old Victorian home like carolers through slush. And she would need time to recover.

Meanwhile, Jeff and Greer lived with their quasi schedule—a malleable plan by which to make sure that someone was always with Sheila, that the household somehow got run, that the bills got paid, and that nobody starved.

Jeff noted Dolores's progress with the wallpaper, then headed up the service stairs. This time he ran into Polly and Lucy Wing, the spinster sister team that he employed as housekeepers. Although the pair had worked for him before he had known either Sheila or Greer, he had turned the supervision of them over to his butler as soon as he had hired him. To their credit, both were taking extra care around Sheila in order not to disturb her or make her uncomfortable.

Greer had offered to take over the housekeeping duties after Sheila's ordeal, so that the number of people entering the home could be reduced, but Jeff had nixed this idea, and Sheila had agreed. She assured both men that the women, who had been cleaning the massive house every Tuesday for years, didn't pose a threat. Jeff was secretly relieved to hear it, and he was sure that Greer was, too, although the well-schooled butler never would have admitted as much. Greer had more than enough on his plate for the week. Thanksgiving was in two days, and, although Sheila wasn't sure whether she could join in, she had insisted that their traditions continue.

Polly and Lucy bowed slightly, and Jeff returned the gesture. Then he hoisted the package and, with a sigh, carried it toward the second-floor bedroom he shared with his wife—the room that had become her cocoon.

Chapter Two

GREER, LUNCHEON TRAY in tow, met him on the landing.

Jeff's brows raised at the site of the empty plates, bowls, and saucers. He shook his head. "She's going to regret all those extra calories she's taking in when she gets a handle on her situation."

Greer nodded. "Most people go to one extreme or the other when faced with crisis."

Jeff pulled his to-do list from his shirt pocket. "I'll pick up dinner," he said as he jotted *Pasta and Co.* on the sheet of paper. "That should free up a little time for you."

"Thank you, sir. I do apologize for asking, sir, but . . ." Greer looked down, obviously uncomfortable with any request that might hint at either weakness or unprofessionalism.

"Don't apologize. Eventually, we'll get back to our regular schedules but, for now, just waive the protocol so that we can all keep our heads above water. What do you need?"

"Would you pick up something for tomorrow, too? As I recall, Miss Gray has no skills whatsoever in the kitchen, and I will be hard-pressed to get everything ready for Thanksgiving dinner."

Jeff glanced at his list. The last chore listed under "Tuesday" was to be at Sea-Tac at nine that night to pick up Sheila's sister, Karen Gray. "Tell you what, Greer. Pasta and Company can cover all of tomorrow's meals. Jot a list and leave it on the kitchen counter. I'll grab it on my way out."

Greer looked relieved. "Yes, sir." He turned and descended the service stairs.

Jeff peeked around the bedroom door. Sheila was curled up on the chaise in the darkest corner of their bedroom, sleeping. She was wearing a gray sweat suit, which Jeff noticed was tighter than it had been a week ago. He was concerned about how much she slept, and had even brought it up with one of her doctors. But the doc had assured him that it was okay for now, as they were trying different medications and methods, and it would take awhile to arrive at the proper balance.

After she had been returned home, Sheila had abruptly stopped just about everything—exercising, cooking, painting, surfing the net. The only activity she'd engaged in since the ordeal was an almost constant lifting of fork to mouth. So, here was the chef of the house—a trained chef, no less—not cooking, yet eating a lot more. And Jeff and Greer were hard-pressed to put good meals on the table. Or the tray, as it were, since Sheila would no longer eat in the dining room. To give both Greer and himself a break from the kitchen, he was steadily filling the Christmas coffers of every one of the Queen Anne neighborhood's eateries—but none more than Pasta and Company, which was best-known for its gourmet-on-the-run offerings.

He quietly propped the package against the chest of drawers, then gently covered Sheila with a chenille throw. He went through a side door and into his dressing room to write her a note:

My Dear Sleeping Beauty,

At last, your farm has arrived. I hope it gives you happy memories of your time spent there as a child. Perhaps you'll want to reminisce with Karen when she arrives. May I join you for dinner before heading to the airport to pick her up?

I'll be back by seven.

Love you,

J—

Jeff secured a piece of tape to the top of the note, then returned to the bedroom and attached it to the package before kissing Sheila lightly on the cheek.

He took extra care not to make any noise as he pulled the door closed behind him, then stood in the hallway for several minutes and thought about the road ahead.

As much as he hated to entertain the notion, he had to accept the fact that Sheila might never be the same. He fought against the vise squeezing his chest, the wall he had built so that he wouldn't break down every time he pictured the worst-case scenario that might be his future. Her future. The rest of their lives together.

He shook his head as if he could physically dislodge the negative thoughts that crowded his brain, then headed downstairs.

Greer set a plate of food on the kitchen table. "I hope this meets with your satisfaction, sir. I'm afraid I can offer little variety until I go grocery shopping."

"I'm really not hungry, Greer."

"With all due respect, sir, we cannot afford for you to take ill."

"Have you had lunch?"

"No, sir."

"We'll be in a lot more trouble if *you* get sick. Now, fix yourself a plate and join me. And don't even think about arguing." Jeff sat down and took an unenthusiastic bite of the hot ham and cheese sandwich.

Greer quickly made another sandwich, then brought it to the table with a cup of tea, two cookbooks, and a grocery list as long as Yesler Way. After jotting a few more items on the sheet, he said, "Mr. Talbot, a technician from the alarm company will be here this afternoon to double-check the system."

"They'd better do more than just check it, after last night's false alarm. It's such a nerve-jangler that I'm starting to wonder whether Sheila would feel safer without it." The installation of an alarm system was another change that had been implemented since Sheila's ordeal. It had gone against Jeff's grain to have the structure of the historical home compromised by installing keypads on every floor, and having wires and sensors secured to every exterior door and window. It was so sensitive that it reacted to every element in the mail carrier's motto. Or, at least, the two that were currently plaguing Seattle: wind and rain.

Jeff exhaled. "I hate to saddle you with the alarm company, Greer, but I *have* to stop by Blanche's and the warehouse this afternoon before I go up to the Rose property. Those antiques are the only thing that's going to keep us liquid over the next several months."

Blanche Appleby, who owned a huge antiques mall named All Things Old, had rented one of her vacant warehouses to Jeff for storage of the merchandise he'd recently purchased from the sole benefactor of Verena Rose.

"No problem, sir. I'll do the grocery shopping for Thanksgiving dinner tomorrow morning."

"I'd tell you to have the stuff delivered, but you probably need the break from the house."

"Yes, sir. A change of scenery would be nice."

Jeff could use a break, too. Not the harried jaunts to conduct business or to run errands but a *real* break. He needed some time with his old bud, Sam Carver, an hour or two to shoot the breeze and down a beer. It would do Sam some good, too, he knew. Sam had been working extra hours since his partner at the furniture restoration business—who was also his daughter—was in countdown mode for her December 21 wedding.

Jeff pulled the list from his shirt pocket, checked it for an open slot, then glanced at his watch. It didn't look promising. By the time he did the shopping, returned home with the food, drove down to the waterfront and conducted some antiquing business with Blanche, checked the warehouse (and rearranged the inventory so that more could be brought in), drove up to Lake Stevens, loaded his woodie with boxes from the Rose property, and drove back to the warehouse, he'd be lucky if he had enough time for a lousy cup of coffee.

Sirens blared and whooped, eating up the silence, along with what little shred of nerves he had left. The big house filled with a sense of panic.

Greer dashed to the keypad located by the back door and punched numbers. The blaring, undulating horns of the faulty alarm system choked off.

A walkie-talkie squawked. Greer, who had begun carrying the thing so that Sheila could quickly summon him, now whipped the transistor radio from his trouser pocket like a gunslinger drawing his weapon and pushed the side button. "Mrs. Talbot?"

The phone rang then, masking Sheila's response.

"That'll be the alarm company," Jeff said. "You go up and assure Sheila everything's okay. I'm going to give this dispatcher a piece of my mind."

The butler shot up the service stairs as Jeff grabbed the phone. Expecting the alarm company's dispatcher to be on the other line, he barked a hello into the receiver and, in return, was informed by a nasally voice that the caller was Mrs. Henrietta Gardner of the neighborhood's holiday committee.

"My apologies, Mrs. Gardner, but this is not a good time."

She continued unthwarted. "Mr. Talbot, I realize you have turned us down every year when we've asked if we might include your lovely home in the Queen Anne holiday tour. But don't you see? Yours is truly the grandest Queen Anne structure in the community, and the tour just never seems complete without it. Can we count on you *this* year?"

Jeff gripped the phone so tightly that his knuckles turned white.

This last entry in his morning's parade was almost more than he could take.

Chapter Three

OPINIONS ABOUT SEATTLE'S rainy climate have filled enough columns, pages, and books to level the surrounding forests. Those not familiar with the area take it down to its simplest equation: Seattle = rain. They fail to acknowledge the fact that several other U.S. cities receive more annual rainfall than the Emerald City; they also seem not to care about changing their tune.

Most Seattleites preferred it that way, Jeff concluded, as it kept down the population and prevented even more congestion on the thoroughfares.

If one wanted to convince them otherwise, he knew, there wasn't a chance of it during the holidays. In spite of the fact that Jeff was a true Seattleite who rarely used windshield wipers and never carried an umbrella, this was the Rainy Season. And this year's Rainy Season was in fine form, seemingly making up for the previous winter's drought. The jet stream was wrapped around the region as tight as Santa's belt. They would all be lucky if they didn't drown.

After declining the holiday committee's request (for the fifteenth year in a row), Jeff darted into the mud room and grabbed a tattered old raincoat. He shoved his arms into its sleeves and snugged a cap on his head before jogging through the downpour to the carriage house. Usually, he dressed better, but today he didn't care. The dreary weather and the unkempt clothes echoed his mood. It crossed his mind that, for the first time, he would actually look like a picker when he visited Blanche's shop. The thought of her inevitable surprise made him smile. It would be good to startle her just a little, keep her on her toes.

He needed to expedite his time, so he climbed into the black Jimmy instead of his woodie, shot over to the gourmet grocery store, quickly filled Greer's shopping list, then returned home in order to exchange the SUV for the 1948 Chevy.

As he pulled into the driveway, he beeped the Jimmy's horn and brought the vehicle to a stop at the back steps.

Greer dashed out and began unloading the packages while Jeff loped to the carriage house garage and climbed into the woodie. He pulled out of the building and gave Greer a quick wave as he drove past, eager to complete his next errand so he could get over to the Rose property. He had planned on being there right after lunch, but, as with every day in the last month, his plans had been altered. Still, he admitted grudgingly, having a written list helped. At least he'd been able to carve out a two-hour wedge for tackling the work.

The Rose property consisted of two dilapidated Victorian homes so cluttered with junk and hidden treasures that one could barely walk through either of them. The movers who had been helping Jeff had hauled several loads of furniture and boxes from the "storage building," as the old woman had called the house nearest the quaint tree-lined street when he had met her years earlier.

Today would be the first time that he would spend any significant amount of time in the home located at the back of the large lot. That one, which was almost completely hidden by overgrown shrubbery, was the one Verena Rose had actually lived in.

Jeff felt some angst over today's late start. He wished he could steer the woodie north and get to work on his recent purchases. But he had promised Blanche that he would drop by her antiques shop near the downtown waterfront with a more detailed list of the Vaseline glass collection he had recently unpacked at the warehouse, and she was itching to add the stuff to her inventory for her holiday shoppers.

The yellow-green glass hadn't impressed him much when Blanche first introduced him to it, back when he started picking full-time. That collection, which she had artfully displayed in a large mahogany china cabinet at her mall, seemed okay enough, if you were into the lime-colored stuff. But when she turned on the blacklights strategically located throughout the cabinet, the glass glowed like Kryptonite, and he had been drawn to it ever since.

Blanche enlightened him, explaining that uranium had been used in the making, thus giving the phosphorescent glow to the transparent Vaseline glass and its creamy cousin, custard glass.

As he drove down Elliott, he coached himself not to be persuaded by Blanche to stay for tea or to look in on her latest acquisitions.

He had considered driving the SUV, thus sparing the car's wooden trim from exposure to the inclement weather, but he needed the extra room the car offered to haul back some footlockers and vintage luggage he recalled seeing in the old houses. With the backseat of the woodie removed, he could fit in more than twice as much as the Jimmy would hold.

The only good luck he had been blessed with lately—and he hesitated to think of it as good luck, since it was bad luck for someone else—was that he'd inadvertently gained some extra time to move his treasures.

He had been given the opportunity less than two months before to purchase the jam-packed contents of two buildings from a man who had inherited the property in the town of Lake Stevens, about thirty miles north of Seattle.

As it turned out, the man—a guy around thirty years old by the name of Nathan Rose—was the great-nephew, and the sole surviving relative, of Verena Rose.

Jeff had met the Rose woman. Sort of. A few years earlier, she had neither given her name nor encouraged him when he had stopped by her place to see if she had any stuff she wanted to get rid of. He left a business card with her at the time, suspecting that she only accepted it so he would leave. After her death, her nephew called to say he had found the card and wanted to cut a quick deal with Jeff for all the contents.

Nathan Rose went on to tell Jeff that he planned to have the structures razed and a modular home erected on the property in time for Christmas.

Jeff had worked fast, arranged a barter with Blanche for storage space, and had begun moving the buildings' contents.

Recently, though, Nathan Rose had called to say that he had had to change his plans. One of his children had been hospitalized, and he wouldn't be financially able to move as quickly as he had hoped. What this meant to Jeff was that he could slow down a bit on moving the contents to the warehouse. He wouldn't waste time, because he still needed to secure a steady income. But to say that the breathing space was welcome would be an understatement. It had given him more time with Sheila during those first few crucial weeks after her abduction.

He recalled the package that had been delivered that morning. The charcoal sketch of a Pennsylvania farm, exquisitely rendered by an itinerant artist, had cost a bundle. And, although he had no doubt about its value, he wondered whether it was worth it in the scheme of things—particularly as compared with a child's need for medical care. Of course, he hoped the art would somehow aid in Sheila's recovery. The traveling artist had perfectly captured the old Pennsylvania farmstead where Sheila and her sister Karen had summered with their mother's parents. Still, it had cost a lot of money.

That didn't mean that Jeff couldn't use some of his own funds to assist the Rose family. He bounced an idea around in his brain, an idea that he might be able to do something to help. He had, after all, gotten a fantastic deal from Nathan Rose. Not that he felt guilty about it. He hadn't swindled the guy. Matter of fact, he had tried to tell him that all those antiques and collectibles in the two old houses had the potential of bringing a small fortune. But Rose didn't care, so bent was he upon putting his family in a new house in time for Christmas.

As Jeff pulled into the crowded parking lot of All Things Old, he put the idea of helping the Rose family on his mental back burner to stew.

Chapter Four

He circled the building before parking in the front lot. Generally, he could gauge Blanche's availability by how many other pickers were at the loading docks around back.

Only two pickup trucks were parked near the platform. Both were dark blue Chevys—each about twenty years old, he guessed—but one of them looked like it had been jerked through a knothole. He knew the old picker who owned the beat-up one. The guy would drive that truck across a burnout if he thought there was anything on the other side that he could turn for a profit.

Jeff stepped inside the huge antiques mall and breathed in the aroma that filled the place. The oils and woods and age blended perfectly with the scents of fresh-brewed coffee and spiced punch that drifted down from the fourth floor tearoom, The Cabbage Rose. Everything carried the scent of having been aged like good Scotch, and Jeff let the smells work their magic on his stressed senses.

He started toward the back, wishing he had time to peruse the aisles. Picker or not, he never lost sight of the restorative effects that were to be gained from a few hours lost among the booths.

Smiling, he nodded to Trudy Blessing, who was busily orchestrating the cashiers at the large, L-shaped oak counter. Trudy was Blanche's personal assistant, and, in spite of Blanche's ability to do anything she set her mind to, Jeff couldn't imagine her getting along without Trudy's services. Jeff would have ample opportunity to visit with both women on Thursday, when they would join in on Thanksgiving festivities at the Talbot home.

He headed down the long corridor toward Blanche's office. All Things Old had originally been a warehouse as well, which Blanche and her husband, George, had turned into a museum with price tags. Jeff had never met George, who had died shortly after the place opened, but from the stories Blanche told, he knew he had missed out on a real corker. The guy would have had to be, to have been Blanche's partner.

As Jeff approached the office, he recognized the old man slumped against the door facing.

"What are you doing out here, Tinker? Blanche got you on hold?"

"Take a number, Talbot. She's got some new guy in there."

"A new picker?"

Tinker raised a shoulder.

Fortunately, Jeff didn't have to worry for awhile—the inventory he had bought from Nathan Rose would carry him for a long time—but he suspected that Tinker's existence depended upon a steady flow of good loot. "Do you think this area can handle another one?"

"I'm not necessarily saying the guy is a picker. But I've heard a word or two here and there. Sounds Oriental."

"The guy, or the stuff?"

"The stuff."

Jeff paused, then changed the subject. "Been finding much?"

"Some," Tinker said without looking up. "Enough to stay afloat."

"That's something to be thankful for."

"That's what my old lady keeps telling me. But, just once, I'd like a real break."

Before Jeff could respond, the door opened and Blanche poked her head out. Her red hair looked more burgundy than copper, and Jeff wondered whether she'd put a holiday-inspired rinse on it. Few women in their seventies could get away with it, but Blanche's personality was strong enough to have colored her tresses from the inside out.

She peered up at the two men. "Jeffrey, I thought I heard your voice." She turned to Tinker. "Sorry to keep you waiting. Won't you both come in?"

"As long as I get to finish my dealings with you first," Tinker said.

"Have I ever slighted you, Tinker?" Blanche said without malice as she led the way into her office. When they entered, a man rose from one of the chairs in front of the large French library table that served as Blanche's desk.

"Mr. Bolton, these are two of my most reliable pickers. Tinker and Talbot."

Jeff raised a brow. "Sounds like Tommy and Tuppence, Blanche. Have you started your Christie-for-Christmas reading early?"

"Not this early, but it wouldn't matter. I know that both you and Tinker are loners when it comes to ferreting out treasures. But I must say, Jeffrey, you look more like a picker on the prowl than you have in some time." She tugged at the sleeve of his tattered shirt.

He grinned. "I thought you'd get a kick out of this getup. I have to load some stuff this afternoon that hasn't seen a dust rag in fifty years."

Blanche circled to her side of the desk and took a seat. "The better for all of us, I say. No danger of reproductions in a lot like that."

"Enough about my grunt work." Although he knew that Blanche wouldn't talk out of school about his recent purchase, he wanted to steer away from the subject, especially in front of a stranger. He extended his hand to the unfamiliar man. "Call me Jeff."

"I go by Max." The man gripped Jeff's hand firmly. His strength surprised Jeff a little. He wondered whether the guy was making some sort of statement.

"I'm just Tinker." He shuffled to a chair without bothering to shake hands with the new guy.

After everyone had taken a seat, Blanche said, "Mr. Bolton is selling off his collection of *inro.*"

"That's a new one on me," said Tinker.

"They're basically Japanese pillboxes," Bolton said, retrieving one from his shirt pocket and handing it to Tinker. After a quick look, the old picker passed it to Jeff.

He admired the exquisite little piece of artwork, which was slightly smaller than a business card case. The lacquered black item had a burnished gold cherry blossom pattern and a silk cord threaded through a channel that surrounded its edges. The ends of the cord were then strung through a small bead at the top, and on into a disk above that.

"This is an amazing piece of artwork," Jeff said.

"I heard my wife describe them to enough people that I can give you the lowdown. Her collection is made up of pieces from the late Edo period, mid-eighteen hundreds. The *netuske*—" he pronounced it 'net-ski' "—keeps the cord together. Its disk shape symbolizes a rice cake. The *ojime,* or bead, slides down to keep the *inro* closed. The *hiramaki-e* is the flat gold of the pattern, which is actually gold dust applied to wet lacquer. Each compartment swivels out and is self-contained. When they're lined up, though, you can hardly tell that there are multiple parts. I won't argue that the concept is a stroke of brilliance. The price tags reflect it, too. They generally bring four figures. Higher than the Smith Tower."

Blanche laughed. "Just about everything is, these days."

Tinker didn't seem to hear her. He let out a low whistle, then reached for the object in order to have a second look. "Seems a shame to hide one in a pocket."

Bolton said, "That's the point. Kimonos don't have

pockets. These hung from the *obi,* or sash, and were used to carry herbs, medicines, that sort of thing.

"But," he continued, "I need to clear out some things; not much space in my little houseboat over on Lake Union. Now that my wife's passed, I don't see any sense in keeping them. Besides, it's hard enough to keep up with my own collection."

"Which is . . . ?" Tinker's obvious interest told Jeff that the old picker was beginning to see dollar signs.

"Tsubas. I started collecting them while I was overseas."

"Now, *those* I know." Tinker said. He looked at Jeff. "They're the little hand guards on Japanese swords."

Bolton's brows shot up. "That's right. I don't meet too many people who are familiar with them. I started collecting when I was stationed in Tokyo. Fought in the Second World War."

Tinker leaned forward. "You don't say? You fought in The Big One? Where were you?"

"Japan. What about you?"

"Same. Island hopping, mostly." Tinker shook his head. "Damn, you look twenty years younger than me. Guess I should've listened when my wife told me to take better care of myself. The woman still nags me about it. Know what I tell her? I say, 'If I'd known I was gonna live this long, I *would've* taken better care of myself.' "

"My wife took care *of* me till she died six months ago. I married an Asian woman while I was stationed over there. Hell, I'm surprised I don't look like a soy bean." Bolton chuckled. "But I turned out pretty good, so maybe there's something to all that health stuff, after all."

"So," Tinker said, "you're not a picker?"

"Picker? No, sir. I'll leave that in the capable hands of gents like you and Talbot."

The relief on Tinker's face was unmistakable.

Bolton went on. "I've opened up a seaplane touring service. I fly people over to Bainbridge or Whidbey, the Juan de Fucas, Victoria. You know, to sightsee, have picnics, whatever."

He pulled a couple of business cards from his pocket and handed one to each of the men.

Jeff read the card, then looked up. "Giving Kenmore and Seattle Seaplanes a run for their money, huh?"

"I plan to offer some amenities that the other services don't. Mostly, though, I'm in it for the fun of flying."

Jeff was doubtful Bolton's endeavor would make it, special amenities or not. Between the two companies, Seattle was pretty well sewn up for floatplane services. He sat back and studied both men. Every time he saw Tinker, he was surprised that he was still alive. The old picker was stoop-shouldered, with arthritic hands and a mass of scraggly hair that looked as gray and dingy as Seattle's winter sky. Max Bolton's hair was white, but the crewcut gave it a youthful appearance. In addition, he was fit and tan, where Tinker was saggy and sallow. Bolton was probably three or four inches shorter than Tinker, who Jeff guessed to be around his own five-eleven. Bolton's ramrod straight posture counteracted Tinker's slouch, however, and made him appear to be the taller of the two.

Tinker has enough trouble just getting around, Jeff thought, *let alone considering an exercise regimen.* He made a mental note to get with the program while there was still time. He had about thirty years before he would hit the age that these two men were, but by the time he got there, he wanted to be in the shape Bolton was in, instead of ending up like Tinker.

In addition, he had been putting off his annual physical. With Sheila's increased medical needs, he hadn't wanted to take the time to call and schedule an appointment, then waste an afternoon in the doctor's waiting room, then schedule a morning slot for lab work, then . . . well, the process could drag on for weeks, even months. After seeing these two guys side by side, though, he promised himself that he'd get to it just as soon as the holidays were behind him.

". . . has quite a collection," Blanche was saying. "I don't have room for all of it. I thought one of you two might have a client who would be interested."

Tinker looked up as if a balloon might appear over his

head with the answer. Then he looked at Bolton. "Can't say as I know anyone offhand but I'll keep my ears open."

Jeff's approach was more direct, but his answer was pretty much the same. "From what you've said, that *inro* collection sounds worthy of an auction. Have you contacted any of the major houses?"

"I suggested that to him," said Blanche, "but he wants to try the local market first."

"I'll pay the going rate, of course, if any of you come up with a buyer." Bolton retrieved a stack of Polaroids from the corner of Blanche's desk, divided them like he was cutting a deck of cards, and handed a stack to each of the men. "Here's a sample of what I've got. I apologize for the photography. Never have been good with a camera." He paused. "That reminds me. Several of my clients have asked for photos. You know, aerial shots, touristy stuff. I don't suppose any of you could recommend a good photographer? Also, I might need someone if I go to auction with the *inro*."

Blanche looked expectantly at Jeff, and he knew what she was thinking. But he decided against recommending his sister-in-law. He wasn't sure whether Karen wanted to mess with any little jobs during her brief stay in the Emerald City. He knew she had swung an assignment in the region, planning to kill two birds with one stone, but it hadn't sounded as if it was going to require much of her time.

"Well," Bolton said when no one offered a suggestion, "you've got my card. If you think of anyone—for the photography or the collection—I'd appreciate a call."

That settled Jeff's dilemma. He would tell Karen about Max Bolton on the way back from the airport that night, and she could decide for herself.

"Just leave the photos with Mrs. Appleby." Bolton rose. He poked an index finger toward Blanche. "*Tsuba,*" he said with a nod.

Blanche looked doubtful. "I'll keep an eye out, but don't hold your breath. Most Oriental antiques end up over in the International District. There's a large Asian faction here, and Orientalia gets snapped up quickly."

"The cup's half full, Mrs. Appleby. It's like any other collectible. There are still a lot of people who don't want the stuff or don't care about passing it along to their descendants. A large Asian community means there's a chance for *more* Oriental wares."

"That's a good way to look at it. I'll call if anything turns up."

"I'm counting on it. And, let me know if you want any pieces from the *inro* collection. I'm going to move the stuff as soon as possible. There might not be any left when I'm through in Chinatown."

He gave a final nod, then left the room.

Jeff studied the stranger's business card. "When did this guy say he started his seaplane business?"

Blanche retrieved a checkbook from the file cabinet behind her, wrote while she talked. "A few months ago. He told me that he had wanted to fly since before he could walk but that he wasn't a pilot in the war. So he saved his pay and took lessons after the war was over." She ripped the check from the book and handed it to Tinker.

He took it, then began to hoist himself from his chair. The check crumpled in the clutch of the arthritic hand. "He should've trained while he was in the service, like I did. Would've saved himself a chunk of money." The words came out pinched because Tinker held his breath while he got to his feet. Jeff could hear the old man's knee joints creak.

"He'd *better* make a killing on his collections," Tinker added. "Another seaplane business in Seattle is about as smart as another friggin' coffee shop."

And with that sage observation, Tinker headed out the door.

After he was gone, Blanche said, "Tinker's right, you know. I don't think Seattle is hurting for seaplanes."

"True enough, but this Bolton fella said he was offering something different." Jeff popped the card with a finger. "Looks like he's going for the high-end clients: catered picnics, sightseeing, guided tours, even hotel packages at the Empress. But the others probably offer all that, too."

"He must like a challenge. Karen's fees might be way

out of his league, though. I wasn't sure whether to mention her or not when he asked about a photographer."

"Neither was I, especially since she'll only be here a week or so. But, hey, this might work out great. She's probably going to need some steady, and reliable, transportation—and he mentioned getting someone to photograph his collection.

"I'm not sure what her latest assignment is," he continued, "but seaplane travel will be a lot faster than either car or ferry crawling. She'll have more time to concentrate on getting decent shots, what with this damned weather."

"You're right. She might be able to barter photography for her fare."

"Karen? No way. She's not going to pay for anything that *National Geographic* covers as part of her expenses. But she might give the guy a cut rate on the photos, if he'll be at her beck and call for her own jaunts. That'll cost a lot more than a barter setup, but she's got a hell of an expense account from what I can tell."

Jeff looked once again at the business card Bolton had handed him. The company's name, along with the pier and telephone numbers, was printed in teal green across the center, with a half-tone image of a vintage seaplane behind it. Jeff stood. "You might've missed a bet, Blanche. If he's purchasing specialty foods, you could hook him up with your tearoom."

"Or, you could dangle this opportunity in front of Sheila. Maybe it would help get her back on track."

Even though his wife had given up her dreams of being a professional chef, she had occasionally done special catering jobs—as long as her clients understood that she didn't deliver. He gave Blanche a doubtful look. "Right now, I can't even get her to come to the first floor. You know, where the kitchen is located?" Jeff didn't want to get into a depressing conversation about his home life.

"Well, what about Thursday? She'll come down for Thanksgiving dinner, won't she?"

Jeff shrugged. "I wish I knew, Blanche. God knows, I wish I knew."

Chapter Five

NATHAN ROSE SAT on the porch of his dilapidated rental house drinking a can of generic beer.

Jeff climbed from the woodie and walked across the wet, spongy yard to join him. The drive along the curvy state roads had taken longer than he had anticipated, thanks to the relentless rain, and he was glad to have finally arrived.

Nathan's feet were propped on the porch railing. Two holes, one in the sole of each boot, stared darkly at Jeff like somber eyes. The man's Carhartt jacket was stained and threadbare. Jeff knew that Nathan was a lineman with the rural electric company, and he suspected that the family was living paycheck-to-paycheck.

Jeff's heart went out to the guy. Here was a typical blue-collar man who worked hard to give his family three squares and change, sentenced to put a dream on standby because of unexpected hospital bills. Jeff was sure that the man didn't begrudge this turn of events; meeting with him to close their deal, he had watched as Rose displayed a quiet yet authentic love for his three children. But Jeff had also seen the defeat in the lines of his face, a face that was too young to have lines. Now, he saw only resignation there. Here was a man who had been taking futile swings at curve balls all his life.

"Talbot, pull up a seat." Nathan reached into a cooler beside his own chair and retrieved another can, which he offered to Jeff.

Jeff started to decline, then realized it might do him good to sit back and relax for a change. The drive up from Blanche's store had been wet and nerve-racking, fighting commuters trying to escape the Emerald City with the same frantic effort that Dorothy had spent trying to leave Oz.

He took a seat in a tattered lawn chair, popped the can's top, and took a gulp. He made a face at the bland taste. His personal favorite was Foster's, and he hadn't had anything this tasteless to drink since his college days. When he realized that his reaction might offend his host, he glanced at Nathan and was relieved to see him busy restocking the cooler from a cardboard case.

Nathan opened a fresh can and siphoned off a quarter of the liquid. His expression didn't change, and Jeff wondered how long the man had been buying cut rate beer. "What brings you over here, Talbot? I figured you'd be busy moving Aunt Verena's museum."

"I'm on my way over there now, but I wanted to drop by and see how you're holding up. Is your son recovering okay?"

"Seems to be," Nathan said with more appreciation than acknowledgment.

"That's good."

"Yep. Doctors say he'll probably be able to go back to school before Christmas break, get in on the parties. That'll cheer him up."

Jeff nodded, and both men continued to drink their beer in silence. He was a little surprised at how comforting it was simply to sit and have a beer. The simple act of sitting on the porch in the company of the quiet man offered more tranquility than Jeff had experienced in a long time.

As if some force wasn't about to let him enjoy too much serenity, a commotion erupted from inside the house, followed by two kids—one boy, one girl—bursting through the door and onto the porch. When the two saw Jeff, they stopped in their tracks.

He didn't know much about ages, but Jeff guessed that the girl was around nine or ten, the boy a couple of years younger.

"Sorry, Dad," the girl said. "We didn't know anyone was here."

"Homework done?" Nathan asked.

"Almost."

"And?"

"*Almost* only counts in horseshoes and somethin'." The girl's voice registered defeat. Without prompting, both children went back into the house.

Jeff said, "Horseshoes and *something*?"

"Damned if I remember what it is."

He had heard the saying, too, but surprisingly couldn't recall the rest of it either. He changed the subject. "Are they holding up okay?"

Nathan nodded. "They're good kids, although they get a little antsy when the weather's like this, and they can't be outside so much."

"Can't blame them there."

Nathan grunted. "You got that right."

Jeff checked in on the thoughts he'd set to simmering in the back of his mind. He wanted to help this family. Sheila, the old Sheila, would teasingly accuse him of catching the Christmas spirit. He liked Christmas well enough, more so in the years since she had come into his life and given his holidays a booster shot. It was different when you had someone with whom to share it, someone who typically relished the baking and decorating and shopping and the hundreds of other activities attached to the holiday. But he doubted that he was "catching" anything.

In spite of all the things that seemed to be out of joint in his own life, he recognized just how blessed he and

Sheila really were. Thing was, with a proud man like Nathan Rose, it was iffy at best to get him to accept what he might construe as charity.

No, Jeff decided, there was no way right now to approach the subject. He scooted the pot of benevolence once again to the back burner.

Nathan finished off his beer and opened up the cooler. He gave Jeff a questioning look, but Jeff declined. "I'd better think about the drive home after I get the woodie loaded up."

"She's a heck of a car. Forty-eight Fleetmaster, right?"

"You've got a good eye."

"You could put her up against anything new that's rolling out of Detroit."

"I'm with you there. My grandfather bought her new, and he was a real stickler for taking care of things. I inherited her, along with my house, after he died."

"Inheritance is a funny thing, isn't it? Sometimes it's a gem, like your car. Hopefully, the place left to you was in better shape than those two dilapidated houses full of junk that Aunt Verena left me. White elephants, that's all they are."

"I still think that junk has possibility."

"Maybe. If you know what's what, and who to trust, and where to take it." The man waved a hand in dismissal. "More than I could mess with."

Jeff decided to keep his mouth shut. He had tried to convince Nathan of the potential value when they had first spoken. To say it again now might only cause resentment. He nursed the beer, hoping to make it last while he tried to satisfy his curiosity about the Rose woman. "Did you know your aunt very well?"

"Well enough, I suppose. But I didn't get to know her till we were the only two left in the family, before I got married. Maybe we got along with each other because she'd had a son at one time."

Nathan took another drink, then continued. "Mel—that's my wife, Melanie—Mel says that parents who have had only sons or only daughters are different from each other, and that both are different from ones like us, who have both."

Jeff thought about Sam Carver, who had five daughters, and wondered how different things would be if Sam had a son. Likely, Jeff and Sam would see even less of each other than they now did. He said to Nathan, "I had wondered whether your aunt had children. Even though I've barely scratched the surface over there, I've come across many items that would've belonged to a young man."

"Well, she kept everything. I'm sure you'll put the puzzle pieces together and eventually get a picture."

"Which is what I'd better get to doing." Jeff stood and stretched. "Thanks for the beer."

"Anytime. Maybe you can drop by after Josh gets out of the hospital. He would go nuts over that car. And, let me know if you need a hand over there."

"I'll keep that in mind," Jeff said as he made his way to the car.

Odd, it hadn't crossed his mind to hire Nathan Rose to help him out. That bothered him a little, knowing how much the man needed the extra money.

Oh, well, like his own Auntie Pim had told him time and again, "You can feed lunch to a stray pup, but he has to dig for his own supper."

Chapter Six

Both buildings on the Rose property were clapboard structures, with paint long since beaten away and black-shrouded windows that looked like gaping holes in a prize-fighter's smile.

The drive around the lake had taken about ten minutes and, during that time, the rain let up considerably. Jeff backed his car close to the porch steps at the side of the house Verena had lived in on the back of the property. He unlocked the back hatch door of the woodie, unloaded boxes and newspaper, then shot up the stairs and onto the porch.

He fished a key ring out of his pants pocket and let himself into the kitchen. He turned on a switch and strained to study his surroundings in the faint light emitted from the bulb. The dimness, in conjunction with the approaching dusk of an already dreary day, would slow his progress.

He retrieved a notepad and pen from his picker's toolbox, and jotted "lightbulbs" on the top sheet. Many more days like this one, and he'd never get anything done. He traded pen and paper for a flashlight, and made his way around the room. To the left of the sink he located a switch and flipped it up, feeding energy to a fixture over the area. He found another light in the range hood, and a small lamp on the old chrome and pale green laminate table on the far wall.

He hung his jacket on the back of a chair and briskly rubbed his arms. After setting the thermostat to 68 degrees, he took in the space atop the cabinets.

There, dozens of pieces of jadite—crowded and stacked and coated with a gummy layer of grease and dust—were joined together by swags of cobwebs strung like Christmas lights.

This was the best sort of find for a picker. You just *knew* that the stuff was authentic, not reproduction, which was getting to be more and more of a problem.

He hadn't thought about needing a stepladder but rummaged around until he located a red and white step stool-chair combination from the fifties. He climbed up and started retrieving the pieces, then realized that the countertops were so crowded there was no place to set anything.

Back down the step stool. He planned his attack. There were some good finds on the counters—a couple of cast iron French fry cutters, several pieces of crockery, and a large and jumbled array of salt and pepper shakers—but the sight of all that jadite in one group was so damned appealing. He didn't want to waste time wrapping the other stuff when it had been his plan to rescue the jadite.

The table where he had turned on the old lamp was stacked with cookbooks. Those were easy enough to drop into a couple of boxes to clear a workspace, so he did, then loaded the boxes into the car, and pulled the table over next to his step stool.

An hour and a half later, he had all the pieces down, wrapped, boxed, and in the back of the woodie. He estimated that, roughly, he would make three grand for those ninety minutes of work. It wasn't hard to accrue a chunk of money when a jadite egg cup typically brought about fifty bucks on the retail market.

After finishing that chore, he made a walk-through, gathering up containers, files, and boxes that already held items. It was quick work, and it made him feel as if he was making progress in cleaning out the house.

Since the bedrooms would require more time than he could afford today—manipulating mattresses and dismantling bed frames—he opted for retrieving the living room rug.

Excitement almost got the best of him as he tried to make out the weave's intricate pattern. He suspected it was an Aubusson, but he couldn't be sure without doing some research. He would pull a few books on oriental rugs from his research shelves when he got home, see if he could unravel the rug's history and determine a value.

Maneuvering around the jumble, he carried coffee and end tables, plant stands, and more boxes from the area, then "walked" a couple of occasional chairs and a couch off the massive rug. The whole project posed a real challenge, because there wasn't enough free space anywhere to do much moving.

Not long into the job, he questioned his decision. His original plan, to lift the corners of a massive barrister bookcase and inch the edge of the rug out from under it, wasn't panning out. Cardboard boxes and old, brown grocery bags, stacked on every conceivable inch of floor space not taken up by solid, heavy wooden furniture, prevented leverage and threatened to rip the rug's weaker areas.

He spent another chunk of time unloading and dismantling the bookcase as he emptied each glass-fronted segment, until at last he'd reached the floor.

Eagerly, he scooted more items out of the way and headed for the opposite corner of the large room. It was there that everything showed the most wear—from the 1920s club chair, its carpetbag upholstery so threadbare that he could barely make out its design, to the dog-eared piles of stained and spine-broken paperbacks to the rug itself, which showed two worn rectangles directly in front of the chair.

It didn't take a detective to figure out that this was where the old woman had spent most of her time.

Jeff shuffled everything aside. He wanted to roll the rug from this end, so that the weakest fibers would be encased. On hands and knees, he crawled along the edge and began rolling up the rug. He was about to make the fourth revolution when he spied a dark saucer-sized blotch on the bottom fibers. He unrolled the rug one turn and checked the top. From what he could tell, the stain hadn't bled through. But the light in this room was worse than that in the kitchen, so he couldn't be sure.

Many liquids can bleed through and ruin a carpet—ink, grape juice, furniture oil, tea. As Jeff hopped up and walked to the kitchen to retrieve his flashlight, his irritation increased. He'd be damned disgusted if he'd gone to all that work to free the rug and it ended up being worth a fraction of what he'd counted on.

Back in the living room, he knelt at his work area in order to get a better look.

"*Something* is on it," he said aloud, and the sound of his voice startled him. He'd been in total silence for almost three hours.

"But . . ." He scanned the room, mentally restructured it as it had been before he'd moved everything around.

Flashlight in hand, he walked to the spot where the bookcase had been. He expected to find a pristine patch of carpet, protected from the traffic, spills, and grime of several years. But instead, he discovered that it was as dingy as the surrounding area. He studied everything more closely.

The traffic patterns, the impressions left by footed furniture, the fading that would have been caused by age—none of it added up in correlation to the locations.

Jeff spoke aloud again, as if hearing his own voice somehow anchored him to logic. "Why would Verena Rose, an old packrat of a woman—with a heart condition, as I remember—have been moving furniture?"

It didn't make sense. Obviously, it wasn't in her nature

to sort or clean or organize. Something nudged his mind. His pulse picked up pace.

He returned to the area where he'd begun rolling the rug. If the rug didn't show signs of having been there for very long, then the wooden floor beneath would. The oak boards hadn't been maintained. There was no glossy, protective wax coating. And unprotected wood showed wear and scratches.

And stains.

He laid down the flashlight and coiled the rug out of the way so that he could study the patterns on the floor.

The dark stain had discolored the floorboards, and the beam of the flashlight revealed its brown-red shade.

Jeff had seen it in its dried state many times before, and, although many things looked like it, he had no doubt that this *was* it.

Chapter Seven

IT WAS BLOOD, Jeff was certain of it.

He crawled to the wall, leaned against it for support. The brittle wallpaper crackled behind him, scratching at nerves that were already on edge.

He had to call the police. He knew that. Their first course of action would be forensics: They would have to establish officially whether or not the stain was blood, and, if so, was it the old woman's? He conjured several explanations, fought against a mental playing-out of any of them. He didn't have the stomach for gruesome images, especially those that might mean an old woman had been bludgeoned.

He thought back: How was it that Verena Rose had died? Had he even been *told* how she had died?

Something about falling in the bathtub? No, he remembered now. Nathan Rose had called after finding Jeff's business card, said that his great-aunt had apparently suffered a heart attack and had collapsed in the bathroom.

Jeff sighed, hoisted himself off the floor, and went to the kitchen. From his jacket pocket, he retrieved the cell phone he'd begun carrying after Sheila's abduction, and punched 911.

He exhaled and hit Send.

While he waited for the cops to arrive, he did a little snooping around to see if he could determine which bathroom the woman had died in. Should be easy enough, he thought. Unless this *did* turn out to be murder and the killer had cleaned up after himself. Of course, in a place as dirty as this, anything that had been cleaned might actually present more evidence of foul play. Was that why the killer hadn't done a thorough job of cleaning up the blood?

He didn't envy the crime scene investigators on this one. True, their field had advanced by leaps and bounds over the last few years. With the state-of-the-art technology at their disposal, Jeff was surprised that anyone could get away with murder nowadays.

There were two bathrooms in each of the two houses—one upstairs and one downstairs. He walked down the short hallway that led to a bedroom and adjoining bath on the first floor.

He turned on the light and stopped in his tracks. The porcelain was gone. He had known that, of course. This was one of the bathrooms from which Maura Carver had chosen the fixtures in exchange for helping Jeff. Maura and her fiancé, Darius, along with Jeff's best friend and Maura's father, Sam, had all put in a fast and furious day of pipe wrenches and battery-powered screwdrivers at the two houses. Jeff had worked out a deal with Nathan Rose for some of the architectural elements of the houses—bathroom fixtures, stained glass windows, door hardware—and had bartered with Maura because there wasn't enough time to do the job alone.

Maura's wedding was four weeks away, but Jeff wasn't sure how her new house was coming along. He wondered which bathroom Verena's body had been found in. If it was the one upstairs, then that part of the crime scene was relatively intact. The group had run out of time that working weekend and hadn't made it upstairs.

But if it was this one—and if Verena Rose had been murdered—then the crime scene evidence had been shuffled about like a set of dominoes.

He wondered whether the woman really had been sick. One way to find out, at least if Nathan's assurance was true that the only thing he'd removed from the house was the contents of the refrigerator.

The simple discovery of a prescription bottle or two might answer a lot of questions.

Easily slipping into protect-the-crime-scene sensibilities, he pried open the medicine cabinet with the end of a rattail comb.

The shelves were crammed with decanters of cough medicine and calamine, seeping tubes of ointments, boxes of fixative for dentures, half-capped bottles of aspirin. But no prescription bottles.

Noting that the countertop was as littered and crammed with items as the medicine cabinet, Jeff poked through the countertop's jumble of bottles and tubes, lipsticks and brushes, cardboard cylinders that had held toilet paper, and wrinkled tubes from which toothpaste had oozed.

At last, he unearthed a brown bottle, its pharmacy label illegible under the grime. He twisted the cap off and was surprised to find that the container was almost full. He shook out a couple of the tiny white tablets, figured they were nitroglycerin, to be placed under the tongue to prevent heart attack. His Auntie Pim had used the things for years, and, as she had aged, he had had to remind her constantly to avoid running out. This full bottle made him wonder whether Verena had died because she hadn't been able to locate it among the disarray.

Then again, if she'd had help falling and striking her head on the tub, the pills wouldn't have made a difference.

He considered the scenario if the stain on the floor turned out to be human blood. Verena's blood. Her great-nephew Nathan was her sole benefactor. On the surface, that looked like a strong motive. But if Nathan Rose was so money hungry as to murder his elderly aunt, then wouldn't he have sold off the fortune in antiques for the big payoff?

Not necessarily. Not if he didn't believe or understand that the loot could be parlayed into big bucks. Despite the fact that the general population of North America—and Europe, for that matter—was more aware than ever before of the value of collectibles and antiques, there were still scads of unbelievers among the flock who regularly and obliviously discarded fortunes.

Jeff knew that none of this would matter to the authorities. They wouldn't care whether Nathan Rose had made ten thousand dollars or ten cents. You couldn't profit from a crime.

Two implications of that scenario hit Jeff: On the one side—and most important in the scheme of things—his Libra-balanced brain saw what the Rose family would have to endure if Nathan was arrested under suspicion of murder. On the other side, his common-sense, mercenary brain said emphatically, "Talbot, you're screwed." Jeff envisioned his newly acquired assets being, at the least, frozen—or, worse, confiscated, only to be auctioned off later by the state.

It would be a hardship, but he had alternatives. If it came down to it, he'd juggle some bank accounts, contact his broker, and have interest on his investments sent in monthly dividends as opposed to rolling it into the principal investments. He'd get back to the grassroots of his profession: pound the pavement, hit the sales—estate, tag, garage, yard, whatever people wanted to call them. He'd review his files, hunt down the bargains at the malls and flea markets, be the go-between, and turn a quick profit. It would take a lot more time than what he was currently working on, but he could make a pretty steady income of it. He would make cold calls, drive the back roads of the region in search of farmsteads and rural homes. Many of the folks living out in the country had junk piled in old smokehouses, attics, basements, barns, garages. If a picker was lucky, the occupants had at least kept the roofs in good condition so as to avoid any water damage to the castoffs. Yeah, Jeff concluded, he could back up and punt. He could save the game, even if it took a few more plays, even if getting to the goal wasn't as neat and tied up with a big red bow and delivered like a gift to the cheering section. But it could be done. He could save the game.

Nathan Rose could not. If he was arrested, if he hired an attorney who couldn't convince the judge that the hard-working family man, father of three—with one in the hospital, no less—was not a flight risk, then what would it do to his family? What would their holidays be like? What would the rest of their *lives* be like?

Jeff thought about the money he had paid Nathan Rose for all the stuff that surrounded him now. What would the authorities do with that? Freeze it, too, probably. Put it in escrow or some such holding cell. That is, if there was any of it left, with the Rose boy's mounting hospital bills, and Christmas a few weeks away.

That brought Jeff to another question: What about the things he had already disposed of? The pieces he'd used for barter, as payment to Blanche for the warehouse rental down on the waterfront? What about the treasures he'd laid back to give as presents? The ones he'd already given?

Jeff wondered whether he would look guiltier than anyone. After all, *he* was the one who stood to make a killing on the whole deal. *Calm down,* he counseled himself. If the authorities weren't aware of the popularity and value underneath the decades of dirt and clutter in the two old houses, then maybe they'd leave him alone.

He had never questioned doing the right thing, and he wasn't questioning it now. He was just allowing the realization to sink in that his life might be hugely affected by the outcome of his discovery. And he'd had enough changes in his life recently.

Chapter Eight

DETECTIVE MIKE GADZINSKI was a stocky man with a ruddy complexion and features more in keeping with a plump twelve-year-old. Jeff guessed the man to be straddling fifty.

After he had introduced himself, Gadzinski pulled a pristine white handkerchief from his hip pocket and smoothed it out on the floor with the same precision Greer would use if he were preparing a luncheon tray for the queen mother.

The detective perched on the linen square with his knees while he tried to keep the toes of his well-polished oxfords from touching the dusty floor. The image put Jeff in mind of a circus elephant balanced on a beach ball. The longer Gadzinski loomed precariously over the strain, the redder his face became, until it looked as if it were soaking up the blood like a sponge.

He hoped the detective was a fast worker. After the two

uniformed officers had quickly arrived on the scene and just as quickly called the detective, it had taken nearly an hour for Gadzinski to arrive.

During that time, Jeff and the two cops waited on the wraparound porch. When, during small talk, the officers learned that he was former FBI, they relaxed and regaled him with war stories about the detective they were waiting for, referring to him several times as "Inspector Gadget," because of his propensity to spend every spare penny of his department's money—and no small amount of his own—buying every newfangled crime scene accessory that came down technology's pike.

Now he watched the detective illuminate a couple of high-powered flashlights, and a part of him wanted to help look for clues. He had long since resigned himself to the fact that being an officer of the law, no matter what branch, stayed in your blood. But he was a picker now, not an agent. His toolbox held special lights, but instead of being used to register traces of blood that couldn't be seen under a garden variety sixty-watt bulb, these were black lights that authenticated Vaseline glass and revealed identifying markings. Instead of brushes and powders for lifting prints, his kit held Simichrome and Goo Gone for removing tarnish and sticker residue. Instead of specimen bags, he carried bubble wrap for protecting valuable finds.

The computerized gadgets in a crime scene investigator's bag of tricks made Jeff's picker's toolbox look like a stocking full of coals. The only item he carried that resembled anything from his days with the Bureau was a magnifying glass. If he took that out now, he would look like Sherlock Holmes.

He sneaked a glance at his written schedule to double-check the time Karen's flight was supposed to arrive. His lips tightened, and he stuck the paper back in his pocket.

Gadzinski looked up as he snapped the plastic end from a pipette that Jeff knew held sterilized water. "Got a date?"

"Family flying in. I'm supposed to be at Sea-Tac before nine."

"Plenty of time," he said as he tinkered with a small

digital gadget. He rose to his feet, and Jeff was amazed that the heavy man did so with no appearance of struggle.

Gadzinski read the gadget's computer display. "It's human, all right."

One of the cops walked in from the back porch. "Detective Gadgetski," he said, emphasizing the second syllable in a not-too-shabby attempt at disguising the sobriquet, "there's a fatality accident on Five, north of Everett. Mind if we assist?"

Gadzinski responded distractedly, with no indication that he'd noticed the swipe at his name. "Go ahead. The body from this one has been in the ground for two months, so there's not much for you to do here. Go where you can be of some use."

After the officer left, Gadzinski eyed Jeff. "From the looks of you, you've been digging around in here quite a bit. What's your business?"

Jeff gave the detective a thumbnail sketch, telling how he had purchased the contents of the two buildings from the old woman's heir, and about the hurry to move everything so the houses could be razed and construction begun on a new home. "He had to postpone those plans when one of his children was hospitalized."

Gadzinski returned everything to his case in an obsessively organized fashion. "So, he's needing money, and you bought all this junk from him?"

"It looks like junk, but there's a lot of value in this stuff, once I get it cleaned up and on the market."

"How much value?"

"Hard to say, Detective. I mean, I'm hoping it brings a decent profit—it's how I make a living—but I've barely gotten started."

"Do you know how I can contact the nephew?"

"Sure. He lives here in town." Jeff retrieved a slip of paper from his shirt pocket and handed it to the detective. "This is the house number."

Gadzinski took a spiral-top pad from his pocket, copied the address, then returned the slip. Next he asked for Jeff's driver's license, and scribbled Jeff's contact information below that of Nathan Rose's. "Your phone?"

Jeff rattled off the number.

Gadzinski jotted quickly, then looked up. "The officers told me you used to be FBI."

"Yep."

"Do you miss the work?"

"Nope."

"Don't blame you there. Felons get more squirrelly all the time." He stuffed the pad into his pocket. "Until I know whether or not we're looking at a crime scene, I'm going to need your keys to this place."

"I was afraid of that." Jeff pulled the key ring from his pocket.

"Your only set?"

"Yes, sir."

"I'll let you know what I find out, and we'll move forward from there."

"That's as good a direction as any."

The detective grabbed a flashlight and headed down the hallway. Jeff followed, explaining that the bath fixtures had been removed. When Gadzinski reached the room, he peered inside and shook his head, then scribbled a note. "If she was found in this bathroom, Talbot, I'll need to see those fixtures."

Jeff nodded. "Hopefully, Miss Carver hasn't had time to clean them up. Her wedding is next month. The fixtures might still be in storage in the back of her shop."

"Shop?"

"Her father's, actually. Sam Carver. He's a friend of mine."

"You know the shop's number?" Gadzinski pulled the cell phone from his pocket.

"Yeah."

"Call them, find out if she's taken Comet to the stuff yet."

Jeff punched the number. When Maura's greeting on the answering machine finished, and the tone sounded, Jeff said, "Maura, if you haven't cleaned that tub and sink from the Rose house yet, don't. I'll explain later." He hit End, returned the phone.

The detective looked wary. "I hope that was enough."

"It was."

"Better be. Is there a basement in this place?"

"Yeah, access is over here." He led the way to a door beside the staircase leading to the second floor.

Gadzinski pulled on fresh latex gloves that he retrieved from a pocket. "You know, don't you, that these are damn near worthless for protecting prints, but they'll keep my own out of the soup." Still, he lightly put thumb and index finger on the top and bottom of the knob, as opposed to the usual way one might grab it, and turned. The door creaked eerily as he swung it open. He hit the switch and a naked bulb shed weak light on a complex maze of spider webs over worn wooden steps.

"I'll be damned if I'm going to coat this suit with cobwebs. Go see if you can find a broom in the kitchen."

Jeff ignored the order and brushed past the detective, knocking down the filaments with his hands as he made his way down the creaking stairs that led to the dirt-floor basement.

The detective gingerly followed, sweeping the area quickly with the beam of his high-powered flashlight.

Earlier, when Jeff had met with Nathan to purchase the stuff, he hadn't bothered with the basement. Now, although the stuff would take a lot of work, he could see dollar signs—*if* he regained his claim on the goods. There were tons of tools, tools that Blanche would go nuts over for the segment of her shop called George's, after her late husband, which showcased antique tools. They were growing more and more popular as a collectible, and Jeff believed this was due in part to the many men who weren't into antiquing but were being dragged to the malls by their wives. The tools gave them something worthwhile, if they were inclined to apply the old saw, "If you can't beat 'em . . ."

The basement also contained several boxes of musty old newspaper, for which there was no hope, and a number of pieces of broken furniture. It made Jeff think of the bully's toys in *Toy Story*. The items in front of him seemed to have a dark, sinister side.

Both men wandered around, peering into dark corners and under tables laden with box upon box of junk. Potential treasures, Jeff reasoned, his mind automatically calculating as he noted the era of an old chair, or the date on a magazine cover.

"What's this?" Gadzinski said as he changed the angle of the beam. The point of something glinted brightly from behind a jumble of hammers, levels, and table saws.

"What?" Jeff joined the detective.

"That." Gadzinski pointed with the flashlight. "It doesn't make any sense that something down here would have a shine to it."

"No, it doesn't."

The detective made no move toward the object.

"I suppose you want me to climb back there and get it?" Jeff said with no attempt to cover his irritation.

"You want to get to the bottom of this as quickly as I do, don't you? In case you don't know it, dry cleaning isn't cheap."

He refrained from telling the detective that he owned shirts that had cost more than the man's suit. He crawled over the mound, items shifting under his feet like a landslide. As he stooped to pick up the object, Gadzinski said, "Try not to touch it."

Jeff glared at him.

The man shrugged. "You know what I mean."

"Hand me the light, then, so I can see what I'm doing."

He took the flashlight, ran the beam the length of the object, and reached for one end.

"What is it?" Gadzinski asked.

Jeff held up the object as if it were a snake.

Before he could reply that he didn't have a clue, Gadzinski said, "Hell, I've seen these. My brother-in-law uses them on his job."

Jeff studied the object. It was an aluminum shank with two leather straps that buckled. At one end was a shiny piece of steel the size and shape of a dinosaur's tooth. "What is it?"

"Hooks. Well, one hook. Should have a mate somewhere."

"When I think of a hook, I think of a pirate. This doesn't look like a hook."

"That's slang for it. Here, pass that light over the gaff."

"The what?"

"The steel tooth."

Jeff did so.

"These have to be kept sharp, and this one has been sharpened recently. It's usually company policy to keep a guard over the business end so a guy doesn't gore himself with it."

Using the flashlight, he looked more closely at the tip. "Detective, I could be wrong, but I think there's a trace of blood on the tip."

"Give me the light. And don't touch anything other than the spot you're holding on to. I've got an idea."

Gadzinski examined the steel tip. "You're right. By damn, Talbot, I think we just found our murder weapon."

"You still haven't told me what it is exactly."

"It's called a pole climber. You know, for climbing poles? Telephone repairmen, electric linemen, that sort of work."

Jeff's heart was in his throat.

Gadzinski shined the flashlight beam in Jeff's face. "You look pale, Talbot. Got something to tell me?"

Jeff's voice was tight. "Yeah. The old woman's nephew is a lineman."

Chapter Nine

"**YOU'RE KIDDING ME**, right?"

"I wish I were."

"I'll be surprised if it ends up being that easy, but you never know."

The two men returned to the living room, where the detective eyeballed the hook, then chose a cardboard box full of magazines and dumped them on the floor. He grabbed his case, and started walking. Jeff followed, careful not to brush the pole climber against anything.

Once on the porch, Gadzinski took the hook from Jeff and propped it at an angle in the box so that all sides of the straps were exposed, then went to work assembling something that looked, for all intents and purposes, like a high-school chemistry experiment. He strung an extension cord out from the kitchen, plugged it into one of those little warming plates used for a coffee cup, and took a tiny tube of super glue from a lidded plastic container that held a couple dozen of them.

"I'll get the hot water," Jeff said.

"Good, you're familiar with cyanoacrylate fuming. It does the job, but I'll be glad when the technology improves for it."

Gadzinski took the cup of water and set it inside the box. It would provide the needed humidity. Next, he made a small bowl shape out of aluminum foil, placed it on the warming pad, and put a dollop of glue in the center. Then he brought the flaps of the box up to contain it.

Superglue fuming, as most people called it, was a tricky procedure, but it was a clever and effective way to "seal" prints for the lab. It was usually used when evidence had to be shipped, and Jeff was impressed that the detective was going to such lengths. This one small process could make all the difference in solving a crime—and perhaps keeping an innocent man from going to prison.

After Gadzinski had successfully set the piece, he opened a large evidence bag and slid the pole climber inside. When he went back in the house, Jeff followed.

"The guy's got three kids," he said when they reached the living room, "and one of them has been in the hospital for a couple of months. I've only been around him a few times, but I just don't see him killing anybody. Especially an elderly aunt. What reason would he have?"

The detective swept his arm in a grand gesture. "Monetary gain. The medical bills must be killing him."

"I told you before, his monetary gain would have been a lot more if he had sold off this stuff properly. He didn't get rich off me. He just wanted enough to put a prefab on this spot."

Gadzinski shrugged. "Who knows how people think?" He pulled the notepad from his pocket and studied the Rose address that Jeff had given him earlier. "I'd better go talk to him."

"Go easy on the guy."

"I will if he *makes* it easy."

Jeff's jaw tightened.

Gadzinski headed toward the kitchen. Jeff turned out

the living room lamp. In the dark, the detective's stark white handkerchief, which he had left on the floor, glowed briefly like a television screen right after it's switched off.

On his way past the thermostat, Jeff shut off the heat. No sense in running up bills when he wouldn't even have access to the place. In the kitchen, he doused the dim lights, grabbed his coat, and followed Gadzinski onto the porch.

He was surprised to discover that night had fallen. The chain of events had been surreal, and he surfaced on the porch with the feeling that he had spent a year in seclusion. He angled his watch toward the shaft of light emanating from a street lamp and cursed. He started down the stairs, calculating how to make up the lost time.

"Fancy car, Talbot. How do you keep the wood from warping in all this rain?"

Jeff turned and looked up, blinking against the raindrops. "I have a butler who dries it off every evening when I pull it into the garage."

Gadzinski looked up and down, then cackled. "That's a good one." He continued to carry on as he cracked open the briefcase and withdrew a roll of yellow caution tape. "A butler," he blurted amid more cackling and sniffling. He reached into his hip pocket and came up empty, then the look on his face registered the abandoned handkerchief, and he pulled another one out of his breast pocket.

A regular Houdini, Jeff thought.

As the man dabbed at his eyes with the fresh handkerchief, Jeff finished descending the stairs and crawled behind the wheel of the woodie.

A glance at his reflection in the rearview mirror answered any questions he might have had about the detective's skepticism over his employing a butler. His face was so grimy and smudged that it appeared his five-o'clock shadow stretched from throat to scalp. His dark hair was strung with a dingy gauze of cobwebs, which gave him a picture of where he was headed if the gray he'd been noticing lately continued to appear at its current rate. To top it off, his flannel shirt and faded jeans were as grungy as they were tattered.

All in all, he was a mess—dirty, exhausted, hungry. And he would have to forego dinner with Sheila in order to shower and shave and have enough time to drive to the airport.

He considered sending Greer to pick up Karen but immediately dismissed the notion. Sheila believed that, in her own absence, her sister had to be greeted by family. And Karen would be miffed if she were relegated to something along the lines of estranged guest. As for Greer, although he would do anything his employers asked, the prospect of his shuttling Karen Gray to the house had disaster written all over it. No, Jeff determined, the day had been bad enough, without his setting off a string of firecrackers.

With that decision worked out, he fished around on the floorboard behind the driver's seat and found his thermos. After a cup or two of coffee, he'd be ready for just about anything.

Or so he thought.

Chapter Ten

HE DROVE THE Jimmy to Sea-Tac simply because the vehicle was right in front of him when he hurried out the back door of his house.

In his distracted and exhausted state, he almost veered right, toward the rental car return, instead of left, which led to short-term parking. Swerving, he narrowly missed another SUV and got the blare of a horn as a warning.

As he walked through the covered walkway that connected the parking structure to the terminal, he glanced at his reflection in the glass, discreetly checking himself over. He had rushed so much getting ready that he felt a sudden need to make sure he hadn't forgotten his pants.

Since the idea of meeting travelers at the gate was now a thing of the past, he joined the crowd gathered around the escalators that would carry passengers up to the baggage claim area. He was trying to avoid colliding with a young man juggling a large bouquet of flowers in one arm and a toddler in the other, when a mass of people poured from the side-by-side escalators like floodwaters.

An uneasy feeling came over him as he scanned the faces of those who rushed by. What if he didn't recognize Karen? He hadn't seen her in almost three years. He wasn't sure what latest affectation she was into. Unlike her sister, who still had the same hairstyle she'd been wearing when Jeff first met her, Karen might have changed the style—and color—of her hair a dozen times since her last visit. Sheila also stuck to the same, classic clothing styles, where Karen was apt to show up looking like a preppie college student one time and a Goth queen the next. He concentrated on the image of Karen and her basic physical traits. She firmly believed in sustaining physical fitness above everything else, maintaining that she never knew when her life might depend on it.

He began drawing a mental image. Just to be safe, he put a ball cap on it. He'd seen Karen in one often enough and, that way, he didn't have to fret over a distraction like purple hair or dreadlocks. Or purple dreadlocks, for that matter.

Someone bumped into him, hard. He turned, prepared to stand his ground.

"Quit your daydreaming, silly! This camera equipment weighs a ton!"

He grabbed the bag, then gave his sister-in-law a brief hug. Her hair was its God-given shade of light auburn but the buzz-cut poked his chin. He backed up and studied the woman whose scalp looked like a cross between a porcupine and a carrot.

Karen Gray was a couple of inches shorter than Sheila, about five-five, he figured, but she was so fit and confident that she actually seemed taller. She had green eyes that glittered and jumped with anticipation, as if she were perpetually seeking adventure, and a smattering of light freckles that shaved ten years off her age.

She smiled then, and one of her front teeth flashed gold. "There's an icebreaker if I ever saw one."

"Yep. I tried to keep my mouth shut so I wouldn't blind anybody, but you know me. That didn't last long."

"I'll bet." As they were swept up with the tide of people flowing toward baggage claim, Jeff asked her what had happened.

"The Bolivian drug cartel thought I was photographing them, so they started shooting at me while I was on the face of a ledge."

"Were you?"

"Not until they started firing."

"How'd you get out of that one?"

"The driver I hired was, shall we say, multitalented. Anyway, I was shooting with my camera and repelling at the same time. I slipped, broke my tooth, and the only dentist I could get hold of didn't have any matrix to work with."

He didn't doubt that his sister-in-law's occupation was often more dangerous than his own FBI career had been. But he also knew that she had an active imagination.

"Drug cartel. Karen, I swear. I never know whether to believe your tales or not." He studied her eyes and decided to call her bluff. "You're getting creative with this one, aren't you?"

"Yeah, but don't tell anybody. Actually, I tripped on my camera strap walking out of a cave. The part about the dentist is true though."

"Your secret's safe with me." He steered her toward the baggage carousel. "How many drinks did you spring for this trip?"

"Only a dozen or so. More family types traveling. Thanksgiving, you know."

"I know."

Although Karen seemed animated, Jeff read the signs of fatigue, jet lag. Even the woman's tan couldn't conceal the dark circles under her eyes, and there was an edge to her wit.

They fought through the congestion around the conveyor belt, and it took the concentrated efforts of both of them to claim Karen's luggage. It seemed to Jeff like a lot of bags.

Finally, they had located every piece, carried it to the parking structure, and stuffed it into the Jimmy.

Jeff headed north. After they were under way, he said, "So, how was your flight?"

"That's like asking, 'So, how was your day, honey?' Does anyone really want to know the answer to that one?"

He had actually considered telling Karen the many things that had happened to him since that morning, something he wouldn't have done in the harsh light of day or airport corridors, but now he didn't dare. Karen clearly wasn't in the mood.

"*Flights,* plural," she said with a sigh. "I'm damned glad to have both feet on the ground. Relatively speaking. I've been on five planes in three days in four countries, taking sink baths and eating God knows what. My last assignment had me going into places where we had to haul our own water, and I doubt that the people living there know what the word *shower* means. Why do you think I pulled a GI Jane on my hair? Now I've got to depressurize but not so much that I go stir-crazy from lack of excitement in your laid-back little city." Her angst increased with each phrase, and when she turned on Jeff with, "How was *your* day?" the sentence carried her full force of sarcasm.

A montage flickered across his mental screen like the reel from a silent film: alarms, downpours, crowds, police, Sheila, wedding chaos, new faces, old faces, a possible murder, a questionable existence. It was almost too much.

He kept his eyes on the pavement. "My wife won't come out of her bedroom."

After a silence so long that Jeff had resigned himself to a new state of aloneness, Karen said, "You win."

Chapter Eleven

"I CAN'T LET her see me like this!" Sheila said in a panic-laced whisper early Wednesday morning when Karen Gray's chipper voice followed a knock on the bedroom door.

Jeff struggled toward consciousness. The night sounds of crickets and water made it hard to surface, but Sheila punched a button on the sound machine and choked off the insects. He squinted against the daylight coming through the trio of windows on the east wall.

Sheila's statement registered, and Jeff sat up in bed. He marveled at how his sister-in-law had recuperated so quickly from her journey. To his wife, he said, "Honey, she's family, and she knows what you've been through. Besides, when she sees that she woke us up, she'll reserve 'first impression' for later."

Sheila grabbed a hand mirror from her nightstand (something Jeff hadn't seen her do since before the kidnapping), looked at her image, and groaned. She smoothed her hair and pinched her cheeks, then jerked open the stand's drawer and grabbed a bottle of Visine. A dose of that to her bloodshot eyes elicited a gasp.

Jeff hoped that having her sister here would jolt Sheila out of the bedroom. Nothing he'd tried had done the trick.

Karen knocked again. "C'mon, Sis, wake up! If it helps, I've got coffee."

That won Jeff over. He jumped up and grabbed his robe, then headed for the door. Hand on the knob, he looked back at his wife for a sign. Her expression hinted at dread, but Jeff knew his wife. There had been several times over the previous weeks that Sheila had wanted to draw from her sister's strength. And, although Sheila expressed an innate desire to look better before Karen's arrival, it hadn't prevented her day-to-day stress eating. Now, Sheila was probably feeling the anxiety of allowing her sister to see her at top-weight. Finally, though, she nodded, and Jeff opened the door.

Karen shot past him and onto the bed, where she enveloped her younger sister in a bear hug. Jeff sighed, which was his first indication that he had been holding his breath. In Sheila's state, he never knew what her reaction to any given situation might be, and he'd tried lately not to second-guess.

He scooped the tray from a marble-topped eighteenth-century commode made of walnut and satinwood that stood outside their bedroom and took it to the table-and-chair grouping in the far corner of the room.

It didn't escape Jeff that Sheila appeared ten years older than Karen, when, in fact, she was almost five years younger.

"Let me look at you!" Karen said, brushing back Sheila's honey-colored hair.

"Please don't," Sheila said, burying her head and allowing her shoulder-length bob to close around her face like a curtain.

"C'mon, it's *me*. Here, I'll let you rub your hands across my buzz-cut. It's pretty cool."

Karen dropped her head, and Sheila ventured a peek.

"What on earth?" she said as she reached out and stroked her sister's head. "Jeff, you *have* to feel this."

Although Jeff had already immersed himself in a cup of strong, black coffee and the entertainment section of the newspaper, he had glanced several times at the women. He wanted to observe Sheila's reactions, her level of angst, her responses to her sister. "What?" he said innocently, in order to mask his eavesdropping.

Before Sheila could say anything, Karen hopped up and crossed the room to where Jeff was sitting. She grabbed his hand and brushed it across her stubbled crown.

"Feels like my face after two days without a razor. And you wonder why you don't have a boyfriend."

"Who says I don't have a boyfriend?"

"Do you?"

Karen didn't respond.

Sheila crawled from bed and made her way to the breakfast tray, where she poured a cup of coffee and grabbed a cream cheese Danish from a plate of pastries. She took a large bite of the Danish and stared at her husband.

"What?" he said. "Do you want me to have my hair cut that way?"

Sheila chewed the Danish, then swallowed. "Somehow, I don't think it would have the same effect."

Karen prepared a cup of tea, and the two women moved back to the bed.

The antique porcelain tea set was the one Jeff had given his Auntie Pim on her seventieth birthday. It matched the Haviland china his aunt had amassed as a dowry, although she had never married. The pattern, aptly called Primrose (Auntie Pim's Christian name) was ivory with dark blue and pink primroses, and was always used for female guests in the Talbot home.

He finished his coffee. "So, girls, what's on the agenda?"

"Well," Karen said, "I know I should get this fixed—" she flashed her gold tooth at her sister and promised to fill her in later—"but I need a day to crash. So, I plan to bore

Sheila to death with photos, dig out chick flicks and chocolate, and pamper her with a pedicure."

Sheila unearthed a video and handed it to her sister. "Have you seen this one?"

Jeff recognized the jacket of *Tortilla Soup,* one of his wife's newest obsessions since she had taken to watching only movies with food themes. He didn't know whether the food films were spurring her to eat more, or if her burying herself in food after her ordeal had eventually led her to watch only culinary movies.

As the two sisters caught up, Jeff headed for the shower, wishing he could call it a throw-away day. But until Detective Mike Gadzinski told him otherwise, he had to juggle bank accounts, generate income, and do whatever else it took to keep the household afloat until he was once again in control of the Rose property. If he ever was.

He dressed in brown cords and an ivory, cable-stitched sweater, then made his way down the service stairs that led to the kitchen. As he passed through, he grabbed a mug of coffee, and took it with him to the carriage house.

When he had driven away from Verena Rose's home the night before, he hadn't given a second thought to the items stashed in the back of the woodie. Now, he toyed with the idea of calling Detective Gadzinski but just as quickly dismissed the notion, concluding that the detective likely would have him pile the boxes back in the old Rose house without even looking at what was inside them. Jeff wasn't going to sell anything while the investigation was pending, so he decided that there was no harm in keeping the stuff for now. And, he concluded, if he found anything that might be pertinent to the case, he would have no trouble handing it over to the detective, along with a suitable explanation.

He turned on the radio he kept on a small work table, then began unloading the boxes onto a large workbench. After suffering through the strains of "Little Drummer Boy," "What Child Is This?," and "Silent Night," he told the radio that he would be back in December. He switched from FM to CD, hit *play,* and livened up the place with some classic jazz.

He had marked the boxes from the kitchen, so there was no need to dig through the newspaper-wrapped jadite. Instead, he chose a box that he had grabbed from an upstairs bedroom. When he opened it, the smell of gun oil reminded him of his service revolver.

Inside the cardboard box were what looked like several jewelry boxes. Carefully, he lifted an item encased in plastic. When he removed the plastic, he found the source of the odor: a swatch of soft fabric that apparently had been soaked in the oil. He unwrapped the cloth, revealing a small casket.

He hadn't come across many caskets in his years as a picker. The one he had read about most often was the marriage casket of Projecta and Secundus from the fourth century. Although the artistry on that one depicted Pagan scenes, the inscription indicated that it had been for a Christian marriage. As he recalled, the casket was currently at the British Museum.

Most people bristled when he used the word, not aware that *casket* had once been an endearing word for a container fashioned to hold precious mementos. The vernacular had changed when, sometime around the end of the nineteenth century, undertakers employed euphemisms in order to soften the language of their trade. Thus, *undertaker* became *mortician* and *coffin* became *casket.*

By his way of thinking, the ruse hadn't lasted. It seemed that most people took to calling marriage caskets "boxes" after the funeral industry took the accepted word for a chest to hold valuables.

When he heard *casket,* Jeff always imagined treasures, not bodies, and he wished the general public would return to some of the old ways. Of course, he still referred to his parlor as a parlor, even though *that* direct offshoot of *funeral parlor* was now a *living room.*

He also wished, as he gazed upon the exquisite piece, that the casket would bring forth a treasure.

This one appeared to be made of chiseled steel outfitted with bronze. It was about the size of a shoebox, with curved bronze acanthus leaves forming its feet and more of the leaves hugging its four corners. Its finial—fashioned after the onion domes that graced St. Basil's Cathedral—told him it was Russian.

He recalled reading something about the gunsmiths of the armory in Tula who had taken their artistic talents beyond crafting weapons and had actually rendered items fit for Russian royalty.

He had no doubt that this piece fit the bill. Etched on the front panel was a detailed profile of an Imperial coach, upon which was superimposed a sash draped to form a heart. Hanging from the sash was some sort of Russian military star. He wouldn't have expected the silver of the faceted steel to lend itself to the warm shades of bronze, but the combination worked, if only because of the superior workmanship.

This, he decided, would be Sheila's Christmas gift. He didn't care whether it should be turned over to the police. He didn't care if it was worth a million dollars. Or a thousand. The value would be in his wife's pleasure upon receiving such a remarkable antique.

He grasped the dome and paused before attempting to open the casket. If it was locked, he might be able to pick it. But the locks on these small works of art were often elaborate, some shooting as many as a dozen bolts. If that was the case with this one, the contents might well remain a mystery.

To his relief, the lid opened. Inside it, he counted eight bolts that would have shot into slots had it been locked. After a moment's hesitation, he leaned in to look at the contents. He felt like Pandora.

Chapter Twelve

THE SCENT THAT emanated from the container made him think of a library vault. That discernible amalgam of ink and parchment, age and dust that could be nothing other than old paper.

Well, I'll be damned, he thought. *Maybe it's Christmas, after all.*

Nesting in the casket was a bundle of letters, tied with a satin ribbon that had faded from its original navy blue to a muted lavender. He'd have a hard time keeping these out of Sheila's collection, that much he knew. Although she preferred hotel stationery from such historic establishments as New York's Algonquin or Victoria's Empress or The Pfister in Milwaukee, correspondence in any and every form called to her.

Carefully, he removed the bundle and untied the sash. The envelopes were yellowed and frail, and appeared to have been handled many times.

He studied the blue postmarks. They were in chronological order, beginning with January 8, 1945, and ending June 10 of the same year. The first one was addressed in a tight hand to Verena Rose, Lake Stevens, Wash. Jeff opened it and read:

Dear Mom,

I am sorry that we fought, even sorrier that I lied about my age in order to join up. I was angry with you and did this out of spite, but now I know that it was a mistake. Please help me get out of here.

My birth certificate is in the old desk in the dining room. I put it in an envelope and taped it to the underside of the bottom drawer so that you wouldn't be able to find it and make Uncle Sam send me back home.

Well, now you know, so get it out and send it to me ASAP.

Boot camp is so bad. Why do GIs come home on leave and play it up so? I cannot take another week. Help me come back home where I can grow up, which is something I likely will not get done in this h— hole.

No "I told you so's" from you, either, when I get my feet back on Washington soil. And I'll mind my business about your male friends.

Your loving son,

Andy

(and, regrettably, Private Andrew Carson Rose)

Jeff carefully folded the paper and slipped it back into its sleeve. *So,* he thought, *Verena's son had been a soldier.* Nathan had mentioned that his great-aunt had a son, but Jeff hadn't given much thought to what had happened to the child. The fact that nothing else was said—along with the more obvious fact that Nathan had inherited everything—made Jeff wonder why Verena hadn't left anything to her own son. Curiosity won over, and Jeff anxiously opened the next letter, postmarked January 30.

Mom,

Yes, I received the birth certificate. I've changed my mind, though. It's jake here, now that I'm being treated like a man instead of a kid. We enlisted men can go into the px and buy liquor and cigarettes without being asked questions, and the girls are hot to go with us to the dance joints. Now I know what all the fuss is about, and I'm going to stick it out. Don't worry about me, Mom. The girls here will take care of me. I've got a nickname, something all the fellas like having. "Andy the Dandy" they call me, because I have got a way with the ladies.

You asked about Christmas. We haven't been told much yet, except that it will depend on what ol' Hitler plans for us.

Your grown-up son,
Andy (the Dandy)

P.S. Here I am, standing next to a movie star and a couple of skirts we picked up at the canteen. Yeah, Mom, it really is who you think it is. Now, what do you think of that?

Jeff opened a third letter, glanced through a small group of photos that it contained—guys in uniform, standing in front of tanks and aircraft—then started to unfold the brittle paper when a knock on the door distracted him. He looked up to find Greer standing in the doorway holding an umbrella.

Jeff grinned. Most Seattleites never messed with the awkward things, but Greer collected bumbershoots and had moved to the Emerald City under the false impression that he would be constantly surrounded by them.

"Sir," Greer said, "A Detective Gadzinski is on the telephone." The butler handed the cordless phone to his boss, then walked back outside.

"Detective, what's up?"

"You mentioned a warehouse last night."

"Yeah."

"Have you been over there since?"

"No, actually. Haven't had the time." Jeff knew where this was going but he played dumb. "Why?"

"I'd better take a look at what you've got there. Where is it?"

"On the waterfront, close to downtown." Jeff wanted to take care of a couple of things before leaving home. "How about thirty minutes?"

"Make it an hour."

Jeff rattled off the address, then hung up.

When he started to place the letters back into the marriage casket, he saw that something else was in the bottom of the box. Carefully, he removed a Western Union telegram and a folded piece of fabric. Underneath those were several World War II pinback buttons, off-white printed with red and navy "V for Victory," "Welcome our Heroes Home," or, simply, the Morse code three dots and a dash that stood for victory. He unfolded the cloth first, realized it was something else he had once read about. The red-bordered rectangle was one of the Service Flags given to families who had loved ones serving in the war. For each person serving there would be a dark blue star on the piece of cloth. If that soldier was killed, then a gold star was placed over the blue one.

As Jeff held the Service Flag, he saw not the old woman he had met a few years earlier but, rather, the mother who had experienced the worst that fate had to offer. His heart went out to her, because he knew the symbolic meaning of the colors. Placed over the blue star of the flag he held was the gold star of death. Only two of the five points were stitched down, and he suspected that Verena Rose had been too distraught to complete the task.

He read the telegram:

THE SECRETARY OF WAR DESIRES TO EXPRESS HIS DEEP REGRET THAT YOUR SON PRIVATE ANDREW C. ROSE WAS KILLED IN ACTION IN DEFENSE OF HIS COUNTRY IN THE SOUTH PACIFIC AREA JUNE 9, 1945. LETTER FOLLOWS.

THE ADJUTANT GENERAL

Tenderly, Jeff placed the items back in the casket, then carried it to the house.

The Wells Fargo safe that dwarfed a room in the basement had belonged to Jeff's grandfather, Mercer Talbot. The senior Talbot had been one of the region's most successful lumber barons, and his distrust of banks had bordered on obsession. He wanted money when he wanted money—and he did not want to rely on a penny-pinching banker in order to get at it.

Jeff hadn't thought much about the massive iron safe before he got into the antiques business. Since then, the thing had proved handy countless times.

He secured his newfound treasure in the vault, then went upstairs and to his desk in the library. He flipped to "R" in his address book, and punched numbers on the phone.

Chapter Thirteen

"HELLO?" THE FEMALE voice that answered sounded strained.

"Mrs. Rose?"

"Yes?"

"Mrs. Rose, this is Jeff Talbot, the man who bought the contents of your husband's—"

"What did you tell them last night?" she yelled.

"What?" Although he'd known that the discovery of the pole climber shed strong suspicion on Nathan Rose, he hadn't really thought about Nathan's wife's response.

"The police. What did you say?"

Jeff remained calm. "I had no choice but to call them when I found a bloodstain on the floor."

"They came over here and arrested Nathan! Did you know that? What am I going to tell my kids? That their father is spending Thanksgiving in *jail?*"

Jeff wasn't sure which approach to take. "Where did they take him?"

"Why should I tell you?"

"I used to be in law enforcement, for one thing. For another, I . . ." He what? Felt responsible? Not completely. Could fix things? He wasn't sure. But at least he could make sure the cops weren't overstepping their bounds. He might even be able to speed up Nathan's release. "Listen, Mrs. Rose, is he going to try to post bond?"

"That's a stupid question."

"You're right, it is."

"Of course he's going to try. That is, if the judge will listen."

"What time?"

"Two o'clock, at the courthouse in Everett. The lawyer said that the judge would probably run everybody through fast so he can take off early for the holidays."

Jeff looked at the clock on the mantel. The meeting with Gadzinski shouldn't take too long. "I'll meet you there."

Jeff wasn't sure why he felt compelled to get in the middle of this, but he realized that part of it had to be because the whole thing had such a direct affect on his own livelihood. Besides, he couldn't see Nathan Rose as a murderer. There were times when you just had to make sure the system didn't kick the underdogs.

Detective Gadzinski's white sedan was parked in front of the warehouse, and Jeff got the immediate impression that the man had been sitting there for awhile. Earlier, it hadn't crossed his mind that the detective would suggest a later meeting time just so he could hightail it down there and prevent Jeff from looting the joint.

He pulled the woodie in beside Gadzinski's car, thankful that he'd had the presence of mind to unload the car first thing that morning.

Simultaneously, the two men climbed out of their vehicles and leaned into the wind as they hurried to the door.

"Been here long?" Jeff asked, debating how far to push in order to let the detective know what he suspected.

"Just pulled in, actually."

"Uh-huh." Jeff unlocked the door and flipped some light switches as he stepped into the small office.

Gadzinski looked up at the sky before he moved inside and shut the door. "More rain moving in."

"It's been a strange year for weather."

"True enough. They're predicting that we'll more than make up for last winter's drought—probably before the calendar rolls over."

Jeff nodded, then opened the door that led into the massive storage area of the warehouse. Although several large loads had been brought in, the grouping of antique furniture, boxes, and crates was dwarfed by the huge building. The two men walked toward the stacks and piles of goods, their footsteps striking the concrete floor and echoing loudly off the metal shell of the building.

The whir of the large dehumidifier that Jeff had placed near the treasures in order to prevent mildew damage shut off. Jeff heaved the reservoir and carried it to the bathroom to empty. After he returned, he said, "You know, Detective, this has to be done every couple days, or the damage to these items will cost a fortune to reverse."

"Yeah, I learned that the hard way in my basement at home. My wife was storing a bunch of old magazines down there—*Life, Saturday Evening Post, National Geographic*. Before I realized it, several of them were foxed."

Jeff was surprised that the detective knew the term for discoloration on books and papers. "I've got an inventory of all this. Can't you check the items against it, and let me continue coming over here to dump this thing?"

"I don't know . . ."

"Here." Jeff pulled his wallet from his hip pocket, took out a business card, and handed it to the detective. "You can call my former boss at the Bureau. He'll vouch for my honesty." Printed on the card was Gordon Easthope's name and phone number at the Bureau's Chicago office. Jeff didn't tell Gadzinski that Gordy was friend and mentor as well, and he knew Gordy wouldn't mention it either.

"Don't wait too long to call him, though," Jeff continued. "There's some pretty valuable stuff in here."

"Hell, Talbot, I don't have time to come back down here." Gadzinski pulled a cell phone from his coat pocket. "Let's get it done."

While the detective stabbed numbers, Jeff inspected the goods. He remembered some of the items, but he'd made such a quick pass-through when he'd bought everything from Nathan Rose that he hadn't realized just how much potential there really was.

He paused to examine something wrapped in a movers' quilt. The item seemed awfully small to be wrapped in a quilt normally used for furniture, so he untied the rope and carefully pulled away the quilt, revealing a gate-leg table. He'd been on the lookout for just such a table to use in the dining room. Folded for storage, it took up a scant eight inches and could be easily stored against a wall. However, when the gate legs were opened to support the leaves, the table would seat four people, or serve as a sideboard during a particularly large dinner or holiday party.

Gadzinski joined him. "If Easthope had sung your praises any louder, I wouldn't have needed the phone." He indicated the table. "What's that?"

Jeff raised a leaf, swung out a gate leg, and stepped back. "It's called a Sutherland table. I saw one recently in *Bulfinch's*—that's one of my reference books. It's named after the Duchess of Sutherland, who was a Mistress of the Robes to Queen Victoria."

"Why?"

Jeff thought about it. "I don't know, actually. But that tells me it's around a hundred fifty years old."

"Is it worth anything?"

Jeff shrugged. "A few grand, I suppose."

The detective didn't show any more interest. "Did you hear from your friend? The one who bartered for the bathroom fixtures?"

"The builders are behind schedule, and Maura's swamped with work and wedding plans. She hasn't touched the porcelain."

"That's good news."

"For you, maybe. Not for her."

"She's alive, right? Any day you wake up alive is a good day. The Rose woman can't say that."

"You've got a point." He covered the table, disappointed that he couldn't take it with him. He could have used it for Thanksgiving dinner the next day.

"Your training paid off, Talbot. Not many people would've paid attention to the details. That was the old lady's blood, all right. Got the nephew in jail already."

"That's what I hear. What makes you so sure he killed her?"

"He was the sole benefactor, did you know that?"

He knew but he didn't let on. "Don't you need more than that?"

"I have more than that."

Jeff's jaw clenched. "I don't want to see you railroad a hardworking father, who's got a kid in the hospital to boot, without good reason."

"Look, Talbot, the M.E. admitted that he had handed the Rose body over to a new kid. It looked like a simple case, and the M.E. had 'em stacked to his . . . well, you get the idea.

"Anyhow, he saw it as a cut-and-dried deal: Old lady living alone, has a heart attack while she's washing her hands after going to the john. Turns out, she was on heart meds, so that part checks out. Anyway, she grabs her chest, does a pirouette or two, and bounces off the porcelain before she lands.

"The M.E.'s trying to gloss it over now, but I got a look at the trainee's report. The kid wanted to be thorough—you know how they are, fresh out of school—so he wrote down everything, raised some questions while he was examining the old woman. Thing is, the kid was asking so many damned questions that the M.E. got to where he was only half-listening.

"The clincher, though," Gadzinski continued, "is the kid found plenty of discrepancies."

"Discrepancies. You mean she didn't have a heart attack?"

"Oh, she had a heart attack, all right. But it looks like it might have been provoked by that blow to the head."

Jeff thought about the stain in the living room. "The marks on the body didn't add up to her bruises from bouncing off bathtubs, did they?"

The detective paused before responding. "No, they didn't."

"She was found in the downstairs bathroom, wasn't she." He stated it as fact, not as a question. *Always start with the most logical move.*

"Yeah. How did you know that?"

"Because whoever killed her in the living room picked the closest place he could carry her—or drag her—then staged the whole thing to look like an accident. Right?"

"Looks that way."

"Why would Nathan Rose kill her with a piece of equipment he used on the job every day, then stash it in the basement instead of taking it with him?"

"Stupid move, wasn't it?"

"Detective, you've talked with the guy. Does he strike you as a candidate for the Darwin Award?"

"Someone's always forwarding that E-mail to me. Goes to show you, there *are* people that stupid."

"Maybe, but not Nathan Rose."

"How do you know?"

"How long has he worked with power lines?"

Gadzinski shuffled papers. "Nine years."

"If he were stupid, he'd have been fricasseed by now, don't you think?"

"Granted, it doesn't scan. But it's *all* I've got, so it's *what* I've got. Know what I mean?"

Jeff didn't say anything, and Gadzinski exhaled. "Well, I need to see that bathtub before I go to the courthouse."

He didn't tell him that he would also be at the courthouse. You never knew when the element of surprise might help.

After Gadzinski had locked up the warehouse, Jeff gave him directions to Sam's shop and told him he would meet him there.

Chapter Fourteen

SAM CARVER'S RENOVATION shop was brightly lit against the darkening sky, and the burnished glow of the warm, polished woods of centuries of furniture gleamed in the windows. Suspended as if in midair was Maura's collection of antique plumb bobs, which formed a sort of valance for the picture window. The polished brass and bronze of the spheres shone as the headlights' beams cut through the rain and bounced off them.

Jeff knew that the artistic touch to the window had to be one of Maura's ideas and, although he admired the beauty of it, he wondered whether the pricey display might invite a break-in. He mentioned this to Sam.

"I tried to tell that girl," Sam replied, "but, you know, it's the least of her worries right now. She pointed out that I pay for an elaborate alarm system, so why not rely on it? I just shook my head and increased my insurance coverage."

Sam's black heritage usually gave him an ageless appearance, but today his face was lined with stress and exhaustion.

"Buddy," Jeff said as he slapped Sam's back, "I see we're overdue for a night out."

"You look the same, my friend." Sam wiped his hands on a stained rag. "Sheila doing any better?"

"She finally found a therapist who comes to the house *and* conducts sessions over the phone and through E-mail. Plus, Karen flew in last night. I think that'll help."

Sam grunted. "Between you and me, I'm happy to be moving one more of my brood *out* of the house."

Jeff knew that his friend worshipped every one of his five daughters, and, although Jeff didn't have any children, he had seen enough people go through the stress of putting together a wedding to know the problems it entailed. "How's the mother of the bride holding up?"

"Damned if I know. She's so busy, I don't feel like I've seen her all month. She spends all her time keeping the peace, and making sure the girls don't kill each other. The two oldest don't like the shoes Maura picked out for the bridesmaids, say they won't be able to dance in them at the reception. The other two say they don't look good in the dress style. It goes on and on."

"Don't let it interfere with you and Helen. Remember: Two of the hardest things on a relationship are weddings and canoe trips."

Gadzinski cleared his throat, reminding Jeff that he was waiting.

Jeff introduced his friend to the detective, who refrained from shaking Sam's tung oil-stained hands.

"The tub's back here," Sam said, leading the way to the back. "Maura's been as busy as a fox in a henhouse, so those bath fixtures are intact. Or, should I say, the grime *on* the fixtures." Sam leaned in, spoke quietly to Jeff. "I told her about your message, and what I figured it meant. I'll warn you, she's mighty upset that all this might cause a delay in finishing her house. Can't the detective take a sample and then release the fixtures?"

Jeff shrugged slightly. "I'll see what I can do, but you might as well be prepared for the worst."

"Maura should've been here by now," Sam said as he led the way past a showroom full of antique furniture and into a workshop that took up two-thirds of the large building. The back room smelled strongly of tung oil and turpentine, supported by the more subtle scents of wood stains and fresh shavings.

Gadzinski produced a crisp, white handkerchief from a pocket—if the previous night was any indication, Jeff suspected that the man carried a stash of them—and pressed it against his nose. "How do you keep from passing out from the fumes?"

"What fumes?"

"I didn't take a close look at these," Jeff told Gadzinski as they neared the fixtures. "We were working against the clock to move things out of the house."

The detective carefully lifted the plastic drop cloth that was draped over a clawfoot tub. "Promising." He took a ballpoint pen from his breast pocket and used it as a pointer. "See this? Looks like blood, all right." He opened a case—Jeff recognized it as the same kit he'd used at Verena Rose's home the night before—and retrieved the little gadget that had indicated that the blood on the living room floor was human. Now, he ran the same test.

"Well?" Jeff said.

"One and the same."

"What's going on?"

The men turned as Maura Carver walked toward them.

Gadzinski said, "Are you the one building the house?"

"Yes, I am."

"We'll have to take this tub in, ma'am."

"Take it in?" She looked from Gadzinski to Jeff and back again. "Where?"

"Headquarters. It's part of a murder investigation."

"How long do you have to keep it?"

"Hard to say."

"Well, can't you just determine whatever it is you need to determine, then give it back?"

"That's not how it works."

"You mean, I can't have it installed in my new house? But my wedding is in four weeks!"

"Sorry, ma'am."

Tears welled in Maura's large brown eyes, and Jeff saw that she was trying hard not to lose it in front of the three men. She held her hands up in an "I can't deal with this" gesture, then turned and rushed from the room.

Gadzinski made a call to arrange pick-up of the bathtub, then turned to Jeff. "Does your friend have a photocopier? We can Xerox that inventory, and I'll be on my way."

Jeff looked over at Sam, who was busy consoling his daughter. He didn't want to disturb them, and he'd been in the small office many times, so he knew that the Carvers wouldn't have a problem with his making himself at home. "It's back here." He led the way to the cubicle in the back corner.

After making a copy of the inventory and handing it to the detective, he took the man to the front door. "You should know, several pieces from the Rose property have been dispersed like this. As I recall, though, all of them were from the storage building." Jeff paused, then decided to throw in, as if in afterthought, "and from the kitchen."

"Is that all?"

"Maybe a few things from one of the bedrooms. An upstairs bedroom."

Gadzinski raised a brow. "Talbot, pretend for a moment that you're still one of Hoover's boys."

His jaw tightened. He didn't like the Hoover analogy but, in the interest of solving the case and eventually being able to return to business as usual, he let it slide. He nodded once.

Gadzinski flicked the sheaf of papers with a finger. "This is more organized than MacArthur's raid on the Philippines, which means you probably have flawless records of everything you've removed from the Rose property."

"Sure, I do."

"Where are they?"

He waited a beat. "In my car."

The detective sighed, checked his watch again. "Bring

them in and make copies for me. That way, I'll have an inventory sheet that I know hasn't been tampered with. When you leave here, put your training to work and gather up the loot. Attack it like you're rounding up the usual suspects. Take it all to the warehouse, and let me know when you're finished."

After Jeff had retrieved his briefcase and finished photocopying inventory lists, pages from his pocket notebooks, and the itemized receipt from Blanche, he straightened the papers and begrudgingly handed them to the detective. "I hope you realize that I want this case solved just as quickly as you do. It may sound mercenary, Gadzinski, but this is the same as my getting laid off without notice. Until you solve this thing, I'm *Scrooged.*"

"Do you think you're the only one? Somebody murdered an old lady, and *not* in a humane way, I might add. Once word travels, the people in town will be *demanding* that I put someone behind bars."

"It could be worse, Detective. They might be callous enough not to care that she's gone."

A flicker of what Jeff took as grim realization crossed Gadzinski's face before he turned and walked slowly out the door.

He watched the detective pull the sedan from the parking lot, then went to the back and told his friends goodbye. Thanks to Gadzinski's demands, he had a lot of work ahead of him—and not a damned bit of it was going to make him any money.

Chapter Fifteen

"GREER, MORE COFFEE, please?" Jeff said without looking up. He was seated at the small desk in the kitchen, reworking his Wednesday to-do list.

He had expedited his time by putting a call in to Blanche while he drove home from Sam's shop. The cell phone's headset was taking some getting used to, but he had to admit that it beat hunting down a pay phone.

He gave Blanche a thumbnail sketch of events and asked her to pull the inventory he had given her from the Rose property, then made arrangements to pick up the stuff after he returned from Nathan's arraignment. He also assured her that he would pay for the use of the warehouse. She had said that was the least of her worries—and should be the least of his, too, considering the complications he was dealing with.

When Greer didn't bring the carafe, Jeff looked around, then caught a glimpse of the butler through the tall windows near the back door. He was hurrying up the steps, packages in hand.

Jeff jumped up and opened the door. "I must have too much on my mind," he said. "I didn't even know you were gone."

"Did Miss Karen not tell you? She came down for a luncheon tray, and I asked her to inform you where I would be."

"Don't worry about it. She told me there was coffee for me down here, then she started talking to Sheila at ninety miles an hour, so I got out while I had the chance."

"Did she inform you of the decision about the alarm system?"

"No. What's up?"

"The missus believes she'll feel less panic without it. She also realizes that Miss Karen frequently goes outside at night."

"Thank God for small favors."

"Yes, sir," the butler said, with more fervor than usual.

Greer unpacked fresh produce into the refrigerator, then went back outside and returned with several more plastic bags full of supplies.

"We won't starve tomorrow, from the looks of all that."

"I'm glad to have gotten the shopping out of the way before the market becomes too crowded. Besides, I'm still restocking from the . . . incident."

"Right." Jeff recalled Sheila's insistence that all open foodstuffs be trashed after her kidnapping, so paranoid was she that something might have been poisoned. He wondered whether other people thought about that when the security of their home had been violated.

"Greer, I'm sorry that Sheila's withdrawal has put such a burden on you."

"It's not a problem, sir. I'm ashamed to admit that I'm out of practice where cooking and entertaining are concerned. If butlers were required to pass an annual exam, I would be out on my ear."

"I suspect, though, that there aren't too many butler-hiring households nowadays that have a chef in the family who oversees the kitchen."

"Yes, sir."

"You know, Blanche and Trudy would be happy to bring some dishes. Do you want me to call them?"

"Actually, I've already spoken with Mrs. Appleby, who left me no choice in the matter. And, Robbie offered to help. That is, if you don't mind."

"Not at all. I've told you from the start that I felt guilty asking you to work tomorrow."

"I'm looking forward to it."

"Is Robbie sure he wants to spend the holidays working? I'll pay him, of course, but—"

"He wouldn't hear of it, sir. He knows about Mrs. Talbot's situation, and he's happy to assist."

Although Jeff knew of Robbie's reputation as a stellar butler, he suspected that Robbie's primary motive was to assist Greer. Affection garnered generosity. "Well, Greer, I can promise you one thing: Your bonus will be sweetened this year."

"That's not necessary, sir."

"Whether you realize it or not, this place would fall apart without you. And I know damn well that Sheila would." Jeff didn't care if he had to cash in a mutual fund. He would never be so stupid as to risk losing the best butler in the country. In addition, he knew that Sheila wouldn't let just anybody in her kitchen.

He gulped the rest of his coffee, then filled a thermos to take with him.

While he headed toward the courthouse for Nathan's arraignment, his thoughts were split equally between two subjects: the problems and headaches that were sure to come with his discovery from the night before, and, more important, the fact that someone had killed an elderly woman.

Did Nathan's wife ever drop by to visit with Verena? Would she have taken the kids over there? In the summer, perhaps, when they could've played outside. Both houses were so crammed that there were only paths connecting one room to the next.

He tried to remember more about his encounter with the woman, but his memories weren't a comfortable place to visit. He had been guilty of labeling her, just like so many people did with the elderly. Then, just as quickly, he had dismissed her. The very fact that someone had murdered her told him that there was more to her life than he had originally considered. He was also aggravated with himself. He had been complacent, and he was a man who despised complacency.

Suddenly, he felt a true sense of loss. It might seem odd but, perhaps, it was because there apparently weren't that many people who *had* felt a loss over her death. At least, he perceived it that way, and realized that he needed to talk with Nathan more about this.

Granted, the detective's assignment to round up the loot would keep him busy—too busy, he hoped, to dwell on his personal problems, the stress at home from walking on unsure ground, the physical desires that must be squelched until Sheila was more like herself.

Chapter Sixteen

THE PARKING LOT of the Snohomish County Courthouse in Everett was dotted with orange construction barrels. After finally locating an empty space that would accommodate the woodie, Jeff hurried inside the building and slipped between the closing doors of the elevator. When he stepped off at the third floor, a woman standing near the water fountain across the corridor turned toward him.

It was Melanie Rose, he could tell from the resemblance to the little girl he had seen at the Rose house the afternoon before. This was the adult version, an adult version who was very pregnant.

Jeff calculated from the looks of her that this fourth child would likely arrive in time to boot the doll out of the manger at the local church's Nativity reenactment. The woman's chestnut hair was pulled up in a ponytail, and, combined with the bangs that brushed a high forehead over frightened doe-eyes, it made her look like a high-school girl who had been shunned by the world.

"Mrs. Rose?"

"You're Jeff Talbot, right?"

He spoke before she could lay into him again. "That's me. Let's see if we can get Nathan home in time to compliment your cooking tomorrow."

They took their seats in the courtroom as the guards escorted Nathan Rose past them and toward a table near the front. Melanie reached out and touched her husband's arm.

Nathan's expression held a mix of emotions: anger, fear, defeat.

The bailiff announced, "All rise for Judge Elizabeth Young," and Melanie grabbed Jeff's hand. He had heard about pregnant women and emotions, so he gave her free rein.

Judge Young was a woman with a harsh expression, one who appeared to have looked forty square in the face and told it to go to hell. Although she gave the impression of someone who had never let a man get close enough to expose her to pregnancy, Jeff detected a touch of empathy in the judge's eyes when she observed Nathan's wife.

But she also had a job to do, so one couldn't hold out hope for miracles.

"Mr. Rose, the body of your aunt will have to be exhumed for further investigation. I'm inclined to hold you, but the cemetery officials are working with a skeleton crew—pardon me. The supervisor gave his workers some extra time off for the holidays, and is unsure whether he can expedite the exhumation. Now, although Detective Gadzinski asserts that you stood to gain the most from Mrs. Rose's death, I—"

"Your honor?" Jeff stood. "That isn't necessarily true."

"Who are you?"

Jeff gave his name. "I'm an antiques picker now, but I used to be FBI."

"Approach."

Jeff approached. When he reached the bench, the judge asked, "Why, Mr. *Ex*-FBI, are you getting involved in this?"

"I bought the contents of Mrs. Rose's home from Nathan Rose. *Homes,* actually. There are two buildings. If he had wanted to make a huge profit from the property, he could have done any number of things differently—called in an auction house and appraisers, contacted specific collectors, even gone on-line and disposed of the contents himself. Instead, he simply wanted the places cleared out so that he could put up a prefab home for his family."

"Now *you're* the one who will make a huge profit."

"I'll make a living, and that will only be after months of work—moving, sorting, finding buyers."

"Why didn't Gadzinski arrest you?"

Why *didn't* he? Jeff wondered. He kept silent, hoping it was a rhetorical question.

The judge thumbed through the packet of papers in front of her. "Do you have an alibi for September 11?"

Who *didn't* know where he had been, or what he had been doing, on that day? He wondered whether it hadn't registered with the judge. "I was glued to my television most of that day, like everyone else. But, because of world events that occurred on that date, I remember some details. My refrigerator gave up the ghost, a repairman came to check it over, pronounced it a hopeless cause, and I had to go buy another one. I paid extra to have it delivered that afternoon, and I was home when it arrived."

"Why are you vouching for Mr. Rose?"

He thought, *you've got me,* but he said, "For what it's worth, he doesn't fit the profile. And, it'll be a real hardship on his family if he's not allowed to be with them tomorrow. You see, one of his children is in the hospital."

The judge arched a brow, looked first at Nathan, then at his representation. Jeff wondered whether the court-assigned attorney hadn't had brains enough to point out this fact.

Jeff recalled Nathan's chaotic schedule from when they had arranged to meet in September. He cultivated the seed of doubt that he had just planted in the judge's mind. "Nathan Rose is not a flight risk, Judge. If you'll check hospital records, you'll learn that this father visits his son at least once a day, sometimes more—that's in addition to working long hours at a demanding job. I remember that we worked around those hospital visits when we scheduled the meeting time to finalize my purchase of the buildings' contents.

"As you can see," he continued, "the man isn't planning on taking off."

Again, she looked at Nathan, then his lawyer. She turned back to Jeff. "How long ago did you leave the FBI?"

"Six years, your honor."

"Who was your next in command?"

"Gordon Easthope. He's still with the bureau, Chicago office."

"You have his number?"

He pulled the small notebook from the breast pocket of his sport coat, and gave her Gordy's cell phone number.

After she had scribbled it on a pad, she said, "I'll be back in two minutes. Nobody move."

Sure enough, she returned in two minutes and said, "The FBI thinks a lot of you, Mr. Talbot. I'm surprised you left."

Jeff remained quiet.

The judge straightened some papers and stuck them inside a folder. "Are you willing to put your money where your mouth is?"

"Your honor?"

"Will you take responsibility for Mr. Rose?"

He glanced at Nathan, then at the man's pregnant wife. The despair on their faces mirrored each other. And, Jeff firmly believed that it was genuine. He locked eyes with the judge and said, "Yes, your honor." But he thought, *What the hell am I getting myself into?*

"You may return to your seat."

Jeff walked back to his place beside Nathan's wife.

"Mr. Rose," Judge Young said.

Nathan quickly stood. "Yes, ma'am?"

"We have an alleged murder weapon, an item that purportedly belongs to you." She motioned to the bailiff, who brought the plastic-encased pole climber to her. She held it up, looked inquiringly at Nathan Rose.

"Yes, ma'am, that looks like mine. I tended to the maintenance of my gear—oiling the leather, sharpening and mending tools—while I sat and visited with Aunt Verena. It was a good way to kill two birds with one stone."

He paused and cleared his throat. Jeff wondered whether the man was thinking that he shouldn't have used the word *kill* when he had been charged with doing just that.

Nathan swallowed audibly before continuing. "Anyway, that day, Aunt Verena was glued to the television, so I was getting a lot of maintenance work done. But then the phone rang. It was my wife—" he turned and nodded toward the woman seated beside Jeff. "She said that Josh—that's our oldest—had just been put in the hospital. I didn't even think about my tools, Ma'am. I just ran to my truck and drove over to—up here to Everett. That night, I tried to call Aunt Verena, but I didn't get an answer. So, I phoned her next-door neighbor, told him what had happened, and asked if he would relay the message. He tracked us down at the hospital a few minutes later to tell us that—" he cleared his throat again—"that she was dead."

"When is your son expected to return home?"

"Hopefully by Christmas, ma'am."

"Go home, then. Go home, go to work, go to the hospital, go back home. Mr. Talbot has vouched for you. If you so much as dream about jumping bail, I'll have Talbot arrested and you hunted down. Do you understand?"

"Yes, your honor. I'm not going anywhere. Thank you."

The judge slammed her gavel against the block, then called Nathan's attorney to her chambers.

Jeff wondered if the apathetic court-appointed counsel was about to get a lesson in the fine points of defense.

As he watched the door shut behind the pair, someone called his name. He turned. Detective Gadzinski was walking toward him, wiping his hands on yet another pristine white handkerchief. Jeff wouldn't be surprised if the detective's home contained a sanitized physician's cabinet, with stacks of sterilized white squares in every drawer.

"Talbot, thinking this guy is innocent is one thing. But taking responsibility for him? You could choke on this one."

"Have you ever gotten a gut instinct about anyone, Detective?"

Gadzinski folded the handkerchief and tucked it into a breast pocket before staring at him. At length, he said, "Yeah, my partner."

Jeff waited, but Gadzinski didn't elaborate.

"And?"

"He put a forty-five caliber bullet in my back."

Jeff caught up with Nathan and Melanie Rose in the parking lot.

"Nathan, I know you want to get to the hospital, so I'll only keep you a minute. Can you think of anyone who would've wanted to kill your aunt?"

Nathan shook his head. "I've turned it over and over in my mind ever since that detective told me there was evidence of murder. Aunt Verena kept to herself, but I think that was just her way of coping. Not many people in town liked her, but they didn't keep it a secret, either. They had been snubbing her for years."

"Why was that?"

Nathan shrugged. "I guess they were a little afraid of her. Mom used to tell me that Aunt Verena went off her rocker after her son died in the war."

"What do you think?"

"Like I said, I think she found ways of coping."

"I can't say that we would do any better," Melanie added, "if we lost one of our kids."

Nathan put an arm around his wife's shoulder. "Aunt Verena was okay with not having friends, always said that she would rather *not* have them if it meant she'd have to put up with the likes of that stuck-up Mrs. Weldon."

"Is she half of that couple next door?"

Nathan nodded. "She *lives* to complain about her neighbors. Been that way ever since I can remember."

"You can be sure that Gadzinski talked to them. Question is, did he learn anything?" Jeff leaned against the woodie. "If any items were taken from the house, the authorities are going to have a heck of a time figuring out what they might have been. Excuse me for saying so, but both of those buildings are wrecks."

"That's okay," said Melanie. "That was our main reason for selling the stuff to you. With Josh in the hospital and two more kids at home and another one on the way and everything else"—her hands flew up in surrender—"I barely have time for the day-to-day, let alone the time or the energy to sort through that mess."

Jeff nodded his understanding. "Well, if someone had intended to loot the place, we would've seen evidence of several things missing. As you know, that wasn't the case. If they took something in particular, though, there's probably no way to tell what it was."

"What about something tiny?" asked Melanie. "Like jewelry, or coins, or . . . ?"

Jeff couldn't imagine that this woman in front of him hadn't gone in to see if she wanted anything of her husband's inheritance. He hadn't finished checking the jewelry boxes and caskets yet, but what he had seen so far didn't indicate that anything had been tampered with. "There again, I didn't find any evidence to indicate that but . . ." His voice trailed off.

"Needle in a haystack," Nathan said.

"That's pretty much it."

Melanie sighed. "Nate, we need to get over to the hospital."

Jeff told the couple good-bye, then said, "Let me know if you need anything, okay?"

"Thanks." Nathan extended his hand. "And thanks for whatever you said to that judge. Maybe I need to fire that jerk they assigned to me and hire you."

Jeff gripped the hand in his own. "I'll just plan on being around when you appear in court." Jeff added with a smile, "Try to enjoy your holiday."

He climbed into the woodie and headed south. He hadn't been on the road five minutes when it started sprinkling. He would be lucky if he got home before the holiday travelers clogged every strip of pavement from Canada to California.

Chapter Seventeen

JEFF TWISTED IN bed so that he could get a clear view of the clock on Sheila's nightstand. Twelve-fifteen. He looked with envy at his sleeping wife, at the same time wondering why he was the only one suffering from indigestion. Both had eaten his most recent kitchen creation for supper, which Sheila had not only stamped with an enthusiastic approval but also had named "Talbot's Three-Can Chili."

He had cooked up the quick and easy meal by opening three cans he had found in the pantry—one each of kidney beans (which he drained), Hormel's Vegetarian Chili, and Del Monte's Chili-Style Tomatoes. He hadn't told Sheila it was healthy, too, and saw it as a small contribution toward helping her cut back on calories.

Now, he suspected that he was being paid back for trying to do a good deed. Taking care not to disturb Sheila, he slipped out of bed, grabbed his robe and a roll of antacids, and headed downstairs.

He had to admit that he would rather be reading those letters he had stashed in the vault, anyway. They had been on his mind all evening, but he had felt a responsibility to spend time after dinner by helping Greer with some of the many last-minute preparations for the next day's feast. Greer wasn't one to accept assistance from his employer, but Jeff had persevered.

He opened the antacids and popped a couple into his mouth as he descended the main stairs, then made his way toward the back of the house. A sliver of pale light emanated from the dining room, illuminating the polished hardwood floor of the immense corridor. As he neared, he heard the soothing blend of two voices intermixed with the occasional light *clink* of silver and china coming from the room. It reminded Jeff of holidays past, when Sheila was typically the one who stayed up late to get everything in order for a holiday feast.

He slid back the pocket doors. This year, the blond-haired person working with Greer was not Sheila but Robbie.

Greer looked up from the ornate serving tray he was polishing, while Robbie, obviously unaware of Jeff's presence, continued talking.

Greer touched Robbie's arm slightly, and the young man immediately paused and looked toward the doorway. "My apologies, Mr. Talbot. I didn't realize."

Jeff waved him off. "No apology necessary, Robbie."

The butler's deep tan seemed out of place, but then Jeff remembered that Robbie had recently returned from a cruise he had been on with the family that employed him.

Greer said, "I'm sorry, sir. May I get you something? A brandy? Midnight snack?"

"No, thanks. I'm on my way to the basement to work on something."

"Yes, sir. Please let me know if I can be of any help."

"I'd say you're doing more than you should be already."

"Actually, sir, polishing silver is therapeutic."

Jeff sighed. "If things get any crazier, I may have to join you."

"Yes, sir," they said in unison.

He grabbed a Foster's from the fridge and went to the basement. While Verena Rose's basement was dank and unkempt, his was tidy and had areas that had been finished off. He retrieved the chiseled steel casket from the safe and took it to a nearby sitting area. He unfolded a letter and two old-style ten-dollar bills fell out of it. Curious, he read:

March 20, 1945

Dear Mom,

The socks arrived, but you shouldn't apologize for not knitting them yourself. Sure, lots of fellas get homemade things but we both know that you've never been domestically inclined. Which reminds me: I hope you're eating properly. I hadn't thought about how you relied on me to do all the cooking.

It's paying off, though. Now, I'm cooking for fifty or sixty at a time! It keeps me off the front lines. They don't give us much to work with, but I've promised the fellas I will make peach cobbler and apple pies for Easter. What I need for you to do is this: Dig out the recipes for those—you'll find them in the file box in the cabinet by the spices—send them to me pronto. Throw in a box of cinnamon, too.

Truth is, we'll be lucky as h— if we get a hot meal for the holiday. I won't lie to you, we've lost many men. And, the way they're moving us around, we'll be lucky if we're able to eat at all.

I don't know why you sent me this money. I'm doing swell and, besides, you'll need it for meals at the café. We both know that you can't cook, and I doubt you have grown a green thumb (not to mention a Victory garden) since I left.

Your son,

Andy

He didn't know what to think about this one, but when he imagined the same scenario happening between his Auntie Pim and himself, he suspected that Verena's feelings had been hurt over her son's refusal to accept her gift.

He slipped the letter back into its envelope, filed it in order, withdrew the next one, and read the tightly scrawled words.

After that, he thumbed through the few remaining envelopes, and noted that all the correspondence written by the young GI was in envelopes addressed to Verena Rose. None to a Mr. Rose. Jeff made a mental note to see if he could uncover any information about Andy Rose's father.

He was feeling an odd curiosity about the young man in the letters. He had heard others say that you could become quickly attached to these unknown soldiers, because of the candor many of them shared through their letters home. Eventually, the reading was like looking in on a weekly television show, like becoming familiar, even friendly, with a celebrity who doesn't even know you exist. But you have a vested interest, and you anxiously await the next installment so that you might learn what these acquaintances are up to.

Although he had recently picked up a book that contained wartime correspondence, he hadn't yet read it, so had never before looked at the war on a personal level. He found himself increasingly curious about the war years.

He wanted to learn more, not only about Verena's young soldier-son but also about that period of history. In a segment of the basement, he kept a small library of books on military—everything from the Civil War to Korea, with both world wars sandwiched between. Oftentimes, they had come in handy identifying and putting a value on collectibles such as uniform buttons, ammo, and weapons. He pulled a book of war letters from a shelf containing volumes about World War II, and read with fascination until his eyelids grew heavy.

When he checked the clock on the table next to his chair, he was amazed to discover that he'd been in the basement for nearly three hours. The beer bottle stood, half-full and warm, next to the clock.

He would have to save the rest of Private Rose's words for another time. After placing them back in the casket and returning it to the safe, he grabbed the beer bottle and wearily climbed the stairs.

It might be days before he could steal another block of time to read the rest of the letters and to go through the other boxes that were stowed in the garage. Already, he dreaded the busy times that were ahead. He should take all the boxes to the warehouse, and he would. In time. If the detective trusted him to transport them, then he shouldn't have a problem with them being stored here for a while longer.

He stopped at the dining room to look in on the butlers, but the room was now dark. He flipped the light switch, illuminating the warm wood moldings, period wallpaper, and ceiling with its salmon and wild game theme that had been painted when the home was built. Greer and Robbie had transformed the room with crisp vintage linens, gleaming bronze candlesticks, and antique china in autumnal colors. Every place was perfectly set for the next day's dinner. The massive table looked as if it had been lifted from the movie set of *The Age of Innocence*.

He made his way through the house, turning off lamps that lighted his way as he went. As he climbed the stairs, he thought about the coming weeks. So many things were out of sorts that, instead of giving thanks for what he had, he considered asking for a miracle. Or, two. But, since greed wasn't his nature, he gave up the notion when he couldn't decide which miracle to ask for.

CHAPTER EIGHTEEN

PRIMROSE TALBOT WAS turning in her grave. Jeff was certain of this fact as he opened the can of cranberry sauce and slid the gelatinous cylinder onto a plate. The barrel shape made a sucking noise as it pulled away from the can.

"Sorry, Auntie Pim," he said quietly.

"Sir?" The Talbots' butler paused mid-stride.

"Nothing, Greer. I was just thinking about Thanksgivings past."

"Yes, sir."

The Thanksgiving dinner was no doubt going to be different from any in the Talbot family's past. Only one of the November holidays had not been spent in the Victorian home in the last one hundred twenty years, and that was the year between the death of his spinster aunt Primrose Talbot and his meeting of the woman who would become his wife.

Greer moved on, quickly transferring a casserole dish

from the oven to the adjacent warming oven before checking on the turkey.

Jeff's stomach growled. The meal might not be what Sheila would've artfully prepared, but he had no doubt that it would be better than most that were being placed on tables across the country.

Or being dished up on plates for people who didn't have tables, he surmised as his thoughts turned to Gordy, now a widower who spent his Thanksgiving holidays working the food line of a soup kitchen to help feed Chicago's homeless.

Greer and Robbie worked well together, and Jeff didn't doubt that the two had put into play a detailed schedule as to who would be in charge of what. When Jeff had insisted on helping, Robbie had instantly handed him the tin of cranberry sauce and a can opener, and Jeff suspected that this, too, had been planned ahead.

Robbie was at the sink, peeling potatoes, while Greer sprinkled miniature marshmallows over a pan of sweet potatoes before moving to a work area crowded with bowls of various ingredients.

They had finally agreed to allow Blanche to bring her famous homemade hot rolls, a couple of pies—chocolate pecan and pumpkin—and a new recipe using tea that she wanted to try from a cookbook she had recently acquired. Trudy was to bring the appetizers and a couple of salads, and Jeff didn't think she could get there soon enough.

Karen popped into the kitchen and noshed her way around the perimeter. "Aren't there usually some appetizers on the sideboard in the dining room?" she asked, snatching a segment of raw potato from Robbie's workstation. She sneaked a hard-boiled egg from a bowl where Greer was assembling sage dressing, then grabbed enough tidbits from the relish tray that Greer had to follow her and rearrange everything.

Jeff wrapped cellophane around the cranberry sauce and balanced it on a can of soda in the fridge. If there were any leftovers, he didn't know where they would stash them. "Trudy's bringing the appetizers this year," he said. "She's riding over with Blanche."

"I'll *starve* before they get here." Karen started to filch another celery stick with a cream cheese concoction piped into it when the front doorbell rang. "Ooh! That must be them!" She shot out of the kitchen.

"Thank God," Greer said quietly. He raised his head suddenly, and looked wide-eyed at Jeff. "Did I actually say that aloud? I am so sorry, sir."

Jeff laid a hand reassuringly on the butler's shoulder. "If you hadn't said it, my man, I would have. I'll see if I can keep the brood out of the kitchen for you."

Greer's expression of relief was unmistakable.

Jeff walked through the house and out the front door to help unload baskets and boxes of food from the car. While the women carried crockpots and trays toward the dining room, he carted baskets with pies and rolls into the kitchen. After leaving the items with the butlers, he joined the women in the dining room.

Blanche said, "I told Trudy that she was overdoing it. Just look at all these scrumptious goodies." Blanche removed the lid from a crockpot that contained barbecued meatballs, then uncovered a silver chafing dish and looked at crab-stuffed mushrooms.

"I don't mind. I don't get to cook like this very often." Trudy, who usually seemed to shrink in Karen's presence, surprised everyone by saying, "Karen, you're going to love this." Trudy ladled a strange-looking mixture onto a small china plate and handed it to Karen.

Karen looked as if someone had just handed her a skunk. When the odor of the stuff hit Jeff, he understood why. It smelled as bad as it looked.

Trudy was nonplussed. She opened a bag of tortilla chips, plopped a handful on top of Karen's plate, then said, "Trust me."

Karen took a bite. "My God, you're right. This stuff is fantastic! Will you give me the recipe?"

Jeff laughed. "Don't waste your time, Trudy. It took Karen a week to figure out how to heat water in the microwave."

"That's not true." Karen followed Trudy and Blanche into the den. "What do you call this stuff?"

"It's sausage-broccoli dip."

Jeff liked those two ingredients, so he filled a plate and led his guests to the den. Macy's parade was marching loudly across the television screen; he used the remote to turn down the volume.

Robbie entered with a tray that held bottles of soft drinks and a tea service from Sheila's Autumn Leaf collection. He placed the tray on a credenza next to a drink station that had been set up earlier with a bucket of ice, antique tongues fashioned like eagle's talons, and a variety of glassware and cups and saucers. "Sir," he said to Jeff, "the pot contains spiced tea."

Jeff thanked the butler. The china, which matched that being used for dinner, had been a premium from the Jewel Tea Company for over forty years. He appreciated the vessel more than its contents.

"I'll have some of that tea." Blanche rubbed her hands together. "I feel a bit chilled today."

"Maybe I should make sure we closed the front door." Jeff set his plate on the coffee table, and poured Blanche's tea before walking to the foyer. The door was shut, but he was double-checking the lock when someone called his name from the staircase.

He looked up and saw Sheila perched on a step about halfway down the flight of stairs, her arms wrapped tightly around two of the banister's posts.

He tried to hide his amazement. As nonchalantly as he could, he said, "Hi, honey."

Slowly, he climbed the stairs and sat beside her. "You look nice. Is that a new sweater?"

She rubbed an arm of the sable brown chenille. "I ordered it in September so I would have it for today."

"Can't let it go to waste, then." He hugged her. "Trudy and Blanche just got here. They'll be thrilled to see you."

"I watched them come in."

"So, you've been here for . . ."

"Thirty minutes."

"That's good. How long did it take you to get this far?"

"An hour," she said, showing no more emotion than a newscaster rattling off the Dow Jones report.

"Not bad."

She took a deep breath. "Will you help me make it to the den?"

"You got it." Jeff wrapped an arm around her, and they both stood. As they stepped in unison down to the next stair, the doorbell rang.

Sheila froze. "No one else is supposed to be here."

"Wait right here, okay? I'll get rid of them."

"I can't." She licked her lips, and he knew from past experience that her mouth had gone dry. She spun and ran back up the stairs.

Jeff's irritation at the doorbell's effect momentarily clouded his perspective. But then, he remembered what Sheila's counselor had said. "Every step, *no matter how small . . .*"

As he descended the stairs, he counseled himself to be thankful for Sheila's attempt to join the group. He also debated cutting the wires to the doorbells.

He jerked open the door, and wished he'd thought of cutting those wires sooner.

Detective Gadzinski said, "Talbot? I hardly recognized you without the dirt on your face."

He stepped aside. "Come in, Detective."

"When I saw this place, I thought you'd given me the wrong address. Hell, you probably *do* have a butler."

At that moment, Greer walked hastily toward the pair. "My apologies for not answering the door, sir. I was removing the turkey from the oven when the bell chimed."

Jeff smiled. "That's fine, Greer. I'll take care of it."

Greer bowed slightly, then retreated toward the back of the house.

Gadzinski stood there with his mouth open.

"Is there a turkey missing, Detective?"

"What? Oh. Very funny." He cleared his throat. "I thought you'd like to know: The fellas went ahead and exhumed the Rose body last night. They decided to get it over with before the holiday rush. If it's not the suicides over seasonal depression, then it's all the overeaters who clog their arteries and stress their hearts."

Jeff wondered whether the detective realized he was

dangerously close to becoming one of the latter statistics. He was huffing and puffing, apparently from climbing the stairs up to the house, and his red face looked like the bubble on a thermometer.

"Anyhow," Gadzinski said, "The M.E. got to work on it early this morning. Probably trying to make himself look good after ignoring that trainee back when the old woman died. Or, I should say murdered, now that we have proof."

"So, the pole climber and the injuries match up?"

"No doubt about it. The trainee was right. She had a puncture wound on the top of her head that didn't match up with anything in the bathroom, and the DNA from the pole climber matches. That was her blood on the gaff."

"What about the killer? Any other DNA? Prints?"

"Found a partial that belongs to the nephew. What more do you want?"

"I want you to make sure no one else screws up like the M.E. did."

"It was a rhetorical question."

Jeff ignored him. "Has your lab checked for any other prints?"

"Yeah. Someone smudged up the metal pretty good."

"Doesn't that tell you something? Why would Nathan Rose smudge the murder weapon, then leave it at the scene of the crime? Especially when it belonged to him in the first place?"

"You've got a point. Whoever smudged the metal might not have realized that new technology is being developed every day for crime scene analysis. Right now, someone's working with Photoshop to separate latent prints from rough surfaces, like fabric, leather, materials like that."

"Photoshop?"

"I should've guessed that you're a luddite—antiques, butler, historic house."

"Get to the point, Inspector Gadget."

The detective gave him a long, warning look, then picked up the thread. "It's a software program from that little company called Adobe. You know, headquartered just east of Fremont Bridge?"

"Right."

Gadzinski stroked his jawline. "Maybe, though, Rose smeared it to make it *look* like he wasn't the guy." He looked up at Jeff. "Somebody did that on that TV show *CSI.* Came up with this elaborate scheme to cover the fact that he'd killed his mistress. Almost got away with it, too, except Blondie lucked out and—"

"Blondie?"

"The ex-stripper who's now an investigator. I can't keep their names straight."

"It's *fiction,* Detective."

"True enough. I just watch it for the new technology."

As if saying "technology" again triggered something, Gadzinski retrieved an electronic gadget from his pocket and punched a few keys. Jeff was just happy that it had gotten the guy back on track.

"Almost time for the first football game." The detective stowed the gadget. "I'd better go and see if the wife has turkey on the table. If I time it right, I won't have to listen to my mother-in-law for very long."

"Wait." Jeff grabbed at straws. "Did they check the leather straps on the pole climber, too? Not just the metal? And what about witnesses? Did you talk to the neighbors? Anyone who saw anyone else coming and going from the house?"

"Whoa. Are you sure you're not in the business anymore?" Gadzinski shook his head. "I'll make sure they checked the leather, of course. That's tricky, but there's some new technology that's pretty impressive for rough surfaces.

"My theory about witnesses," he continued, "is that anyone who *is* one also has the potential of being a suspect. Therefore, I've covered that facet.

"Finally, there weren't too many neighbors who had a clear view of the Rose place, what with all the overgrowth. I talked to a family across the street from the old lady's home this morning—a couple with three teenagers. Just listening to their schedules made me tired."

"Did their alibis check out?"

"Alibi, singular. They were scheduled to fly home from L.A. that morning. Finally got back here September 15."

"What did they say about their neighbors?"

"They don't take time to breathe, let alone take an interest in any of their neighbors. All they said was that they knew a 'crazy old bat' lived back there, and that an old couple lived on the adjoining property."

"Why would they notice the old couple?"

"Said that the old woman in that house jumps and runs to the window every time one of the kids pulls into the driveway. The Lake Stevens cops said she calls in complaints every week about those teens and their driving."

"Well, have you talked to her?"

"Tried to. Nobody's home. Probably gone to a relative's house where they can sit in the corner and be ignored."

"You have a healthy attitude about the holidays, Detective."

"Yeah, well, my own kids treat their grandparents that way, in spite of my lectures. It's a damned madhouse at my place today. Why do you think I'm taking a break to work on this case?"

Jeff didn't have much use for the do-as-I-say-not-as-I-do discipline. He considered pointing out to the detective that, perhaps, his own disregard for family on the holidays had influenced his children. Instead, he said, "Why, Detective, I thought it was your dedication to your fellow citizen."

Gadzinski grunted, then peered around Jeff. "Your place is pretty quiet."

"No kids."

"That explains it." Gadzinski snugged the cap back on his head.

"Happy Thanksgiving, Detective."

"Right." He hurried down the steps.

Jeff closed the door and returned to his guests.

Chapter Nineteen

As Jeff approached the entrance to the den, he heard Greer announcing that dinner was served. Everyone rose and moved toward the dining room.

"Jeffrey," Blanche said, "will Sheila join us today?"

"Actually, she came close." Jeff told the group about finding her on the staircase, and how the doorbell had scared her away.

"But it's an improvement," he concluded. "I expect to see her make some real headway over the next few weeks, especially since Christmas is her favorite time of the year."

As he took a seat at the head of the table, and each guest searched out his name among the place cards, Blanche said, "Jeffrey, I almost forgot. You were in the paper last night. Did you know that?"

He sighed. "Because of finding evidence of a murder, right? I wish they had left me out of it."

"They didn't." Blanche retrieved her purse, dug around

until she located a clipping. "Matter of fact, you're in the lead sentence."

She handed over the clipping, and he read aloud the short article.

> "The Lake Stevens Police Department reports that evidence of foul play was found last night in the home of Verena Rose by former FBI agent Jeffrey Talbot.
>
> Rose, who died on September 11 of this year, had lived in the home since 1931. She was 86.
>
> Snohomish County Sheriff's Office Detective Michael Gadzinski is assisting the Lake Stevens Police with the investigation. Gadzinski stated that the Rose body will be exhumed and turned over to the medical examiner's office so that concluding evidence might be determined in connection with the death.
>
> Nathan Rose, sole surviving relative of the deceased, as well as benefactor of her estate, has been arrested.

When he was through reading, Blanche said, "What do you think? Did he do it?"

Jeff looked up from the clipping. "From what I've seen, the man's not a killer."

Trudy, who was admiring the antique oyster plate in Greer's gloved hand—in spite of her obvious disdain for the slimy, shelled creatures that were hammocked in the plate's oval indentations—declined the butler's offering. "Isn't there some way you can help him?"

"Actually, he already has," Blanche said. "Jeffrey vouched for him in court yesterday."

"If you clear him," Karen said, "then you get your antiques back, right?"

"Always the mercenary, dear sister-in-law."

"That's not true. But everything else about the subject has been said. I know it's not your first priority, but it must be on your mind at some level."

"Sure. But only because it's such an intricate part of the

whole. I'm not sure what I can do, other than try to make sure the authorities don't railroad the guy."

"Sometimes, that has to be enough." Blanche slurped an oyster from its shell, tilted her head back, and allowed the meat to slide down her throat. Trudy turned away.

"Maybe," Jeff said, "but I have a feeling there's only one way to clear Nathan Rose's name."

"Which is?"

"Prove that someone else killed his great-aunt."

After a brief period of absolute quiet, the group spent the next several minutes filling their plates from the offerings brought around by Greer and Robbie.

Blanche was the first to break the silence. "So, Karen, where do you fly off to next week?"

Jeff had been wondering the same thing. Karen always lit out sometime during the week following Thanksgiving. One never knew whether she would end up in France or Fiji.

Karen formed a deep crater in her mashed potatoes and concentrated on Robbie's movements as he ladled gravy into the impression. "I'm staying through New Year's, actually."

Jeff almost choked on a bite of fruit salad. "How on earth did you get that much time off?"

"Oh, I quit." She looked up and blinked. "Didn't I tell you that when you picked me up at the airport?"

"No, you didn't." He wondered how this woman could be his wife's sister, and yet be so completely different in every way imaginable.

"I won't get in the way or anything."

"I'm not worried about that, and you know it. But how are you going to make a living after that?"

"Greer will feed me, won't you Greer?" she said teasingly, then her expression turned serious. "I've decided to freelance. I'm always getting offers from the other travel magazines, travel segments of food magazines, that sort of thing. Now, I can pick and choose where I work."

Blanche leaned toward Jeff and whispered, "Why don't you tell her about Mr. Bolton?"

"You know, you're right." Jeff filled Karen in on the new seaplane service.

When he was through, she looked thoughtful. Finally, she said, "Let me think about it."

Blanche spoke up. "I wouldn't waste any time, if I were you. He's a real go-getter." She winked at Jeff, then added, "For an old guy."

"Are you telling me that I should hurry, before he keels over?" Karen accepted a second helping of turkey and dressing from Robbie.

Jeff wondered how she could eat so much and stay so slim. "Heck, I'll probably keel over before he does. He might actually give you a run for your money."

Karen's expression was easy to read. That girl was always ready for a challenge.

"Karen," said Trudy, "we just got in some wonderful cameras at the shop. You might want to take a look."

"Really? You know, I've been interested in adding some more equipment to my arsenal. I'm thinking about buying one of those tiny, old Airstream campers and a pickup, and bumming my way around the West and Southwest, photographing working cowboys and dude ranches, stuff like that. Did you know that there are groups of people who still go on bonafide wagon trains, following the old trails? I'm thinking about trying my hand at some of the more artistic approaches, using older methods and equipment."

Blanche said, "I have a chicken-or-egg question for you. Which came first, your photography or your penchant for collecting cameras?"

"Oh, I'm not a camera collector. Matter of fact, I don't collect anything."

Jeff, who had been raising a glass of wine to his lips, stopped midair. "Give me a break, Karen. I damn near got a hernia from hauling all your equipment through the airport."

"So? That's just the stuff I need for my profession."

"I don't care what you need. I've seen your cameras, and I'll wager that there are more old ones than new ones."

"So? That doesn't mean I collect them."

"I don't run into many closet collectors, do you, Blanche?" Jeff gave her a wink.

The antiques maven took the high road. "What are your favorite cameras, Karen?"

"Oh, I don't know. It depends on the type of photography I'm doing. I like my Speed Graphic for certain black and white shots. Did you know that Rosenthal used a Speed Graphic for his image of the flag raising on Iwo Jima? I use a couple of different ones—Pentax, Nikon—for color shots, but the film is the thing on those. For the western journey, I want to add some of the wet-plate cameras from the turn of the twentieth century. I'll do a lot of sepia shots, like Edward Curtis used to capture the warm brown tones of Native American skin, and the dust and deerskin—"

"So, the older cameras tend to be better for the older-looking photos?"

"It's what I like."

"And, the newer ones are what you used for your last magazine job?"

"Not necessarily."

"So," said Blanche, "you're saying that most of your cameras are vintage."

"Well, they are, of course, but . . ."

Jeff grinned. He was enjoying watching his sister-in-law hang herself, and he decided to feed the group some more rope. "Don't you have some photographs *not* taken by Karen Gray? I recall a recent binge for Curtis prints, as well as Thomas Belden and F. Jay Haynes. That collection parallels your West by Southwest interest."

"Wouldn't you agree that it's smart to study those who captured that type of photography so well? Besides, they're so . . . appealing."

Trudy piped in. "We have several books that show the works of those photographers. Can't you just study those books?"

When Karen didn't have an answer, Jeff sat back and exhaled. "Face it, Sis. You're a collector."

Karen made a face, then asked Greer why it was taking so long to bring out the dessert.

During this feast (which was stretched over two sumptuous hours), between the small talk and the teasing, the catching up on one another's lives and the eating too much, the group scheduled visits with Sheila—each taking a turn and delivering one or two courses to the lady of the house.

Sam and Helen would stop by the house later, along with at least one or two of their daughters and their families. All of them would need the break, according to what Sam had told Jeff earlier: Maura and Darius had drafted the entire family to paint their new house on Friday.

Meanwhile, the Talbot traditions would continue. They would watch Chevy Chase's *National Lampoon's Christmas Vacation,* play Monopoly or Scrabble or both, check out a ballgame or two, and beat an endless trail to the leftovers.

Even now, as Jeff looked around the room at the small gathering of friends and family, he felt as if he were suspended between last year's warm memories, and those that he hoped next year would bring. But, for now, he was simply marking time until Sheila returned to her place at the hub.

Chapter Twenty

THE DOORBELL RANG and Jeff picked up his pace. He wasn't sure who would be visiting this early on Friday morning, and he knew that Greer would answer the door, but he wanted to head off any distractions that might interfere with his plans for the day. If he was going to have to generate income by applying strategies from Picker 101, then he needed every spare minute.

Lots of people would be home—couples cleaning out garages, guys tending toddlers and honey-do lists while their wives shopped the sales, grandmothers attacking in earnest the chores they wanted done before December company arrived in a few short weeks. Yes, it was a perfect day for picking: People would be home, and they would welcome the extra money for the holidays. He was surprised to realize that he couldn't wait to hit the road and see what kind of junk he might scare up. Finding treasure affected him the same as finding crooks: A certain thrill for the hunt got in his blood, and it stayed there.

He grabbed his wallet and checkbook, and kissed his sleeping wife lightly on the forehead.

Typically, the days following Thanksgiving found Sheila fulfilled, unpacking her vast collection of antique Christmas ornaments and decorations, decorating theme trees throughout the house, followed by baking, and baking, and more baking, until the kitchen and pantries and dining room looked like a bustling workshop for Santa's elves.

But not this year. Oh, she'd seemed a little more . . . relaxed . . . since Karen's arrival. And she seemed increasingly comfortable with her latest therapist, a female who went simply by Doctor Jen, and who not only came by the house twice a week but also visited with Sheila every night by either phone or E-mail.

Jeff had even heard Sheila's end of the conversation a few times and had noticed that she sounded like she used to when she talked with friends. It was an encouraging sign. Still, the only move she had made toward leaving the second floor of the house, or executing any of her traditions, had been the start down the stairs the day before.

Jeff opted not to push. The most important thing, obviously, was her health. But, in all honesty, he had to admit that he wouldn't mind some breathing space between the two holidays, for a change.

He descended the stairs, anxious to get going, when a sharp, fresh scent hit his nostrils. A moment later, he saw the parade of freshly cut Christmas trees being brought trunk first through the double front doors.

Even though he had been thinking about Sheila's normal post-Thanksgiving activities, he had completely forgotten that the trees would arrive *today*. They were a standing order, and Sheila typically spent every waking minute of the three days following Thanksgiving decorating them.

One of the four delivery men—Jeff recognized him as the ramrod of the operation from years past—sent two teenaged workers out for the garland, then he and the remaining worker checked tags on the trees and started dispersing them among the rooms.

Jeff watched as they lifted the twelve-foot Douglas fir and carted it toward the front parlor, where it would be placed in front of the turret's large windows. If the teens thought they had the easier job, they'd be surprised. Sheila always ordered enough garland to swag the home's five fireplaces and to wrap around as many staircase banisters.

If he hadn't been so stressed lately, he might have had Greer cancel—which made him wonder why Greer hadn't pointed out the impending arrival.

As if reading his employer's thoughts, Greer said, "My apologies, sir. Since the missus always sees to the details of the trees, it didn't occur to me that we might not need them this year."

Jeff sighed. "I didn't think about it either, Greer. But maybe the scent will stir something in her, and she'll decide to decorate. At any rate, we might have made things worse if we had canceled her order."

"A good point, sir." Greer excused himself, and set about making sure that the trees went to the right rooms.

Jeff snaked his way around the trees and made his way to the breakfast nook. He didn't care for the dark colors Sheila had imposed on the little alcove, but, since it faced east, it was more apt to offer light than the dining room on the opposite side of the house.

After pouring a large mug of coffee from the service Greer had set up on the butler's table, he skimmed the classifieds in both the *Times* and *Post-Intelligencer* for anything that looked promising.

He had recently subscribed to the *Puyallup Herald* as well, after discovering some real finds at the antiques expo held at that town's fairgrounds. Lately, he had heard several complaints from people who didn't think they could do any good at antiques shows, but he had proven them wrong. If you have a basic knowledge, and a few bucks for speculation, then you might net a considerable return by investing a few hours at a weekend show.

His most profitable find during his last visit to that show had been an early Wedgwood bowl. When he first started picking, he learned that the general public thinks of the popular blue-and-white jasperware when they hear Wedgwood, the name of the company founded by Josiah Wedgwood in the eighteenth century. Or some are familiar with drabware, which shot up in price when Martha Stewart mentioned that she collected it.

He knew why he had been able to purchase the tiny bowl for three dollars. Everyone had assumed it was a fake. The piece was glazed, not matte, with a brightly colored design on a white ground, and the mark was a rusty red stamp as opposed to an impression made into the base. He had taken it to a resident expert and had learned that it was one of the earlier pieces made by the company. And he had sold it the next day for fifty times what he had paid.

Now, he worked quickly, circling in red the estate and garage sales that he wanted to check out. After folding the sections and tucking them under his arm, he hurried toward the back door, grabbing the thermos of coffee that Greer had waiting for him in the usual spot on the countertop.

Five hours and thirteen home places later, Jeff was tired, and his clothes were spotted with sprinkles of rain. It made him think of Auntie Pim's ironing day, when she would dip her fingers in a bowl of water, then liberally sprinkle the clothes before pressing them. Now, he felt as if both his clothing and his body needed a good, hot pressing.

He drove cautiously along the winding state highways, his destination one of the antiques shops in Snohomish. He hoped to turn a nice profit on the sterling smalls he had bought from a young couple trying to make money for a trip to Cancun. As he pulled down the alley, he saw Tinker's run-down, dark blue pickup backed up to the double doors.

Tinker and a young man were unloading a primitive jelly cupboard from the truck.

"Need a hand with that?" Jeff called out to them.

Tinker jumped as if he'd been shot. Then his face registered recognition. "My grandson and I can manage without the likes of you."

"The likes of me?" It had been—what?—three days since Jeff had seen Tinker, and the older man never let on that anything was bothering him then.

"What the hell are you doing up here, anyway, a nosin' around my territory? Ain't it enough that you got that Rose woman's loot?"

Territory? Jeff paused. He hadn't been a picker nearly as long as Tinker, but he wasn't about to work like an Avon lady with a mapped out sector.

"I had been working on that old bat for *years,*" Tinker went on, "trying to get her to let go of some of that horde. Then you swoop in like a friggin' vulture and take the whole damned lot of it."

"That's not how it happened."

"Yeah? Then how *did* it happen?"

"You're overstepping your bounds," Jeff said evenly.

The old man grunted. "I didn't figure you'd tell me anything, but I'm gonna tell you something. A lot of us pickers didn't get any mansions handed to us on polished platters. We get out and work our asses off just to make ends meet. You'd better watch your step, and you'd better stay the hell out of my part of the woods. Now get out of my way. Some of us has got a living to make."

As Tinker and the kid hauled the cupboard through the propped-open doors, the old picker said, "Kyle, you bring the truck around front while I get my money for this stuff."

Jeff knew that anything he said, any explanation he offered, would sound lame. He stepped aside and watched Kyle pull the truck away from the doors.

Tinker's attitude told him one thing: The guy was having a harder time making ends meet than he had first suspected when they had seen each other at Blanche's shop a few days before Thanksgiving.

He never liked learning that people in his profession were having a hard time, and it was something he heard more and more. A heightened awareness of the possibility that there were treasures to be found in every attic, basement, and storage building had made every picker's job more challenging.

But there was something else bothering him a lot more than that: Tinker had known the victim.

Did it mean anything? He couldn't be sure. Had Detective Gadzinski found out this important (and, potentially crucial) piece of information? He would call him and let him know, just in case.

But any question that he—or anybody else connected to the case, for that matter—might have led back to the one problem with the entire investigation: Why would anyone, especially someone like Tinker, kill the Rose woman, then leave without stealing anything? Had he been scared away before he could take anything? If so, would he have tried to return later for the loot? Or, had he hoped that he could stage her death to look like an accident, with some preconceived idea, or promise, that he would be contacted by the benefactor upon the event of the old woman's death? Of course, there was also a chance that Tinker had called Nathan after reading Verena's obituary in the paper—and had been turned down. And, finally, there was the chance that Nathan didn't even know about Tinker, or his attempts at buying Verena's belongings.

He glanced at his watch. He wasn't too far from Nathan's house, and he didn't have anything better to do with the rest of his afternoon. At least he might get an answer to one of his questions—the last question in a whole string of them that needed answering.

After conducting a quick business deal with the shop's owner for the silver items he had acquired earlier, he headed toward Lake Stevens.

Chapter Twenty-One

No one was home at Nathan's place, and Jeff realized that they had probably taken the rare opportunity to visit Josh in the hospital as a family, as opposed to breaking it up into shifts.

He drove around the lake, through downtown, then a little beyond, toward the old woman's place. He wasn't sure why he was compelled to go by there, but before he completely realized it, he was parked at the curb near the end of her driveway. He settled back to look at the houses, plan his approach if and when he regained access to their contents. He bristled at the sight of the police caution tape: The bright yellow was as good as announcing that the buildings were vacant and the contents were there for the taking. He counseled himself not to worry about it; the buildings had been empty since September, and no one had bothered anything inside them yet.

As he scanned the neighborhood, with its older, clapboard houses that haphazardly dotted the hilly landscape, he was continually distracted by activity across the street. Four cars in as many minutes pulled into the driveway and back out again, the teenagers in them whooping and spinning bald tires on the wet pavement. These, he decided, were the kids that the detective had been referring to.

He saw a movement in the sliver of light that shown at the picture window of the modest home that adjoined the Rose property, and focused just in time to catch a glimpse of an old woman's face.

He remembered Gadzinski's mentioning an old couple that he hadn't gotten to question, and Jeff wondered now whether he had been back to try again. He also remembered meeting the old man on the Saturday when he had worked at the Rose property with Sam, Maura, and Darius. Now he tried to recall the man's name but couldn't get it to surface, despite the fact that Nathan had mentioned it only two days earlier.

He climbed from the car anyway, and went to the front door, hoping the man would recognize him. He rang the bell and waited.

As the elderly man opened the door, a woman—Jeff recognized the face from the window—hurried toward them.

He hadn't planned what to say, but, as it turned out, it didn't matter.

The woman was thin and made up of jagged edges and sharp points, except for the bouffant hairstyle. When she elbowed the man aside, Jeff was tempted to check whether she had cut him.

"It's about time you showed up!" She peered at him through large glasses. "I've been calling about those hoodlums across the street all morning!"

"Erma, leave him alone. He's not a cop."

"And how would you know that?"

"Because he's the fella who bought Verena's stuff from Nathan a few months back."

Jeff introduced himself to the woman. "I'd like to visit with you about your neighbor, Mrs. Rose."

"Mrs?" the woman said sharply. "*That's* one word that was never attached to her name."

The old man sighed. "Erma, would it hurt you to show some respect for the dead?"

"She did nothing to *earn* my respect, Mr. Weldon." The woman wheeled and disappeared into the house.

Weldon, that was it. Jeff said, "Mr. Weldon, if I could have just a moment."

"Sure, son. Let me grab a coat, and we'll sit on the porch."

Before Jeff could warn him that it was too cold to stay out for very long, the man had retrieved a coat from a hook beside the door and was snugging into it as he limped out to the porch. Jeff figured the old guy probably came out here a lot, just to get away from his wife's caustic tongue.

"Sad news about Verena," the man said after they'd taken seats, "but she was getting up there." He shook his head. "I shouldn't say that too loudly. She only had ten or twelve years on me."

"Were you neighbors very long?"

The man chuckled, a sort of *heh-heh-heh* that sounded as if he was trying to reserve energy. "I grew up right here in this house, stayed on with Mother when my father went overseas during The Good War, as they're calling it.

"It was a tough time to live through," he continued. "You ever been to war, young man?"

"No, Mr. Weldon, I haven't."

The man scowled, and Jeff suspected he was being judged until the man said, "Call me Marty. I hear *Weldon* too much as it is." He jerked his frail, white-fringed head toward the house. "I didn't serve, either. I've had this limp since I first learned to walk, so I stayed on the homefront and kept working at the theater downtown. I had been there for years, doing everything from selling tickets to threading reels onto the projector to sweeping the lobby after the last show.

"Anyway, back then there didn't seem to be a shortage of soldiers. Damn near everybody signed up: singers, movie stars, young, old. You don't see that today. And they weren't as strict about being of age back then. Lots of fellas lied about their age so's they could join the war." He waved a hand toward Verena's house. "Her son was no different."

"Was he a friend of yours?"

"Nah. A few years' difference when you're that age is a world, you know. He thought he was hot stuff, anyway, always mouthing off to her, showing no respect. It broke her heart, I could see that. She might've gotten herself in trouble, but she raised him, worked hard to do a proper job."

"So, you married, and your wife moved in here with you?"

"That's right."

"How long ago was that?"

"Let's see . . . fifty-six years ago. Got married in forty-five." He pointed a gnarled finger at Jeff. "Don't you go tellin' her I had to calculate. I'd never hear the end of it."

"She won't get it from me."

"You're a good boy." He patted Jeff's arm.

"Did you know that there's evidence of murder?"

The old man's eyes widened, and his jaw dropped slightly, but then he quickly regained his composure, and shook his head. "No. No, I hadn't heard that."

If this old man was telling the truth, then it meant that Gadzinski hadn't been around yet to question the couple. "Did you ever see anyone hanging around over there?"

"Maybe I jumped the gun when I told Erma that you weren't a cop. You're beginning to sound just like one."

"Sorry. Old habits die hard. I used to be one. Now, I'm interested in finding out who would've brought harm to your neighbor."

"I can't imagine why anyone would. Admittedly, there weren't many people who would have anything to do with her. You see, she went a little loony after her son died. On the other hand, she didn't bother anybody, didn't stir up trouble or anything. There was hardly ever anyone over there, except for Nate, of course. He's a good boy, too, that one. Did her grocery shopping for her, drove her to doctor appointments, such as that."

"What about Nathan's wife? Did she come around much?"

"It was a rarity. But she's got a passel of kids. The missus and I never had kids, but from the looks of the family across the way—" he pointed toward the house where Jeff had earlier observed all the activity—"one or the other of 'em is always having to be somewhere else.

"Anyway, I don't think Nate's wife was bringing slight to Verena, and the old gal never judged her for it. She was proud to see that Melanie was a fit mother."

"You said that Verena Rose was a good mother, too?"

The old man twisted in his chair and looked Jeff square in the eye. "Not a doubt about it, son." He sat back and added, "You'll hear otherwise. Don't pay it no mind."

"Really? Why the split school?"

Before Jeff could get an answer, the front door opened with a jerk. "Mr. Weldon, your dinner will go in the trash if you don't get in here and eat it so I can clean up the dishes." The old man's wife shut the door.

"Sorry, son, but if I don't eat, I won't have the energy to put up with the woman." He sighed heavily and rose from the chair.

Jeff fought asking him why he *had* put up with the woman all these years, but it was none of his business so he kept quiet.

Weldon seemed to sense the question. "I was a rascal in my day, young man. You've heard the expression, 'You pay for your raisin'?' Well, mark my words, you pay for your grazin', too."

He started to open the door, then paused. "Erma goes to the beauty shop every Thursday afternoon without fail. Come around again, if you have the time." He gave Jeff a pointed look.

"Thanks, Marty, I'll do that."

Chapter Twenty-Two

LUCK WAS WITH him, and that afternoon he purchased a hodgepodge of furniture for next to nothing—both primitive and country pieces (the primitive being more crudely made than the country): three little pine hutches; a maple rocking chair—Shaker craftsmanship, if he wasn't mistaken—and a couple of rope beds, also Shaker, that were stored in a smokehouse adjacent to an old frame farmhouse.

The guy who sold him the stuff had been thrilled to do so. He had said his wife was always complaining about the clutter and that she wanted it cleared out. With Jeff's offer, the man could, as he put it, "get rid of the junk, *and* recoup some of the money she's out spending on Christmas presents for grandkids who already have more toys than their parents have sense."

Jeff hauled it all to Blanche's in five trips, with a bonus that the guy threw in with the last load: a dilapidated cardboard grab-bag box full of what looked like sewing supplies.

He left the box with Blanche while he unpacked the beds, and when he returned, found her with a jeweler's loupe screwed to her right eye and an absolutely sparkling brooch in her left hand. Scattered across the desktop were spools of craft ribbon and cards of seam tape and ric-rac. Directly in front of Blanche, however, was a jumble of jewelry: screw-back earrings, brooches in every design and shape imaginable, and enough Christmas tree pins to rival the real trees that had been hauled into his house that morning.

Blanche plucked the loupe free and swept her hand in a grand gesture over the display. "All this was stashed below the sewing notions. Jeffrey, it's a potential fortune."

"In other words, they're all signed."

"Every one of them, from Eisenberg's Swarovski crystals and Christmas trees to Coro's enameled birds and whimsicals from the thirties to Miriam Haskell's horseshoe-marked pieces that are bringing a fortune right now. Also Marcel Boucher, Schiapiarelli, Hattie Carnegie—it's simply amazing."

"You know as well as I do, Blanche: Most people don't have a clue that they should look for a mark on costume jewelry."

"Even if they did," she said, "most of them wouldn't be caught dead wearing 'grandma's junk jewelry.' But it's fast becoming *the* thing, and this group is just in time for the holidays. I don't have to tell you, it'll sell like mad."

She began punching keys on her adding machine, working faster than a ticker tape, then ripped out the paper and looked it over. She jotted a figure on a notepad, and handed it to him with a question. "Fair enough?"

"*Generous* is the word I would use."

"You've been my best picker this year. Consider it a Christmas bonus."

He bowed slightly, and she grabbed a checkbook while his own mental calculator told him that he had made enough profit on the day's finds to cover his upcoming insurance premium on the woodie. Coverage for a classic car was a killer bill.

She handed him the check, and he put it in his wallet without looking at the amount. "I guess I'd better get that Rose property moved over to the warehouse. Sorry I have to pull inventory from you, especially during the holidays."

"It's certainly not your fault." Blanche sipped tea from a cup with a holly berry motif. "Any new developments in the case?"

"Not that I've been told. But I hope they turn up something soon. I don't know how much of the *real* picker's life I can handle. I'm beat."

Blanche laughed and started to say something, but her phone rang, so they exchanged quick good-byes and Jeff headed back toward the loading dock.

After hauling three loads of antiques from the shop to the warehouse down the street, he emptied the dehumidifier, then started toward home.

Although it had been a financially successful day, it had been a long one, too. Now all he could think about was a hot shower and even hotter coffee. And, maybe a little Kahlua; he had earned it.

He climbed the stairs, uncomfortable in his damp clothes, his joints aching, and opened his bedroom door.

There, he found Sheila and Karen curled up in bed with Ben and Jerry.

He didn't have to read the label on Sheila's ice cream carton to know which flavor she'd chosen. Cherry Garcia was her favorite. He glanced at the container in Karen's hands and learned that she was a fan of New York Super Fudge Chunk.

"If I didn't know better," he said, "I'd say you two haven't moved since I left this morning."

"Uh-huh," Sheila said around a mouthful of ice cream. She didn't look at him, but, rather, at the television screen where Hector Elizando was setting containers of food on a table surrounded by women.

Jeff walked through to his dressing room, grabbed his velour robe, then walked back through toward the bathroom. "Didn't you just watch that movie? I seem to recall that scene from—when? Yesterday?"

Karen rolled her eyes. "And two hours ago. My nutty sister rewound it and started it over."

"It's *Tortilla Soup.* My new favorite."

"Look at these." Karen held up a stack of videos, and read the names off the spines like she was announcing race horses. "*Big Night, Babette's Feast, Like Water for Chocolate.* It's bad enough they're all foodies, but she keeps watching that one"—Karen pointed at the television—"as if the outcome's going to change." She emptied the ice cream carton, then plopped it onto a silver tray on the nightstand. "I swear, she's obsessed."

"No, I'm not. Sometimes I like to do something just because I *can.*"

"Ah," Jeff said knowingly. He had been subjected to Sheila's occasional obsession with a certain film, and more than once had been in Karen's shoes—or, side of the bed, as it were.

He noticed, though, that his ever-adventurous sister-in-law was already beginning to show signs of restlessness. He crooked a finger and beckoned her to follow him. Once they were in the dressing room, he slid the seaplane business card from the top of his bureau and handed it to her. "You know, it's only been a few days since this Max Bolton said he needed a photographer. Why don't you give him a call?"

She grinned at once, and her gold tooth twinkled. Just as quickly, the smile faded. "But what about Sheila?"

"She won't care. Really. Matter of fact, it might actually help her. You know, remove some of the comfortable crutches that are keeping her cooped up in the bedroom."

"Do you really think so? I mean, I've loved playing hooky, but I can only take a few days of this couch potato game. Plus, it's starting to hit me that I quit my job. Freelancing is going to take more work than I first realized."

"I can vouch for that." He laid out a pair of corduroy

trousers and an old pullover sweater. "You have to keep at it."

"Yeah, and you look as if it's already wearing you down." She absently scraped the card against the palm of her hand. "Maybe, if I'm gone during the day, I can offer to help Sheila decorate the trees at night."

"You hate decorating."

"Yeah. But I'd do it, if it meant getting her out of that bedroom."

"I appreciate that."

"I think she's ready, you know. I heard her tell her therapist over the phone that the scent of the Christmas trees had her absolutely itching to decorate, but that she hasn't been able to make herself go downstairs."

"So, the test will be whether the doctor can come up with a way to get her past that."

"Seems to be. Her desire to get back to normal has probably been building for the last couple of weeks; she just didn't realize it until something triggered it."

"I've thought so, too. Expected, really. Her M.D. said that the response to antidepressants is gradual. Hopefully, this Doctor Jen will come up with a plan of attack tailor-made for Sheila."

"Maybe she already has. Sounds like she's using a one-two punch: cognitive-behavior therapy with biofeedback. But the key, I think, is that Sheila found someone she feels comfortable with."

Was that *it?* He wondered. More than anything, he wanted his wife to get well. It seemed a little far-fetched, though, that it might boil down to something as simple as how comfortable she felt with her doctor. He opened the bureau drawer where his socks and underclothes were stored, then turned. "Karen, does it bother you that she wasn't comfortable enough with either of us?"

"You mean without the doctor? God, no. You and I both have had a lot of training in our work. Your FBI training included the antiques world, and my photography includes experience in travel. Add to all that our survivalist training for fieldwork. None of it, though, is a match for the psyche."

"I suppose you're right." He shivered, then wished he had shed the damp clothes as soon as he'd gotten home. "I'm glad you told me about her talk with the doctor, though, because I have an idea for something that might tie in. It could jar her into action by way of a distraction."

"Really? What is it?"

He paused. "Let me run it past her first, before I get anyone's hopes up."

"You mean, it's something we'll all like?"

"No." His grin was mischievous. "Actually, you'll hate it. But that hasn't stopped me before."

Karen held up the business card. "In that case, I'd better make this call and see if I can drum up something to get me out of the house."

Jeff followed his sister-in-law back through the bedroom. The only indication Sheila gave that she was aware of their presence was a slight shifting in order to see the television around them as they walked past.

Chapter Twenty-Three

After he showered, he wrapped himself in the heavy robe and joined his wife in their room. Fortunately, he caught her as the movie's credits finished rolling. He stretched out on his side next to her, tucking a pillow under his head for support. "When is your sister going to get that tooth fixed?"

"After Christmas, I think," Sheila used the remote to mute the TV. "She says it looks festive."

"That's one way to see it, I suppose."

"Do you want to watch a movie with me?"

Although they had had a standing date for Friday night movies ever since Sheila had become housebound, he didn't know if he could sit through another food movie. "How about *White Christmas?* or *Jingle All the Way?*"

"It's still November, and *you're* going to watch a Christmas movie? Yeah, right."

"Hey, I watched one last night."

"Chevy Chase on Thanksgiving doesn't count. It's just sort of *there,* in the background."

"Well, it's not that I don't want to watch them. It's just that—" How could he say it? "—once you do, you're committed. Everything is Christmas after that."

"Okay, sure. If you're willing to watch a Christmas movie, then I am, too."

"You are?" He made no attempt to hide his astonishment.

"Why do you act so surprised?"

"Because I didn't think you would upset your food pyramid."

"Ha, ha," she said flatly, then handed him the movie inventory notebook she kept in her nightstand.

He thumbed through the segment on holidays. Nothing called to him, so he picked one of her favorites. "How about *It's a Wonderful Life* at eight o'clock?"

"It's a date."

He handed her the notebook, and after she had put it away, he said, "I told you about Nathan's wife and kids, didn't I?"

"Three kids, a fourth on the way. Wife's name is . . ."

"Melanie."

"Right."

"I have a feeling they're not going to have much of a Christmas. You know, with their oldest coming home from the hospital soon, and the mother due to deliver around the same time, and the fact that they didn't get to build their new house in time for the holidays." He took a deep breath, then continued. "Well, I was wondering . . ."

"You want to invite them here for Christmas dinner?"

"That's part of it, yeah."

She turned and looked at him. "What's the other part?"

"*Parts,* actually. Christmas isn't built in a day, you know." He grinned. "If you agree to inviting them, then we need to make it a special Christmas for them, right?"

"Jeff, don't tell me you're going to wear a Santa suit."

"God, no. I think we can pull this off without my resorting to any nonsense." He repositioned himself so that he could see her reaction. "I think it'd be nice if you did some on-line shopping, so the kids would have presents to open while they're here. Would you be willing to do that?"

She sat up and leaned her head back against the headboard. "A few days ago, I would've said no way. I couldn't bring myself to even think about going up to my office, even though I can't stand the thought of being on the phone with the catalog companies. But today, Doctor Jen came up with the best idea. She's going to move my computer down here from the third floor."

His instinct was to ask whether the doctor shouldn't be coming up with a plan to get Sheila back to her computer room upstairs, but he didn't want to upset his wife by saying so. Instead, he asked, "I wonder why we didn't think of that?"

"Probably because we've been tying everything together, like one big package that contains an emotional bomb. Doctor Jen says I'll gradually get back to normal if I untie the package and separate it into segments. That way, I take a segment of something I used to like—in this case, my computer—and put it in a place where I'm comfortable, like our bedroom."

He turned all this over in his mind and, on the surface, agreed that the concept made sense. At the same time, he hoped that Sheila wouldn't become fixated with the computer, and end up using it as a substitution for other things. Of course, one could argue that she was doing that now with the food movies. He was toying with the idea of sneaking some romance flicks into the sleeves of the food films, in hopes that she would become interested in *that* part of their bedroom life again, when she interrupted his fantasy.

"You haven't said what you think, Jeff."

He cleared his throat, stalling for time while he got his thoughts back on track. "You know, I think it just might work."

They were quiet for a moment before he said, "So, what do you think of my idea?"

She repeatedly flicked a button on the remote, watched the red light blink on and off. "I'll try."

"Good." He took her hand in his and kissed it. "You

know what else we could do? Invite the kids over early, let them help decorate the trees, and make some cookies, maybe even wrap a few presents. I don't know whether Melanie has been up to much baking, that sort of thing."

"Oh. I hadn't thought about my antique ornaments and . . . and *children.*"

"Do you think that's a problem?" Jeff tried to maintain an innocent tone, so his wife wouldn't realize he was leading her to a productive conclusion.

"That's a stupid question, coming from you. I don't mean to sound like Cruella DeVille, but many of my decorations are over a hundred years old. You of all people should know that antique Christmas ornaments are getting more and more scarce—and you want to turn them over to a bunch of *kids?*" By the time she had finished, her voice was a good octave higher than normal.

"Okay, okay. I know that there are ways to involve a kid without handing him a German Kugel worth several hundred bucks." He didn't keep up with Christmas ornaments—he had always consulted her when he came across them while picking—but he suspected that the large, glass Kugel bells and strawberries and clusters of grapes topped her list for value and rarity.

Sheila brightened. "How about this? What if I come up with a way to get all the trees decorated but one? Then, you can pick up some new ornaments the kids would like—snowmen, candy canes, I don't know—and they can decorate that last tree when they get here Christmas morning."

"Fair enough." He knew he had been manipulative, but he felt that it was in Sheila's best interest. Fortunately, her reaction told him that Karen was right: She *was* ready to take the next step toward normal, and this nudge proved that she was willing to start trying.

She clicked the TV remote and the screen went black. "Doctor Jen suggested that I could stay in one room on Christmas, like the kitchen, for instance. What do you think?"

"That actually sounds like a good idea."

"I thought so, too. That way I could do the cooking, if

you wouldn't mind keeping everyone from inundating me while I'm in there."

"That's doable."

"And, I'll need for you to talk to Melanie, and find out what the kids want, or need, or . . . well, however she wants that done."

"Not a problem." At least, he *hoped* it wouldn't be a problem. He knew that the Roses were proud people and that he would have to persuade them to let him and Sheila do this. That should be easier than what he had just accomplished, because, although it would be tremendous therapy for his wife, he had had to operate with an ulterior motive.

He dressed, then used the phone line normally reserved for the Internet to call Nathan and Melanie. Getting them to come for Christmas took some doing, but, finally, he had their approval, along with the promise that Melanie would provide a detailed list of items for the kids. If Sheila didn't know what a kid might want to decorate a tree with, then he knew they would all be happier if she had specific guidelines where presents were concerned.

After all that was taken care of, he said, "Nathan, I ran into a picker today who goes by the name of Tinker. Have you ever heard of him?"

"Yeah. Matter of fact, I've seen him a time or two over at Aunt Verena's. He used to bug her every few months, try to get her to sell him stuff."

"Did she?"

"No, and she told me not to, either. He was pushy, and that always irritated her."

"Did it ever get out of hand?"

"I don't think so. I mean, she would've told me if it had. You don't think he's the one who . . . do you think he was over there that evening?"

"You have to admit, it's a possibility."

"I wonder if that detective checked for other evidence? Or, did he just assume after he'd found my pole climber that I did it?"

Jeff thought about the fuming procedure Gadzinski had done to set the prints. "He took some extra measures. I'll give him a call. By the way, did you tell him about Tinker?"

"I didn't even think about that old guy until you mentioned him. I mean, he was like your worst idea of a high-pressure salesman, but he never seemed like a real threat. How'd you find out that he knew Aunt Verena?"

"He apparently read the newspaper article that told how I had bought the property. I ran into him today, and he blew up about it."

"Yeah, that sounds like him. But if he wanted her stuff bad enough to hurt her, wouldn't he have stolen it while he was there?"

"You'd think so, unless something scared him away." Jeff fiddled with a pulled thread on his sweater. "I went over there today, sat in my car awhile and watched the neighborhood. You were right about that woman next door being the nosy type."

"Yeah. Hey, do you think she saw anything? She bugs the hell out of me, but her snooping might pay off. You didn't happen to talk to them, did you?"

"I talked to Marty, the old man. He wasn't aware that there was a question about your aunt's death, so that tells me that Gadzinski hasn't been by there yet. Sorry, but the old man also said they hadn't seen anything unusual. Funny thing is, though, he agreed that his wife would have been a likely witness."

"But, you didn't talk to the woman?"

"No. She wasn't too happy about my being there."

"She won't have much of a choice with that detective, though."

"Nope, and neither will Tinker. I guarantee you that Gadzinski will pin him down. In the meantime, hang in there, and try to put this mess out of your mind."

They rang off, and he put a call in to the detective. When voice mail kicked in, Jeff left a message, then hung up and tried to follow the same advice he had just given Verena's nephew.

He went to the kitchen and put together a plate of leftovers, then carried it to the library. He needed to study the classifieds and the atlas, decide his plan of attack for the weekend.

When he walked in, he saw Karen seated at his desk, busily scratching something into a datebook.

"Sorry," he said, turning to leave.

"Get back in here." She jumped up and gave him a hug, which set the dishes to rattling. "I can't thank you enough for hooking me up with this Bolton guy.

"I am so *pumped!*" She went on. "He sounds so adventurous, so . . . fun! He only has a couple of clients so far—he's just starting up the business—but he wants to meet me in town tomorrow, show me the floatplane, look at my work, stuff like that."

"Sounds great." He set the tray on the credenza, and poured a glass of wine. "Don't increase his adventure level too much, though. Remember, he's in his seventies."

"Are you sure? I mean, I know you said that earlier, but he does *not* come across like he's an old man."

"Old or not, I don't know a whole lot about the guy." He settled himself with the tray in a wing chair near the fireplace where, thanks to Greer, some well-banked logs popped and flickered. "I can run a background check on him if you want me to."

"Don't you dare. I'm a big girl, and I can take care of myself. Besides," she said as she leaned over him and grinned teasingly, "if he's really as old as you say he is, I can probably outrun him. Or, at the very least, out-wrestle him."

That was an image he didn't need. He buttered a hot roll as she left the room, thinking that it was sure easy to see how so many females got themselves into compromising situations.

Chapter Twenty-Four

THE MANTEL CLOCK chimed softly, stirring him as he dozed in the wing chair. Simultaneous with the clock's fourth chime, a bell jangled off-key. His brow wrinkled, and he wondered if angels got their wings when the bells were faulty. He opened his eyes slightly, saw that the fire had died down to a few embers, which cast a soft, orange glow onto the stone hearth. He had come back to the library after his date with Sheila two hours earlier. The clock tolled again—step five of its twelve paces toward midnight—followed by the phone ringing. The angel image dissipated as he answered the call.

Gadzinski said, "I appreciate the lead, Talbot, but how am I supposed to find a guy with one name?"

He caught up to speed after a couple of seconds. "I haven't heard Tinker's real name in so long I can't even think of it. I'll tell you someone who can, though." He gave Blanche's name and number to the detective.

"Do you think I can call her this late?"

"You called me, didn't you?"

"Yeah, but I don't care if I irritate you. It's these women who will rip you to shreds."

"What makes you say that, detective?"

"Generally speaking, it's true. Specifically speaking, it's Erma Margaret Weldon. I questioned both her and her husband this evening, and I don't mind telling you that I stopped on the way home and picked up a bouquet of flowers for my wife."

"I can see how Mrs. Weldon might have that effect on a guy." Jeff rose, stirred the fire with a poker. "Did you learn anything?"

"Shouldn't I be asking you that question?"

"Fair enough. Verena didn't have any friends, and Tinker tried his used-car-salesman tactics on her a time or two. But I didn't learn that last part from the Weldons."

"Yeah?"

"Yeah. Matter of fact, that's why I put in a call to you. Like I said, I ran into him today. Thanks, by the way, for giving my name to the newspapers."

"You got something to hide?"

He ignored the question. "Tinker wasn't too happy to learn that the nephew had sold her belongings to me."

"Not a bad motive."

"Except that the stuff is still there."

"Lots of reasons for that, and you know every one of them."

"Yeah." When Gadzinski didn't offer a catchy comeback to that, Jeff said, "What about your murder weapon? Any prints show up?"

"Yeah, as a matter of fact. The thing's filthy with them."

"No kidding?"

"No, thankfully. I don't have to tell you what a mess it would be, trying to dig up evidence in that place."

Secretly, Jeff was grateful because of other reasons. Foremost, it promised to back up his belief that Nathan was innocent. Also, it took the onus off him for woefully compromising a crime scene—even if he didn't know that it *was* one. "Who do they belong to?"

"You know as well as I do that the *eff bee* of *eye* has bigger fish to fry. We're at war, remember?"

It would be easier to name the times when we weren't, thought Jeff. After a fitting acronym—Frightening But Indisputable—popped into his head, he said, "In other words, you don't know yet."

"I don't know yet."

"I can always call Gordy, ask him to pull a few strings."

"Give him a call." Gadzinski blew air. "So, can I call this Appleby woman?"

"Sure, Detective. She's like the Pinkertons. Never sleeps."

"Name me somebody who does."

They rang off, and Jeff walked to the back of the house, toward the door that led to the basement. He wouldn't be able to sleep now, either.

June 4, 1945

Mom,

You're getting married? This is because you're still upset with me for joining up, isn't it? I told you, I'll be back there real soon. We can talk about it then.

We're on the move . . . no sleep, no food. Didn't even get to do that baking I promised the gang—damn Japs bombed the mess tent, and we bugged out in eight minutes. Been moving ever since.

I only have a couple minutes to write this and try to talk some sense into you. I'm lucky we stumbled onto a unit shipping out for special detail. I gave up my last pack of smokes, and a little gold trinket box I had found on a Jap with his legs blown off—all for one lousy piece of paper, and the promise that this will get posted.

What do you mean, I deserted you? Do you know how it made me feel to sit at home every night, without any family? Without a father? For years I did that. Why didn't you marry my father?

You know, I can't believe you would burden me

with this. We're exhausted here, fighting like heathens so that you people over there can get a peaceful night's sleep. Does anybody know what we're going through? Does anybody care?

Maybe you all wrap yourselves up in the false sense of security blankets. Hell, you probably don't even know what we have to do, so that you can feel secure, what we see, what we have nightmares about.

More than a few of my bunkmates—that's funny, since we don't even have bunks at this point—anyhow, they can't even doze off without the nightmares making them scream out. One minute, we're holding each other, crying like frightened children, and the next minute we're in hand combat, slicing through smoke, choking, giving some Jap a gaping red smile from ear to ear.

So, how can you think about marrying some stranger, when I'm risking my life for your safety?

Cool your heels, Mom, and don't go replacing me as the man of the house when I'm not even there to meet this guy. I'm trying to swing a leave. My C.O. understands, as he has to see to running his own mother's affairs (and I'm referring to financial affairs, Mom, not the kind you get yourself into). Anyhow, that means that I should be back there for my birthday.

Don't make a move on this till I get there, do you hear?

Andy

Jeff stared at the stained and tattered sheet of paper, recognized in the text the drastic changes from earlier letters written by the boy. A boy who was quickly being forced to become a man. Andrew Rose's penmanship, always tight, restricted, had in this letter a jaggedness about it, emphasizing the boy's anger.

He folded the letter and slipped it back into the envelope, then wearily climbed the two flights of stairs up to his bedroom, thinking that Verena's lot in life had not been an easy one.

Chapter Twenty-Five

The next morning Jeff woke to an empty bed.

He checked the clock and cursed himself for oversleeping, then grabbed his robe, and shuffled down the corridor in search of his wife.

She was standing at the top of the stairs, attempting to peer down to the first floor. She turned as he approached, and she was smiling. Smiling nervously, he thought, but smiling just the same.

"What's going on?"

"Doctor Jen should be here any minute."

"Huh?"

"Honey, you need coffee. Why don't you go—"

"I will, after you tell me what's going on."

"Greer told me the trees are the most beautiful he's ever seen. Is that true?"

Jeff wondered whether it was true, or whether the astute butler was using the same tactics he himself had been using to draw Sheila out of her limited surroundings. "I hadn't thought about it, but I'd have to say that he's right."

"Good. He and Robbie are stringing my vintage bubble lights on the tree in the parlor right now. You know how long it takes to get those to stand up properly? Anyway, then they're going to put the garlands on the mantels and unpack my decorations. Doctor Jen—who, as it turns out, loves Christmas as much as I do—is going to spend the day with me, get me down the stairs, then take me from room to room and help me do the actual decorating. If I start to falter, she'll be right there to help me through it."

Jeff mentally tallied *that* doctor bill, doubled it on account of it being Saturday, and was determining what he could sell to cover it when Sheila added, "And you won't have to worry about her fee. I bartered her services for a couple of my Victorian Santas."

"Hon, you don't have to do that. The Rose property might be frozen, but I *can* pay your therapist."

"I know that, but working this out made me feel . . . oh, I don't know how to explain it. It's like I'll be responsible for relying on *myself* to follow through with the sessions. Do you know what I mean?"

Jeff took his wife in his arms. "Yes, actually, I do. Just don't give away anything that you'll regret later."

"Don't worry. I may be a mess in some areas right now, but I haven't lost my bargaining skills."

After a moment of silence, she blurted, "I can't *stand* not knowing what's happening down there. Would you check on things for me?"

"You got it." He kissed her forehead, and descended the stairs.

In the dining room, containers stacked two high and two deep formed a border around the room, where they waited to be unpacked. A four-foot-high Victorian feather tree stood in the center of the table, surrounded by antique Santas in coats of dark velvet, and angels, which were their contemporaries, in capes of gold. Nativity sets crowded around those, and vintage ornaments of every conceivable theme and color filled the rest of the surface.

He picked up a brightly painted partridge with a spun

glass tail that could have been the inspiration for the fiber optic filaments currently in vogue, and secured it by its clip to the top of the little tree. He stood back.

The room looked like a mountain of Christmas.

After reporting what he had found to his anxious wife, he coffeed up, and quickly got ready for the day. He hadn't planned anything specific, but he wasn't about to hang around for this three-ring circus.

It was just like buying a house. Once you picked out the one you wanted, and while the bank was busy drawing up papers and putting together figures to determine how much blood they would drain from your arteries, you couldn't stay away from the thing. You drove past it after dinner, during your lunch hour, and on weekends. You parked out front and envisioned yourself living there, envisioned that house full of your stuff. You gazed upon the "sold" placard attached to the top of the real estate sign, and thought: *It's mine; that word says so, makes it real.*

Jeff found himself, once again, sitting in front of the house in Lake Stevens where all that stuff—his stuff—was waiting. It was an inventory he couldn't get to until Gadzinski's high-tech crystal ball revealed who was holding the key.

He poured coffee into the thermos's lid, drank it down, then poured another.

The door of the Weldon home opened. Marty limped outside, dropped into one of the porch chairs, and began rubbing his eyes so sluggishly that he seemed to be in slow motion. When at last he looked up and surveyed the neighborhood, his gaze stopped on the woodie, and he motioned for Jeff to join him.

Jeff rummaged around in a plastic bin of contingency items that he kept on the back floorboard, and retrieved a couple of styrofoam cups. He put them over the bottle's stopper, and took it with him.

"Don't mind if I do, young man," Marty said as Jeff took a seat.

He poured the hot liquid. "I should warn you, it's strong."

"All the better." He took a sip, and his brows raised appreciatively. "I didn't expect to see you back up here so soon. You just missed the detective that's working the case. Were you supposed to meet him?"

He couldn't help wondering what Gadzinski was up to on a Saturday.

"No, I'm just killing time while my wife does the Christmas decorating. I learned a long time ago that it's best if I vacate the premises."

Marty nodded knowingly.

"So," Jeff said. "Did he have any news?"

"Who, that detective? I doubt he would tell anyone if he did." He took another swig of coffee. "He was fingerprinting everybody. He set up a regular Fingerprint Central, you know. One of those teenagers across the street said it reminded her of when the technicians did that at the school when she was little."

"He printed everyone?"

"Everyone who gave permission. And, we all did. He said it was for process of elimination. I had gone over to check on Verena when Nathan called and asked me to, so, naturally, my prints would be on the door and the telephone. I called nine-one-one when I found her, then I phoned Erma. She came over and waited with me for the ambulance to show up, so her prints were probably around, too."

Jeff wondered whether Gadzinski had dusted for prints on doorknobs, tabletops, bathroom fixtures. He also wondered if it meant that none had shown up on the pole climber.

"I'll bet you'd like to be over there digging through Verena's junk."

"You'd win that one." Even if he got the property back, it would always be "Verena's junk" to somebody. He started to contemplate what would happen to all those antiques and collectibles if Nathan's name wasn't cleared, but the outlook was too grim, so he changed his course.

He didn't want to reveal too much but he was curious

about the old woman's life. "Say, I found some letters that Verena's son had written to her. In one, he mentioned that she was supposed to get married. Do you remember anything about that?"

Marty thought a moment. "Vaguely. As I recall, she had gotten pretty tight with a mechanic down at the auto repair shop. Then, all of a sudden, he wasn't around anymore. Not long after that, she got word about her son's death."

It sounded to Jeff as if the most recent letter he had read from Andy to his mother had accomplished what the young man had set out to do.

"Were there bad feelings between her and your wife from the beginning?"

"Not at first. You see, I was already living here when Erma and I married. It was hard on her, moving from Seattle to a small town. You know how people are in a small community; takes them awhile to warm up to strangers.

"Verena's case was different, though," he went on. "Once you've been branded, you might as well forget it. And, the deeper we got into the war, the more fault they found with her. She wouldn't grow a Victory garden, for instance, and many a person judged you harshly if you didn't do things for the war effort."

His heh-heh chuckle was so soft that Jeff barely heard it. "Thing was, she couldn't have grown a plant if her life depended on it."

"Lots of people have brown thumbs. Why were they particularly hard on Verena?"

"I'll get to that." He held out his cup, waited until Jeff had refilled it before he continued.

"See, they didn't recognize the areas where she skimped, they didn't know that she had used V-mail faithfully when she wrote to Andy. People only see what they want to see. They never understood that she had given the single most valuable thing she had—her son—and that no one had the right to ask her for anything else."

"Why didn't she have any girlfriends?"

"Several reasons, I suppose. At first, the 'upstanding' women of the community judged her for showing up in town with a baby, but no husband. Time passed, and they eventually eased up some, but then she had to start working nights, and those early prejudices resurfaced—that time with smug justification."

Jeff's mind was swarming with questions. He picked one. "She never married?"

"I doubt it." The old man waved a hand of dismissal. "Oh, she said that the boy's father had been killed in a farming accident down in California. But . . ." his voice trailed off.

"Lots of girls in trouble made up that sort of story," he said. "They would tell it so often that they usually began to believe it themselves. Had to, if they wanted to get through the day to day. And, who can blame them? Life's hard enough as it is."

Jeff couldn't argue with that.

Marty took a deep breath, let it out with a sigh. "Then there were the war years. It didn't help that, while most women went without stockings, or drew fake seams up the backs of their legs with face paint, or, hell, even wore Victory stockings—those shriveled-up fishnet looking things—Verena always had the sleekest nylons on the market." Marty leaned forward. "Could've been the black market, for all I know, but I sure as hell didn't care."

He leaned back again and smiled. It shaved forty years off his expression.

"Like I said, she was a real dazzler. Kept herself fixed up, always looked like a million bucks when she walked out that door. I could've waited for hours if I'd had to, just to get a glimpse of her, all dolled up in a form-fitting dress—filled out in all the right places, if you know what I mean—with her hat angled just *so,* and her stocking seams as straight as a plumb line, click-clicking along in those spectator heels.

"But you know all that. You hauled a lot of junk out of her house. Likely, those trunks are *full* of her shoes and clothes."

"Possibly. I was having to move so fast that I didn't take a look inside any of them. Now, the cops have it all under lock and key."

"Doesn't matter. You won't get the same effect without Verena in them. That is, Verena before she lost Andy.

"She was never the same after all that," he went on. "I persuaded Erma to go over, take food, tried to get her to befriend Verena. They never meshed, though."

Jeff suspected it was more than that. Not being friends was one thing, but Erma's open hostility when Jeff first met her was altogether different. He let it slide. "I found a lot of stuff that had probably belonged to her son: marbles, comic books, cowboy-and-Indian getups, toy cars and airplanes and trains. I guessed when I found the stuff that she had hung on to everything from his childhood."

"Hung on to, and added to, after he died. It was her way of coping, I suppose. She just kept buying things, as if she expected him to return home. She kept his room just like he had left it for a long time afterward, until her dementia advanced, and she started filling it with all the things she would have bought for him when he was a boy."

Jeff recalled the rooms upstairs, stacked to the rafters. Now, he understood that she had never been able to stop herself from the purchasing, the collecting. Marty Weldon was right: Buying for her boy had been a coping mechanism, a way of tricking her brain, her soul, into believing that if she kept getting ready for Andy's return, then she didn't have to face reality.

"Did you say that both you and your wife were home the day Verena was killed?"

He nodded. "Sad, isn't it, that we had no idea she was in trouble? Of course, that sheds even more suspicion on her nephew."

"How's that?"

He turned up his palms. "No forced entry. She trusted him. And, even he has admitted he was there."

To Jeff's way of thinking, there were more reasons why Nathan *wasn't* the killer. "Was the door locked when you went to check on her?"

"No. Otherwise, I couldn't have gotten inside."

"You don't have a key to her house?"

"Don't, and didn't. No reason for one; Nate checked on her almost every day."

"So, there wasn't anyone else around besides Nathan?"

"No one that I saw. And I would've told somebody if I had seen anyone. I took a nap late that afternoon. Can't seem to go without one."

"Your wife told the police that she didn't see anyone, either?"

"That's right. And, believe me, if there had been someone sneaking around, Erma would've known about it. Rare is the time that she doesn't have her nose poking out of the curtains—and into somebody else's business."

As if his saying this about her sent up some sort of antenna, she pulled into the driveway.

"There's my cue to shut my pie hole and carry in the groceries. Don't rat me out to her."

"I won't. Thanks for the visit." Jeff grabbed his thermos.

"Do you ever put hot chocolate in that thing?"

"I think it could be arranged." He started down the stairs.

"Remember what I said about Thursday?"

Jeff acknowledged with a wave of his hand as he walked to his car.

He drove toward home, going over the many questions that had gone unanswered. He wondered whether Verena had called off her wedding simply because her son had disapproved. And, he was curious: Had she *ever* been married? Also, it seemed to him that a young bride such as Erma would have appreciated having a friend like Verena around; someone who was older, who could be counted on for a little guidance.

But the most intriguing question was this: What had happened to turn Erma Weldon so bitterly against Verena Rose? The answer could be damn near anything.

He looped around to Fisherman's Terminal and purchased some Dungeness crab to take home, certain that he wasn't the only one who wanted a break from turkey leftovers.

It was dark when he pulled up his driveway, and, by all appearances, the day had been a success. Lights designed to look like icicles hung from every gable of the large, Victorian home. Inside, the place was decorated like a Holiday spread for *Architectural Digest.*

Karen arrived right behind him, returning from her first meeting with Max, and appearing even more excited than she had been the day before. She joined Jeff and Sheila in the bedroom and distributed snapshots onto the bedspread like a Vegas dealer while she gave an account of her day.

She told how she had taken her camera equipment along and had shot the photographs—everything from Max with his seaplane to the VW-clutching Fremont Troll under the Aurora Bridge to a cruise ship docking at Bell Street Pier. They had then dropped the film at Ken's on Union, and had gone across the street to eat Chinese food at Genghis Khan while the film was being developed. She said that when Max saw the shots, he went nuts over her composition, and they worked out a deal.

Jeff glanced at the shots while his sister-in-law chattered on, until at last she wound down and—scooping up the photos and saying goodnight—left them in the wake of what was most definitely Hurricane Karen.

And so it was that life-changes dictated new and exacting schedules in the Talbot household.

Both Karen and Jeff rose every morning and hit the road, she to photograph bird's-eye views of the Northwest, he to scare up any item that might turn a profit; Doctor Jen the therapist came to the house every afternoon, and Sheila steadily made headway under her expert care; and, every evening, while an exhausted Jeff returned to the quiet sanctuary of home, Max Bolton wined and dined Karen on every island within a manageable distance from the Emerald City.

Chapter Twenty-Six

ONE AFTERNOON, ABOUT a week before Christmas, Karen joined Jeff at the kitchen table where Greer had laid out a lunch of grilled cheese sandwiches and homemade split pea soup. It was rare that the whole clan was in the house at one time.

Greer was at the sink, cleaning the griddle. "Sir? The missus has been receiving calls in regard to her annual cookie donation for the holiday food baskets."

"Really? She hasn't said anything to me about it."

"Actually, sir, I've been screening them, making notations as to who has called. I tried to keep the reasons vague, but I told them that Mrs. Talbot wouldn't be able to provide the cookies this year."

Karen set down her glass. "Why not? She could dangle another old Santa Claus under her therapist's nose and get her back over her."

"*Meow,* Karen." Jeff took a swig of coffee. "What's

wrong? Are you jealous that they had so much fun decorating the house?"

"No. It just seemed, I don't know, silly."

"Like you've never done anything silly."

Karen made a face. "Seriously, though, Sheila might want to do this. Has anyone asked her?"

"With all due respect, Miss Gray, she would have had everything baked by now. Nothing has been done according to tradition."

"Greer's right, Karen. Sheila always bakes the cookies around the middle of November. Then she spends the week after Thanksgiving decorating and packaging them."

Karen dipped a triangular corner of her sandwich into the soup, then bit off the soggy chunk. She looked at her watch and, around the mouthful of food, said, "It's one-thirty but I have no idea what day it is."

Jeff caught the faint look of surprise that swept over Greer's face. He grinned slightly. Poor Greer. He would never learn how to react to the bohemian attributes of Sheila's sister. Jeff himself wondered how the woman ever managed to stay on schedule, meet deadlines, and arrive in whatever part of the world she was supposed to be in at any given time. She never seemed to have any indication as to the day or the time. Or the month, for that matter.

Greer cleared his throat lightly. "It's Tuesday, madam. The eighteenth of December. The missus has ventured down here a few times, anxious for gifts to be delivered for the children, but she has made no indication that she will be making cookies this year."

Jeff had witnessed his wife's visits to the first floor and was relieved to see that she handled the excursions fairly well—as long as she didn't get near any windows or exterior doors.

"Well," Karen said, "why don't *we* do it?"

Jeff and Greer looked at each other with astonishment. Jeff knew he was speaking for them both when he said, "Are you nuts?"

"I see no reason why we shouldn't. I mean, how hard can it be? I remember when Sheila and I made cookies with Mom when we were kids. It didn't seem that hard.

And, Greer obviously knows how to cook. The food's been great since I've been here. Not like Sheila's, of course, but . . ."

"Thank you, madam, but I must admit that most of it has been brought in."

Karen's face registered doubt, but Jeff couldn't be sure whether she thought Greer was being modest or whether her cookie-baking resolve was waning.

"Well," she said at last, "can't we give it a try? I'm going crazy between photo shoots, and, with all three of us working together, why, I bet we can whip 'em up in a single day."

"Sounds like a Superman ad if you ask me: 'Leap stacked cookies in a single bound.'" Jeff sat back, gazed out the window. It hadn't escaped him that, for all of Max's enthusiasm about the new business, he had slacked off calling Karen except to go out evenings. It was still raining, and Jeff had been out in it all morning. An afternoon in a warm kitchen with a fresh pot of coffee and no cold calls sounded inviting. He looked questioningly at Greer.

The butler said, "Perhaps if we cull the list, choose the ones most dear to the missus." He raised a brow slightly. From anyone else it would have been an elaborate shrug of the shoulders.

"I'm willing to try," Greer said. He looked directly at Karen and added, "if you're *sure* you want to commit."

Karen clapped her hands gleefully. Jeff raised his own hands in surrender.

For all of Greer's training, he admitted to his culinary cohorts, he had never baked a cookie. And Karen didn't know how to cook at all. Jeff had learned from Sheila that baking was an art in and of itself, and that any top restaurant worth its salt had a pastry chef in addition to the regular chef. She had even told him of restaurants that served only desserts.

But here they were—Greer, Karen, and himself—about to attempt production of twenty dozen fancifully decorated cookies according to the aesthetically stunning standards that Sheila had maintained for years.

Oh, and they had to be edible.

We're screwed, Jeff thought.

Greer quickly pored over Sheila's Christmas notebook, found in the cookie segment a laminated shopping list to rival St. Nick's, and sent Karen to the grocery store for provisions.

Then the two men dug out supplies: measuring cups and spoons, whisks and bowls and baking sheets, rolling pins and, finally, Sheila's massive collection of vintage cookie cutters. Jeff had learned not to be too nervous when these came out. Just because they were valuable—from thirty for the small ones to upwards of six hundred dollars for the large, detailed reindeer—was no reason not to put them to use.

When they were through, the ancient refectory table that stretched most of the length of the large kitchen was groaning under the weight of crockery, rolling pins, and confectionery supplies.

After Karen returned, the trio unpacked the bags, Greer organized an assembly line, and gave the chefs a basic rundown. "Here, we have the staples: flour, butter, a variety of spices, and all the sugars—granulated, baker's, confectioner's, and brown."

"Sounds like a law firm." Karen moved forward and snitched a pecan half from a small blue crockery bowl. Next to it were more bowls, containing chopped walnuts and hazelnuts, along with cartons of eggs, bottles of oils, vanilla, and extracts.

Beyond those were the cutters—stars, trees, candy canes, holly, and ornaments, next to a dozen varieties each of the Nutcracker and Santa Claus. Finally, beside a stack of cookie sheets, were glittering containers of crystal sugar, silver dragées, sprinkles in every imaginable Christmas color, snowy coconut, and bottles of red and green food coloring with which to dye the coconut.

The large butcher's block was prepared for packaging the finished goods. It held squares of foil in gold and silver, as well as the traditional red and green, and clear cellophane baggies next to spools of curling ribbon in every holiday hue.

Jeff shook his head. “Greer, if we can’t turn this into cookies, it’s not because you didn’t prepare us.”

Karen, who had retreated to her room, returned with a camera and was busily snapping photos as she oohed and aahed over the display. “My God, Greer, I could hire you as a stylist. Of course, we’d have to fake it up if we were using these in a magazine spread, but I can use these shots later for reference.”

“Fake it up?” Greer said.

“Yeah, you know. Like dish soap in coffee so that it stays bubbly, self-tanning spray and a blowtorch to create a browned and glazed turkey, stuff like that.”

Wide-eyed, the butler said, “I had no idea.”

Karen took one last shot, then stowed the camera. “So, how did you know what to do for today?”

Greer’s expression registered the obvious relief of being back on familiar ground. He held up a notebook. “Mrs. Talbot’s organizational skills put mine to shame. She has it all laid out in here: diagrams, recipes, shopping lists, packaging details, recipients’ contact information. The rest was just common sense.”

Jeff unbuttoned his cuffs and rolled up his sleeves. “Let’s hope the next step is.”

Karen poured eggnog that she had picked up at the store, then questioningly held up a bottle of bourbon.

Jeff said, “It can’t hurt, right?”

Greer ceremoniously provided each with chef’s hat and apron, and the three got to work.

Three hours later, the kitchen was a wreck. The table and floor wore a fine coat of flour, egg shells crunched under Karen’s feet every time she moved, and the trio had succeeded in mixing only four batches of cookie dough. After much experimentation, Greer had finally rolled out enough to cut out a decent variety of shapes. Two dozen were almost finished baking in Sheila’s reproduction Elmira oven, and as many more were awaiting their turn.

Karen giggled for no apparent reason, then snatched another bite of dough. Jeff slapped her hand. "Karen, I swear you've eaten half of what we've mixed."

"I can't resist these with the Jello in the dough. Besides," she added with a sly grin, "I have to taste test."

"Actually," Greer said, "I've been gauging our success by the fact that Miss Gray hasn't succumbed to food poisoning."

Karen slapped playfully at Greer, who smiled in return. It appeared that the butler was beginning to adjust to the eccentric woman.

"I'm surprised she hasn't gotten sick from mixing alcohol with this stuff." Jeff surveyed their work. He wasn't sure whether they were accomplishing as much as they should, but he had to admit that the task had been therapeutic. For the first time, he understood why Sheila enjoyed it so much. He hadn't spent one minute all afternoon thinking about making money or paying bills or how Gadzinski was coming along with his investigation into the murder of Verena Rose.

Greer, who had gone to the basement in search of containers in which to stow the gift bags of cookies, ran up the stairs. "Do I smell something burning?"

Chapter Twenty-Seven

"OH, NO!" KAREN wailed. "I was supposed to take the last batch out of the oven."

Before she could finish admitting her mistake, Greer had jerked open the oven door and was fanning smoke. He pulled the tray from the top rack and threw it on the range top.

Karen stared wide-eyed at the charred Santas. "Sheila's going to *kill* us!"

"Us?" Jeff coughed. "You're the one who was supposed to remove them."

"Why didn't *you* smell them burning? You're the one who's *trained* for emergencies, aren't you?"

"Me?" He jerked the chef's hat from his head. "You're the one who says she can handle anything. You've had more survivalist training during your last year on the job than I had during my whole time with the Bureau. People refer to you as Captain Cook with tampons, and yet you can't even count to ten minutes and take a damned cookie sheet out of the oven."

"Uh, something's burning."

The trio turned in unison to find Sheila standing in the hallway. She looked upset. After a few seconds, though, she snickered, and everyone relaxed.

"Jeff," she said, "I can't believe I was worried about a few harmless children helping me hang Christmas ornaments. They couldn't do this much damage if they tried."

"No kidding." Karen took off her apron and tossed it to her sister. "If you expect to have a kitchen left in this house, you'll do what's good for all of us and help these guys."

The doorbell chimed, saving Karen from chastisement. "That'll be my date," she announced as she headed toward the front door.

Sheila donned the apron and began scraping burned discs from the cookie sheets.

Jeff wrapped an arm around his wife. "Are you okay? I mean, down here."

"As long as I stay away from the windows and doors, sure."

"What about Max?"

"He's been here several times while you were working. Doctor Jen was with me."

Jeff nodded, then surveyed the room.

"Sorry about the mess. I guess things got out of hand."

"That's okay. It was worth it, just to see the three of you trying to work together. I think."

Karen returned a moment later with Max Bolton. Animatedly, she was filling him in on the cookie fiasco. He stepped into the kitchen, greeted Jeff, then looked around and shook his head. "This is why you're the photographer, and I'm the pilot."

"Maybe so, but which one of us makes more money at it?"

"If what I'm paying you is any indication, you are."

Karen laughed like a smitten schoolgirl, and Jeff and Sheila exchanged a knowing glance.

Jeff started reorganizing the work area. "Isn't it a little dark for outdoor photography?"

"Oh, didn't I tell you?" Karen went to the sink and began washing the flour from her hands. "Max is taking me on one of the Argosy Christmas cruises tonight. They're serving dinner."

Max shook his head. "She says 'serving dinner' like it's a lunch line when, in fact, this is a gourmet event—Dungeness crab, filet mignon, a tower of chocolate something-or-other for dessert. I hope she's planning on changing clothes."

"I can hear you, Max."

"Good. Then you'll get cleaned up so we aren't late?" He tapped the face of his wristwatch. "They leave the pier in forty minutes."

In ten minutes, Karen had transformed herself stunningly by punching up her makeup and changing into a red-and-black-sequined sweater set over black slacks. Jeff watched her and Max leave, then went back to the kitchen.

Sheila had reclaimed control, with Greer's help.

Jeff took a broken cookie from one of the sheets and popped it into his mouth. "Something about him seems familiar."

Sheila attacked a batch of cookie dough with a rolling pin. "Who, Max? Of course, it does. Karen has talked about him nonstop for *days*."

"Yeah, but there's something in the expression."

"I've noticed it, sir," said Greer as he measured flour into the bowl of a stand mixer. "It matches Miss Karen's. Both of them have that same *carpe diem* attitude."

"They have a 'carp the day' thing going, all right. Sounds like they've been together day and night for—what?—two weeks."

"There's nothing wrong with that." Sheila cut out star shapes. "I think he's the first love interest she's had since that guy in Paris who turned out to be married with five kids."

"I still don't get it. Why would a good-looking young woman want to date an older guy?"

"And what if I had felt that way, Jeff Talbot? Where would we be right now?"

"A dozen years is nothing compared to—what?—forty years. I told her earlier he's old enough to be her father. Actually, he could be her grandfather."

"From what she tells me, he doesn't *act* it. And that's what counts."

"I suppose."

"Why don't you make yourself useful, husband, and order us a pizza?"

"Sounds good."

After he had called in the order, he settled down in the library with a cup of coffee and his latest copy of *Antiques and the Arts* to wait for the delivery person. The coffee tasted suspiciously like dish soap.

The phone rang. He checked Caller I.D. and saw that Nathan Rose was on the other end.

When he answered, Nathan said, "Good news. Josh gets to come home from the hospital tomorrow."

"That *is* good news."

"Yeah. The way it looks, though, we'll just about get him home when it'll be time to admit Melanie."

"So, the baby's not going to wait for Christmas?"

"Not according to the doctor. 'Course, he hasn't been right yet, so I don't know why we're putting any store in what he's saying now."

"That's a point," Jeff paused. "You know, I'd like to talk to you about something. Do you mind if I drop by tomorrow?"

"Well, I have to go to work as soon as we get Josh home." After a beat, he said, "I guess you could come up to the hospital. We have to be there at eight, but the doctor might not come around for another hour after that to release him."

"Fine, if you're sure it's not a problem."

"Shouldn't be. Everything all right?"

"Well, I thought we could put our heads together, see if we might come up with anything to give the investigation a kick in the butt."

"I'm all for that. For the most part, I can deal with what people say about me, but Maggie and Logan are getting a lot of heat over it from their classmates."

Jeff hadn't thought about that. "They'll be more than ready for Christmas break then. If it's any consolation, my wife is outdoing herself for the big day."

"We appreciate it, even if it isn't easy to let you go to all the trouble. It'll be good for the kids, though, and it'll take a huge load off Mel."

"That's what it's about. I'll see you tomorrow." He rang off, and the doorbell chimed. As he went to answer it he wondered offhandedly whether Nathan's kids liked pizza.

Chapter Twenty-Eight

It was a study in opposites. The delicately flourished handwriting, against the utilitarian V-mail form, was elegance and grace in the face of a world at war.

Because it was the only correspondence he had found *to* Andrew Rose, as opposed to *from* him, Jeff concluded that it held special meaning. It had to, for Verena to have kept it.

A wash of loss came over him now, and he debated for a moment whether or not he should read it. Somehow, it seemed different from reading those that had already been read.

There were none of the telltale signs that this letter had ever been sent. Instinctively, Jeff knew that this was because news of Andrew Rose's death had arrived before it could be mailed.

The woman was gone now, though, and he wanted to learn more about her. He wanted a three-dimensional image of her. He unfolded the pages and read the words of a young mother, words written a half-century earlier.

June 10, 1945

Dearest Son,

Your last letter hurt me more than I can say. How could you possibly suggest that I have never loved you? Do you honestly not know that you have been my life ever since I learned that I had conceived you? Don't you know that everything I have done for the last fifteen years has been in order that we might survive?

I'm not complaining, so don't try to misconstrue my words: I could easily have worked twice as hard, been twice as poor, suffered twice the loneliness of a single mother's life, and never complained. I suppose you wouldn't be aware of that, because I never wanted you to know of the hardships. Why would I? It would only have caused you worry, and it has always been one of my main goals to protect you from worry.

I wanted you to have a normal childhood—or, at least, as normal as one parent can provide. At least those men—whom you now refer to as my . . . I can't even repeat what you said—at least they tried to befriend you! It's more than I can say for those hypocrites you dragged home from church!

That's not to say that they are all hypocrites, and I'm sorry if it sounded that way. I know they aren't. But the few who weren't, those men who tried to set a proper, Christian example for you, never lasted long because it upset their wives for them to be around me. They felt threatened, I suppose, although I never gave them any reason to feel that way. The other men, those who don't care what their wives think, also don't respect them—and would rather spend their time in our home making passes at me instead of being devout, male role models for you.

I tried going to church when you asked. But you

don't know what it's like, going to a place that promises love, only to be snubbed by most of the women and pressed up against in dark corners by half the men. So don't judge me, Andrew. Don't call me the names that you're learning, now that you're in a man's world.

True, I was only fourteen when I had you. But I kept you! I could have given you up for adoption. Or, even gone to a has-been doctor with a dull knife who was more than willing to help girls out of their messes. I had money. My father may have disowned me when he learned about you but my mother didn't. Not totally. She had brought her own money into their marriage, and she saw to it that you and I had a decent chance in the beginning. So, you see? Your idea that women are inferior doesn't wash with me.

Most of that money went to this home, this property, so that we would never lack for a roof over our heads. Yes, I worked as a lounge singer. I had no choice. You say that you were ashamed because of it, yet you now spend all your free time in the bars. Who's the hypocrite now?

Would you rather I had dressed you in rags and sent you to school with an empty stomach? Or, worse, gotten rid of you at the start?

I have never asked you for anything. I have never demanded help, or insisted upon love. But I have earned respect, Andrew. Everything I have done since the moment I knew I was going to have you has been because I love you.

You are my life. Don't you know that by now? But don't run away and then try to deny me the right to male companionship. Your selfishness shocks and saddens me.

Yes, of course, I want you to come home on leave. I miss you more than you will ever realize, and I have always loved you more than anything else. Perhaps I have loved you too much, although I never thought that was possible.

Don't give me an ultimatum, though. Don't de-

mand that I prove I love you by breaking off my relationship with Tom. He's a good man, one who respects me, and wants to get to know you. You're being unreasonable, and you're being spoiled. You left to spite me, and it broke my heart. But you chose your life. How can you ask me not to choose one, now that you're gone? Am I supposed to sit here and waste away, hoping that you'll pay me a visit now and then? Can't you see how unfair you're being?

I will plan on seeing you soon.

Love, as always,

Mom

No wonder Verena went a little off her rocker, Jeff thought as he put the letter back in the marriage casket. She had chastised her son—possibly for the first time—and he had been killed. And, she had irrationally blamed herself.

The words she had written had apparently lodged themselves in her mind as the last thing she had said to him. It didn't matter that he had never read the letter. Unless Jeff was mistaken, her mind had fixated on only one thing: He was not there, so she couldn't take them back.

Now he knew what had changed her from the stunning beauty Marty Weldon had described into an old woman only once removed from being a bag lady.

The next thing to do was to find out who had put her out of her misery.

Chapter Twenty-Nine

As HE DROVE toward the hospital in Everett on Thursday morning, Jeff thought again about something Nathan had said the afternoon they had shared a beer on the rental house's front porch. It had given him an idea the evening before, and he had drafted Greer to help him reinstall the woodie's back seat.

He parked, went inside, and headed toward a nurse's station for information. On the way he spotted Nathan and Melanie walking out of a room, pushing a wheelchair. The thin, pale boy in it would be Josh.

Jeff introduced himself. "Don't tell me you're already checked out."

"He's anxious," Melanie said. "We thought it would be easier if we got out of the room for a while."

"Mel?"

"You go ahead, Nate. We'll meet you back here." Melanie took off, pushing the wheelchair.

"Is he going to be okay?"

Nathan nodded. "Good as new before we know it."

"Glad to hear it." Jeff wondered what illness the boy suffered from, but Nathan offered no information, and Jeff didn't want to pry.

The two men found a couple of empty chairs in an alcove, and Jeff continued the conversation. "Has Gadzinski been in contact with you?"

"Not till this morning. He came by the house around seven. Asked me if anyone at work had been using my hooks."

"Had they?"

"No."

"Would someone else have had a reason to touch them? Say, to move them out of the way so he could get to something else on the truck, or in the field?"

Nate looked at him and raised a brow. "He asked me that, too. The answer's no." He pulled a penknife from his jeans pocket, used it to trim a ragged fingernail. "Did you know they could lift prints off leather?"

"It's tricky, but they're developing new technology all the time." As he said it, he thought about the cops on the porch the day he had called about the bloodstain, making fun of Gadzinski's penchant for high-tech gizmos.

"He already told you all this, didn't he?"

"I haven't talked to him. Some of this stuff's like riding a bike. Once you learn it, it's with you for life." Jeff paused for effect. "Detective comes to your house early like that, it usually means he's got a new lead, or new info. It's something solid, and he's itching to see where it takes him. I'd say he found somebody else's prints."

"I'll go you one better. Try *two* somebody elses. And that's not counting mine."

Jeff stared. "They found prints belonging to *three* different people?"

Nathan nodded.

Let 'em make fun of their Inspector Gadget now, Jeff thought.

After pondering this latest development, Jeff knew exactly how Gadzinski felt. If prints from Nathan Rose's coworkers could be ruled out, it meant that two more people could be added to the suspect list. Now, all they had to do was identify the owners of the prints. He realized it wasn't that easy. But, perhaps, they were a step closer to solving the thing.

He saw Melanie and Josh at the end of the corridor, making their way toward where he and Nathan were seated. "Nathan, remember when you told me that Josh would like to see my car? Well, why don't we go one further? How about I give him a ride home in it this morning?"

Nathan stood. "I'm capable of driving my son home from the hospital."

Jeff felt pressure building. He hadn't prepared for this kind of reaction. He stood, too.

"Well, hell, I know that," Jeff said. Maybe he should have thought things through. Now, he saw no way out, except to push blindly ahead. "I just thought . . . honestly, I didn't intend to cause a problem."

Melanie parked Josh outside the door of his room, and walked up to the pair. "Is everything okay?"

Jeff spoke up. "Your husband mentioned last week that Josh would get a kick out of my forty-eight Chevy, so I was offering him a ride in it. Bad idea, I guess."

Nathan said, "That's not it."

Both parents looked at their son, who was busy trying to corral a helium balloon bouquet.

"My car might not be much, but it'll get us home just fine."

"Nate." Melanie touched his arm.

"I mean it, Mel." He pulled free, and went back to his son.

"Don't take it personally, Mr. Talbot. Nate has his pride, and he already feels you and your wife are doing way too much for us. People are calling him a killer. There's only so much a man can take, you know?"

Jeff hated it when fate had a man by the throat. From what he had seen, Nathan Rose was a man who worked hard, toed the line, tried to do right by his family—and was probably a guy who still had to swallow his pride for one reason or another on a daily basis.

To make it worse, there was likely somebody always reminding him that no matter what he did to try and get ahead, it would never be enough.

"Tell him something for me, Melanie. Tell him, sure, I've got a great car. But it's worth nothing compared to what he has, what both of you have. See, Sheila and I can't have any kids, and that's not always an easy thing for us to deal with." He paused as a group of nurses walked past, then continued when they were out of earshot. "Nathan said something the other day about lifting the kid's spirits, and I thought this would be a great way to do it."

"Thanks for trying."

"Yeah. Well, tell him I didn't mean anything by it." Jeff turned and went back outside.

The wind had picked up in the short time he had been in the hospital. He pulled his coat tighter around him.

As he approached his car, someone yelled his name. He turned. Nathan was walking toward him.

"You got seat belts in that thing?"

"My wife insisted on it."

"Yeah, they have a way of doin' that about things." Nathan seemed lost in thought for a beat, then he gave a nod. "Pull her up to the door, then."

Jeff watched Josh's mouth drop when he saw the car, then heard the boy whoop, obviously in response to his dad's news.

When Jeff got out to open the doors for his passengers, the nurse standing by the wheelchair cautioned the boy to stay calm. Melanie planted a kiss on her husband's lips, then climbed in. Nathan gently tucked Josh into the seat at the back of the long wagon and then went to pick up his own car.

Jeff kept an eye on the rearview mirror as he drove, and he would bet that Josh turned around a hundred times to wave at his dad and give him a huge grin.

Many things about that day left their impression on Jeff: A child whose biggest thrill wasn't which car he rode in, but in sharing his excitement with his father; a wife's touch that reached beyond words; his own joy in getting to play a small role in the boy's happiness. But the most lasting imprint would be the look in a man's eyes when he swallowed his pride for the sake of his son.

A man like that didn't kill people, and Jeff was more determined than ever to help clear the young father's name.

Chapter Thirty

After Jeff had safely delivered the excited patient to his home, he remembered Marty Weldon's invitation to visit on a Thursday afternoon. He had four hours to kill, so he drove down to Snohomish to depressurize among the antiques shops before heading back up to Lake Stevens.

He had a soup-and-sandwich lunch in a café and ordered two hot chocolates for the road. If he wanted Marty to tell him more about the past, it wouldn't bode well to forget the old man's simple request.

Marty opened the door, saw the large styrofoam containers, and rubbed his palms. "Chocolate, right?"

"Yes, sir. I wasn't sure about whipped cream, so I—"

"No, no, that's fine." His hands fluttered. "Bring it to the kitchen, and we'll pour it in some real mugs."

The mugs were waiting on the countertop. "I was counting on your visit. Erma says that chocolate's bad for me on more levels than she cares to name."

"Is it?"

"Nah." He dragged out the word.

They took the mugs to the living room, where Marty settled into a plump recliner and Jeff sat opposite him on the couch. They drank in silence for a few moments, while Jeff contemplated his best approach to prime the pump.

"What kind of work did you do, Marty?"

"I owned the movie theater. Started there when I was just a shaver. Worked my way up through the ranks, then bought the place when the owner passed away in nineteen sixty."

"You must like movies, then."

He moved a shoulder. "Not so much anymore. But you get a different perspective when you're worried about the reels arriving in time, or not at all. Not to mention keeping the whole operation afloat."

"Only one profession your entire life? That's impressive." *Look conversational.* He sat back and crossed an ankle over a knee. "You had mentioned the other day that Verena changed jobs."

"She'd worked for an attorney in town for as far back as I could remember. It was a decent job, allowed her to be home at night with Andy. But things have a way of changing."

Jeff couldn't argue with him there. He nodded, and Marty continued his story.

"Her boss decided to retire, and, since he didn't have anyone to leave the firm to, he just locked up. Say, I'll bet you could go down there right now and find all his law books and desks and such still up there, in that second-story office. I always figured climbing up and down those stairs every day was what made Verena's legs so shapely."

Jeff made a mental note to follow up on that antiques lead. Barrister bookcases were always in demand. For now, though, he needed to find out if anything in Verena's past would clear up what had happened—and, in turn, free up the antiques he'd acquired.

"Where was I?" The old man thought a second, then picked up the thread. "She had to start over. This little town didn't offer much, so she went to work at the diner on weeknights and sang in one of the local bars every Saturday. She had one of those whiskey-soaked voices, you know, like Lauren Bacall.

"Andy was probably eleven or twelve by then, so it wasn't like she was leaving a baby at home.

"She never had much opportunity to go to the movies. Back then, the studios made a film a week. Did you know that? You had your three major studios—and no telling how many smaller ones—so several new features were shown every week. Well, the owner liked the lobby cards because they didn't take up much space. He gave me the one-sheets—those were the advertising posters that fit our glass case out front. I didn't have any use for them, but, back then, you didn't turn down anything that was free, know what I mean? Besides, I figured I had earned them, being a jack-of-all-trades around the movie house like I was. Well, Verena loved those posters, so I always gave them to her."

Jeff's hopes flared. "What do you think she did with them?"

Marty moved a hand in dismissal. "Long gone, I'm sure. For all I know, she used them for tinder in that old wood heat stove."

A vise clamped around Jeff's chest. He wondered whether such news could actually bring on a heart attack. The chances that the old lady had preserved any of the posters were one in a million, he knew that. But learning that a prime part of American culture hadn't survived could . . . it could be fatal.

"Are you all right, son?"

Jeff found his voice. "Maybe she kept the posters. You said yourself she loved them."

"She didn't like the cutesy stuff, though. Preferred the tough-guy private eyes, the gangsters. George Raft, Dick Powell, Bogey. I didn't think about it at the time, but that fits with the image most women around here had of her. *Femme fatale,* you know."

The vise tightened.

Marty started up again. "The diner was just down the street from the theater, so we walked home together most evenings, her looking snazzy, even in her uniform and sensible shoes, and me juggling stacks of folded posters.

"I was smitten with her, just like every other male between the ages of thirteen and—heh, heh—eighty. But, for a kid, or someone like me, who had turned twenty but had never been with anyone before he got married, she represented everything we had been told to steer clear of: the older woman, the one you hankered to get a look at, the one who would flatter you, and laugh with you, and do all the things you were told to stay away from.

"If she saw me as the shy kid with a limp who lived next door, she never let on. She was always nice to me, always interested in what I had to say. And she always offered me something to drink when we got to her house; coffee, usually, but sometimes she would pour a touch of liquor in it. We would wind down together like that. Eventually, it got to be our routine."

The old man's expression said that he was in a different place and time.

Jeff had a hunch. "Marty, may I ask you a personal question?"

Several seconds passed before the old man surfaced. "You want to know if I had an affair with her."

"It might change things if you did."

"You could say that I had an affair with the *idea* of her."

Jeff wondered if he had read the signs wrong. "But you didn't have an affair *with* her?"

The old man grunted. "Would you call one time with a woman an affair?" He shrugged. "Depends on who you ask. My wife would.

"I don't know why I told you that. I promised to keep it secret. But doing so has always seemed like a grave disservice to a brief and shining moment in one long, dreary existence.

"As I said, it was only the one time, and the world had gone to hell, and . . . well, you'll see." He repositioned himself in the recliner.

"It was a Wednesday night, and Erma was at prayer meeting. Church nights were typically slower at the movies, and that night was worse because the reels hadn't arrived. We shut down early, and I started for home.

"I checked the diner on the way past, but Verena wasn't there. I figured she'd had a slow night, too, and hitched a ride home with somebody who had just gotten his gas rations and was feeling generous. So, I walked on home. Her house was dark—all of them were, on account of the blackout—but, as I walked past, I heard her crying. I went up to make sure she was all right.

"When she opened the door, I thought she was wearing a mask. Startled the hell out of me. Her features were all crumpled, distorted-like, and her face was red and smeared. And she was clutching a telegram." He paused, remembering. "Worst thing in the world, you know. Sometimes, you would see that black sedan crawling down the street, looking for a particular house number. Other times, you'd hear that it came in the form of a telegram."

He sighed heavily. "So, I scooped her up and got her to the couch. I fixed a pot of strong coffee and spiked it with whiskey like we'd done those other times, and made her drink it.

"I told her everything you can think of to tell a person when they've had a blow like that. I begged her to let me call a doctor, but she wouldn't. I didn't know what else to do, so I lay down beside her, and rocked her, and cried with her.

"When you're holding on like that, holding on for your lives, it's like your bodies *fuse*. When that happens, you truly don't know where yours stops and the other one begins."

He looked at Jeff. His eyes were bright. "Do you know what it's like, when neither one of you says a word, when you know that nothing *needs* saying, and, even if it did, it's in a language that nobody's written yet?"

Jeff nodded. He knew.

The old man continued.

"Afterward, I knew that it would kill Erma if she found out. We had only been married a few months, you see. So, I sneaked out of Verena's house and left the back way through the old iron gate; you can't see it now because it's covered up with vines. I walked a couple of blocks while I worked out a story, then circled around and came home.

"As soon as I walked in, Erma asked why I smelled of perfume. So, I told her about this gal who came into the theater lobby, drunk as a lord and demanding that we let her in for free. I said my boss and I were trying to keep her quiet and figure out what to do with her when she passed out. I looped my arms around her, like this—" Marty sat forward, and demonstrated "—and was trying to hold her steady, while the boss ran to the back room for a chair."

He grew animated, warming to his story. "Her dress was made of this slinky fabric, something that might remind you of parachute silk, and I was trying to hold her sort of tight-like so that that dress wouldn't slide up and reveal anything. Before I knew it, she had slid right out of it, and was lying on the floor in a heap, and naked as a picked bird." He slumped back, breathless.

Confession is an exhausting bedmate. When Marty didn't continue, Jeff prompted. "So, what did you do?"

"I made it up, remember?"

Jeff blinked.

"You see? It's so ludicrous, it's believable."

The old man told a good story. Jeff wondered if he could believe anything else Marty Weldon had told him.

Jeff didn't want Marty to know his suspicions. "How did Erma find out?"

"Stupid move on my part. At some point, I had stuck Verena's handkerchief in my coat pocket."

"And Erma found it."

"No. Not there, anyway. I found it the next night, and it still had Verena's perfume on it. Call me sentimental; I wrapped it up in tissues and hid it. My wife found it two months later. I told her we'd gotten sloppy drunk, and that I had been a fool, and all those other things you say to save your butt. Truth is, I was as sober as I am right now.

"Don't get me wrong. Erma's been a good wife for more than fifty years. I admire the hell out of her." He looked down, rubbed at a purplish blotch on the back of his hand. When he looked back up, the determination in his eyes was evident. "But I'll tell you right now, son, if I had it to do over, I wouldn't change a thing. Verena needed me, and on some level, I needed her. Did I kill her? Son, I couldn't have killed that woman if she begged me."

He pulled his sweater closer around him. "She did, too, when I first got there. But I have to believe that I somehow helped prevent her taking her own life."

"And," Jeff said, "you promised her that you would keep it a secret."

"Who, Verena? No. I promised Erma. As you can see, Erma wouldn't have killed her, for fear that this would all come out."

"Why did you tell me?"

"Don't you see? What Erma is most afraid of is the one thing that exonerates her."

Jeff placed the mug on a nearby coaster. He was overwhelmed by all the information he had just had thrown at him. How had this odd triangle lived side by side all these years?

One thing was certain: The ripples had dictated Erma's life, had fed the bitterness, the contempt, the constant spying on people.

There was no getting around it, motive was here somewhere, Jeff knew, but it had been here for more than half a century. What, if anything, had changed the equation?

The doorbell rang, and both men jumped.

The old man made no move toward it, though.

"Sir?"

Marty looked up. "Would you answer it, son?"

"Sure."

Detective Mike Gadzinski stood on the porch, his face grim. When Jeff opened the door, the detective said, "Didn't expect to find you here."

"I expected you." Jeff stepped aside. "You've matched the prints, haven't you?"

"One of them, why? You got something?"

Jeff thought about the old man's secret. "Will you allow me to see how this plays out first?"

Gadzinski studied his face, gave a nod. He shed his wet overcoat and hung it on one of the hooks by the front door.

"Did Tinker let you print him?"

"Finally." Gadzinski retrieved one of his trademark handkerchiefs and mopped the back of his neck. "He put up a squawk till I threatened to take him in as a material witness. He said he couldn't miss the time off work."

"Sounds just like him." Jeff closed the door. "No word from Gordy on the third set, huh?"

"Not yet. Thanks for putting a word in to him on that."

"I want to see this cleared up, too."

They walked to the living room and had seated themselves on the couch opposite Marty when the back door opened. Erma Weldon stepped inside.

Chapter Thirty-One

SHE PAUSED AT a wall thermostat and dialed the control a good half-inch to the right before sitting in an armchair near Marty's recliner. She looked expectantly at the detective.

Gadzinski skimmed a sheet of typed notes. "Recapping your earlier statements: You were here together all afternoon. Nathan Rose called. Mr. Weldon went to check on Verena Rose. Door was unlocked, you—" he pointed at Marty "—found the victim in the bathroom, unconscious. Called nine-one-one, then your wife, who joined you to wait for the paramedics." He looked up at the pair.

Both bobbed their heads. Mr. Weldon added, "That sounds about right, Detective."

"It needs to sound *exactly* right."

Marty's gaze dropped. He nodded slightly.

Erma looked quizzically from her husband to the detective. "Mr. Weldon was gone no more than three or four minutes when he called me."

"Are both of you willing to testify to each other's whereabouts that afternoon?"

They looked at each other, but didn't answer.

Jeff took the opening. "Marty, how long was your nap that afternoon?"

"About three—" He glared at Jeff. "You're pulling that good-cop-bad-cop trick on us, aren't you?"

"You were asleep for three hours?" Gadzinski exhaled. "Okay, folks, let's cut to the chase. Mr. Weldon, your prints are on the murder weapon."

Erma gasped, and her hand flew up to stifle it.

Marty looked up, wide-eyed. "They can't be. I wiped it clean."

"The metal, perhaps. Not the leather."

Erma said, "It's a trick. They can't get prints that way."

Jeff clasped his hands. "Actually, Mrs. Weldon, they can."

She looked doubtful. "Marty?" Erma reached for her husband, her hand trembling. "Are they telling the truth? Did you kill her?"

"I couldn't have killed her if I'd wanted to."

"Of course not," Erma snapped, jerking back as if she had been burned. "You were still having an affair with her, weren't you?"

"Even if I'd wanted to have an affair, when would I have done it? You haven't let me out of your sight in fifty years."

"You disgraced me, Marty," she cried, plucking a tissue from a box on the table separating their chairs. "You disgraced me with that woman, and then you made me spend my life living next to her."

Marty buried his head in his hands. "After all these years, you still don't believe me. It was one time, Erma. *One time!* And, even that wasn't about the act. I'm just thankful that you've never suffered a loss so great as to tear you apart like hers did."

"Don't you preach to me about loss. I lost you six months after we got married."

The room fell quiet.

Jeff sluiced beads of perspiration from above his lip with his thumb and forefinger.

Detective Gadzinski mopped his brow. "Why don't you two tell me what really happened that afternoon?"

Marty cleared his throat. "After I called for an ambulance, I saw that metal contraption on the floor. I went over to take a look, and that's when I saw the blood. Real quick-like, I rubbed down the metal, threw the thing in the basement, and moved some stuff around in the living room to cover up the blood." He looked at his wife. "I thought you had killed her."

"You *what?* If I were capable of killing anyone, I would've killed her fifty years ago. Why on earth would you think I did it that afternoon?"

"Because when I woke from my nap, you weren't in the house."

"Oh, for heaven's sake." Erma's edge was back. "How many times have I told you? I was running between the flower patch and the basement that afternoon, getting things ready for winter."

Her expression changed from irritation to realization. She bolted from her chair. "You're trying to make it look like I killed her! Why would you turn on me like this?"

Marty stood and faced her. "*Turn* on you? I'm trying to protect you."

"By doing what? Telling these men you were asleep while I killed your lover?"

Gadzinski jumped up. "Both of you settle down, and sit down."

They did as they were told.

"Mrs. Weldon." The detective was all cop now. "Did you go to Verena Rose's house that day, before your husband called you?"

"What? No! Why would you ask such a thing?"

"You obviously had a lot of hate for her."

"I-I despised her for what she did. But I couldn't kill anybody. I just couldn't."

"Somebody did," Jeff reminded her.

Marty knelt on one knee beside his wife's chair, took

her hand in his. "Erma, honey, don't you know that you're the one I've loved all these years? Please believe that."

In her other hand, she gripped the tissue tighter and tighter until she was shaking. Finally, she brought it to her face and sobbed, "Oh, what have I done? God forgive me, what have I done?"

"Erma, don't say another word. We'll hire a lawyer, a good one, and I'll stick by you, just like I have all these years."

"What?" Slowly, realization showed on her face. "I told you, I did not kill her. But . . ." She looked at Gadzinski. "I wasn't honest when I said that I didn't see anyone."

Gadzinski sat down across from her. "You saw someone at her house?"

Erma nodded. "There was a man, skulking through the brush toward the back alley. It was getting near dark, you know, and her nephew had left quite awhile earlier. I was in the kitchen about to start supper, but I hadn't turned on the lights yet. It's easier to see out, don't you know, when the lights are off at dusk."

"Are you sure it was a man?"

"Yes, quite sure."

"Could you tell much about him?"

She frowned. "Older, I think, because he was stooped over, kind of shuffled along. Of course, that could have been because he wasn't supposed to be there, couldn't it? I see that now. At the time, I just thought she was up to her old tricks, when men moved through there like parts on an assembly line. I worked during the war.

"Boeing," she continued, with a determined nod. "Surprises you, I can tell by your expression. I am no one's idea of Rosie the Riveter, least of all, my own. I despised it, too, *despised* having to work a man's job. I married Marty so I could get away from it. I had so looked forward to living in a small community. Then I get here, only to find Verena, dressing up like a tart and parading up and down the streets, tempting every man in town. Ask anybody. They'll tell you." She raised her head, then turned it, locked away in a green cage she had sentenced herself to.

Marty looked down and shook his head.

Jeff grabbed his jacket and went to the front porch. The cold wind felt good after the stifling warmth in the house. He stood still and let it blow over him. And he wished it could blow through his thoughts, as well. It would take a lot of wind to sweep away what he was feeling.

He had learned a lesson that day.

For all his love of antiques, they were cold, inanimate objects. But the elderly were living links to the past—and he had been guilty of dismissing them, treating them like one-dimensional has-beens. Not even has-beens, really, because he hadn't given them credit for *being* anything. He had forgotten that these were once teenagers, facing the same decisions, the same temptations, that teenagers face today. He had forgotten that they had fought wars, shaped futures, loved one another, *survived.*

He wasn't alone, either, although realizing it was no comfort. He had treated Verena Rose like . . . no, it was worse than that. He hadn't *treated* her like anything. He hadn't looked upon her as someone who had experienced passion, or grief, or youth. Yet, he knew now that she was once a vibrant, beautiful, desired, and loved woman. A girl, really, who had supported herself and her baby against overwhelming odds, a mother who had raised her child alone, and a woman who had lived through the event most feared by any parent: a child's death.

A child is born. A son is given.

And, *that* had altered her forever.

After several minutes, Gadzinski joined him. He mopped his face again, then stuffed the white square in a coat pocket. "I knew we were in for it as soon as she cranked up the heat."

"In more ways than one."

"You got that right."

Jeff watched a driver slowly pass, craning his neck to take in the action at the Weldon house. "Are they okay in there?"

"Yeah."

"Are you going to arrest them?"

"I should. He tampered with evidence, she withheld information. I don't know. Maybe your partner will match that third print today. It was top-list this morning when I spoke with him." Gadzinski shook his head. "Of course, I've been operating on the premise that whoever matches that third print is the murderer. But that print isn't so exciting now, since it doesn't belong to that old picker, and—"

"And Erma Weldon's description does," Jeff finished. "What about Tinker's grandson?"

"Long shot, but . . ."

"Why don't I ask Nathan whether Tinker's grandson was ever with him when he dropped by?"

"You do that, and I'll—" Gadzinski frowned. "Hell, Talbot, I'll ask him. You're not on the case, remember? Besides, you probably need to scare up some junk to make up for the fact that this unsolved murder has your inventory in hock."

Jeff nodded once. "And, now is as good a time as any." He descended the stairs, then turned. "What'll you do if the same thing happens with the third print?"

Gadzinski lifted a shoulder. "For all we know, there was a fourth set, before Marty Weldon wiped down the weapon. If the killer touched only metal, then we're back at square one."

Chapter Thirty-Two

THE OLD HOMESTEAD obviously had been a farm for many years. To the back and left was a burnout, evidenced by the charred but still standing chimney. Beyond the blackened foundation were three large outbuildings. Jeff's heart beat a little faster when he saw them. Lots of potential loot could be waiting behind the doors of those buildings.

He needed a distraction after the scene at the Weldon house, and nothing distracted him like antiques. He pulled the woodie in on the gravel drive behind a white pickup with built-in toolboxes and tall side rails.

Most of the exterior work on a new dwelling was finished. As he approached the structure, the echoes of hammer blows reached him. The door was ajar, so he called out, even though he figured the sound of his voice was absorbed by the echoes. He let himself in. The scent of new-sawn wood was warm and sweet. It appealed to him, and he wondered offhandedly whether it had something to do with his ancestry in the lumber trade.

He followed the sound to its source. A carpenter who had to be at least six-five was balancing on his shoulder the carcass of what would eventually be a kitchen cabinet. A second carpenter stood back, apparently to observe the effect.

Jeff leaned against the door frame. The tall man said, "Got a lot done today, Boyd. Whadayya think?"

"The name's Talbot, but it looks good to me."

Both workers craned their necks to look at Jeff, and he saw that the smaller one was a woman.

The tall man said, "Thought you were the owner. What can we do for you?"

"I noticed the barns out back and wanted to see if there was any junk in them for sale."

"You're the fifth one this week," said the female. "Everybody and his cat reads Kovel's column and, *poof!* He's cookin' up a get-rich-quick scheme."

Jeff shrugged. He was always learning something new from Ralph and Terry Kovel, as well as from the increasing number of television shows about antiques, but he had to admit: His job had been a lot more challenging since John Q. Public had become informed. "Did the owner let go of anything?"

"Yep," said the woman. "Lock, stock, and barrel—"

"*Barrels,* plural." The man interrupted his partner. "And, literally. There were several barrels packed with old china. You know, that heavy stuff like they used in diners and hotels, and on trains?"

"Naval china, too," the woman added.

Jeff had recently read a newspaper article about collectible restaurant ware once commissioned by the Navy. The pieces, white with navy blue anchors and other military insignia, appealed to many people. He worked to hide his disappointment. "That stuff's popular, all right."

The guy balanced the cabinet on a sawhorse. "That's what the old man said."

"Old man?"

"The one who bought it." The man chuckled. "He

looked damn near as stove-up as that blue Ford of his, but he got those barrels loaded up quick enough."

Jeff arched a brow. A mental list of pickers and what they drove popped into his mind, but he didn't need it. He had recently seen the dark blue truck, and he knew that Tinker had been here.

"How long ago?"

"Way before lunchtime. You guys ought to get together, work out a territory system so you aren't playing second string all the time."

He considered offering them some advice, but thanked them for their time instead and went back outside.

As he walked toward the car, he couldn't help but wonder. If Tinker was responsible for Verena's death, why hadn't he stolen something while he was at it? The guy always appeared to be so damned mercenary. Moot, for now, he thought. If Gadzinski had come up with any evidence at all, Tinker wouldn't still be out among them, ferreting out loot.

The cell phone was ringing when he climbed back into the woodie. He grabbed it from the passenger seat and flipped it open. Gordy was hollering before he could get it to his ear.

"What's that?" Jeff held the phone away from his eardrum.

"What are you and your Inspector Gadget trying to pull? Trick or Treat's come and gone."

"Gordy, what the hell are you talking about?"

"I ran your prints. The ones from the pole climber?"

"Yeah?"

"Yeah. What's the game?"

Jeff started the car, turned on the defroster. "Gadzinski might be playing some game, but you know damned well I'm not."

"Are you anywhere near his office?"

Jeff thought. He was probably fifteen minutes east of I-5, but it might as well have been one of those "you can't get there from here" scenarios. He had a couple of choices. Either way, he could hook the interstate and be in Everett in around twenty, twenty-five minutes, if the traffic wasn't jammed up to its eyeballs.

"Talbot!"

"Half an hour out. Why?"

"Because I don't like pranks."

"Talk some sense, Gordy."

"Sure, I'll talk some sense. And your inspector had better do the same. Those fingerprints you sent me? They belong to a dead man."

Jeff jotted down all the information his former partner provided. He tried Gadzinski's number, but lost the signal before the call went through. He found that aspect of his new cell phone the most irritating. One minute, you could be talking to someone, the next, nothing. So much for technology. He snapped his seat belt and pulled onto the road.

The drizzle started again, picked up quickly, and seemed to be settled in for a long night as he made his way south. The curvy stretch of road wasn't too busy, something he became even more thankful for when nightfall dropped like a shoe.

He strained to see the pavement through the now-heavy downpour that hung like a veil over the inky black night. His shoulders tensed as he leaned forward and watched for the cutoff road that would take him over to Everett.

It was getting harder to see, and he punched the dimmer switch with his foot, only to discover that the headlamps had been on bright. As he started to punch it again, he glanced in his rearview mirror and caught the glare of a vehicle's bright lights bearing down on him.

Where the hell did he come from?

The vehicle closed the gap fast and rode the woodie's bumper, all the while failing to dim its lights. It was either an SUV or a truck, because the beam cut right through the woodie's back glass.

"You damned fool," Jeff said, as if the driver could hear him. "Are you trying to blind me?"

When the driver whipped into the oncoming lane to pass, Jeff breathed a sigh of relief. Probably some stupid kid who hasn't learned that it isn't worth it. Trouble was, they usually learned that lesson the hard way.

Instead of going on around, though, the vehicle hung back, alternately gunning and braking, staying in Jeff's blind spot.

An image of Dennis Weaver in *Duel* flashed in his brain, set his heart to pumping harder. It went against the grain to give in to the jerk, but it wasn't worth risking an accident just because he was in the right. So, he let up on the gas, giving the guy a wide berth.

The moron wouldn't take it.

Jeff looked in the side mirror.

Suddenly, the headlights went black.

Jeff knew it wasn't an accident. The driver had turned off his damned lights.

A sensation like cold fingertips played at the back of his neck. He shivered as gooseflesh shot down his spine and bottomed out with a dull, spreading blow to his groin. His legs felt weak, as the eeriness of the invisible truck sank in.

"Get a grip, man," he said, and the act of speaking helped. He wasn't sure how to react if the other driver became more aggressive. Although he had been through defensive driving courses as part of his FBI training, he hadn't been driving a car from the forties. Handling the woodie wasn't like anything else. It was a damned boat, rocking in a storm. No antilock brakes or power steering, no fuel injection, no tight little axle made to turn on a dime.

They came up on a curve, and his heart pounded against his chest wall.

Then the lights were back. The vehicle ducked in behind him again and rode the woodie's bumper around the loop as if they had been welded together.

Back on the straight stretch, the guy played blind-spot again. Occasionally, he doused the headlamps.

"Stupid punk," Jeff muttered. He didn't want to turn in order to keep the guy in his sights. The conditions were too tricky. So, his gaze darted from his side-view mirror to the road to his rearview mirror, all the while adjusting to either the bright headlights or the fact that he couldn't locate the vehicle at all.

They passed a yellow and black warning sign that indicated a left curve ahead. Jeff watched for the vehicle to duck in behind him.

It didn't.

Jeff's jaw tightened as the vehicle came up nose and nose with the woodie. At last, Jeff saw that it was a pickup.

A pickup driven by someone who was going to get them both killed.

In an instant, a beam illuminated the curve, followed by blinding headlights from a car rounding the curve toward them.

The pickup driver cut his wheel and came at the woodie.

Jeff swerved, his mind a frantic jumble of thoughts, images, as he fought the wheel. At the same time, he tried to see who was driving the truck, but there was no way. It was too dark, too much rain.

There was nothing he could do. The pickup slammed into the woodie, sideswiping it. If Jeff tried to ride along—a move that might minimize the damage to his car—they would end up in a three-car crash, followed by a short ride in a long black car with curtains over its glass.

He squashed his brakes. The truck's right front bumper clipped the woodie and rode along its side, splintering wood, scraping paint, and mangling chrome. Tires screamed, then the big car dropped off the pavement. The pickup driver gunned it, and sliced through the slim corridor between the woodie and the oncoming car. Jeff saw a blur of red taillights as the pickup made the corner.

Jeff squashed the brakes again as rows and rows of green stalks slapped the car's windows. The tires pushed spongy, rain-soaked ground ahead of them, building a makeshift dam and causing the rear of the car to whip around like a dog chasing its tail. The big car's weight gave it momentum, and it slid backwards for years. Jeff fought against the wheel, tried to right the heavy, long car, but it was too late. The rear fender struck something hard, and the last thought Jeff remembered having was: Thank God this is a big old boat.

Chapter Thirty-Three

HE WAS A kid again, lying on his back on a merry-go-round, Auntie Pim's anxious voice calling from a thousand miles away, warning him to sit up before he made himself sick.

He gripped the wheel and held on until the vertigo subsided several minutes later.

He walked unsteadily—fighting against his own tremors and a wet terrain that sucked at his sneakers like a vacuum—following the destruction left behind by his little joy ride over hill and dale and cornfield. The woodie had slid to a stop with no small amount of help from a cornerpost and five rows of barbed wire that had, moments before, resembled a musical staff.

Fortunately, he had located his cell phone with the help

of a flashlight he kept in the glove compartment and had called 911.

Now, with the flashlight in one hand and his thermos in the other, he picked his way toward the pavement.

Whoever had put him—and the driver of the oncoming car—in danger, had ice in his veins. The maneuver had been coldly calculated. Although Jeff didn't think that the person he knew to drive a beat-up truck was capable of anything so cold-blooded, Tinker looked ominously suspicious—on several counts.

Flashing lights—red, blue, and yellow—vacillated in the distance. It took him several more minutes to reach them.

A young woman stood at the edge of the pavement, talking with an officer. Between bouts of crying, she told him what she had seen.

Jeff would've cried, too, if he hadn't been so shell-shocked. He handed his driver's license to the patrolman, along with his version of the accident, and threw in his suspicions for good measure.

"You said it was an older Chevrolet. Did you get a look at the headlights?"

"Get a look?" Was this guy *kidding?*

"Round or square?"

Jeff replayed a couple of mental slides, which upped his angst a notch. "Round. Why?"

"Pre-eighty," the patrolman stated. He wrote it down, then added, "In nineteen eighty, Chevy trucks introduced square lamps."

Jeff raised a brow, then screwed the lid off the thermos and poured coffee into it.

The patrolmen leaned in and took a whiff. "Need me to take you home?"

"This is *coffee.*"

The patrolman looked off into the distant field, then back. "You don't have a car, sir."

Oh. He was more rattled than he had first thought. "Sure. Thanks."

During the ride home, Jeff used his cell phone to let Sheila know what had happened, to tell her that the woodie was in the hands of the wrecker driver, and to assure her—several times—that he was okay. By the time he was delivered to his front door, he was more than ready to leave moving vehicles behind.

Greer swung open the front door as Jeff kicked off his muddy shoes. The butler turned. "Yes, madam, it's him."

Jeff stepped inside. Greer said, "Please let me know if there is anything I can do, sir. Anything at all."

"Thanks, Greer. Maybe a martini in the library. A little later."

"My pleasure, sir."

Sheila was perched on the second-floor landing, already dressed for bed in a pair of flannel pajamas. She looked cozy. He could use some of that coziness.

He climbed the stairs slowly. Soreness was setting in, and it felt like he was coming down with the flu more than anything else.

"Honey?" She met him halfway, helped support him. "Are you sure you shouldn't be at the hospital?"

"I'm fine. Really. Just a little achy."

When they arrived in the bedroom, she said, "Let me look at you, make sure you don't have any cuts or bruises."

She carefully undressed him, then moved her hands over his body, checking for sore spots. She squeezed, and prodded, and gave him more action than she had in a hell of a long time.

Torture. He wrapped his arms around her, pulled her onto the bed.

She squeezed him—a light, comforting squeeze. "I'm so relieved that you're okay."

"More than okay," he whispered as he kissed the crook of her neck.

She rubbed his back. "That's the most important thing. And don't worry about the car. You can get her in to a top-notch restorer, and you can rent or buy something else in the meantime. I mean, I know it'll take months to—"

"Sheila, honey, the car is *not* what I'm thinking about right now."

"I just know that . . . well, you really should get some rest. I'm afraid you're going to feel pretty rough tomorrow."

"Then you'd better take advantage of me tonight."

He slid his hands under that cozy flannel top, and the feel of her skin damn near singed his fingers.

She exhaled. "Jeff, can't we just hold each other for now? Okay?"

He swallowed, tried to relax. He held her for several minutes without responding. By the time he whispered, "Okay," she had fallen asleep.

He slipped away, threw on drawstring pants and a robe, and went downstairs.

He was seated on the couch in the library, having his second martini as he absently watched the toy train circling the Christmas tree. It was an American Flyer, post-war model (which put it between 1945 and 1969), and was one of three vintage sets he owned. The two pre-war models were set up, too: the Lionel in the parlor, and the German Marklin in the den.

The click-click of heels on the foyer floor accented the rhythm of the train. Karen entered the library and dropped her coat and purse on a chair while she kicked off a glossy pair of spiked high heels. She wore a short black dress that shimmered as she walked a crooked path to the credenza. After pouring a glass of red wine, she plopped down in the chair opposite him and flashed a lopsided grin.

He nodded. "You look like you had fun tonight."

"That makes one of us," she said, adding and extra "s" or two. "You look like someone kicked your dog."

Drunks do have a way of nailing it, don't they? "I heard a car drive off as you came in," he said. "Didn't your knight in antique armor walk you to the door?"

She siphoned off a third of her drink. "I took a cab. And, Max is not an antique."

He chastised himself for yet again stereotyping seniors. He was wondering whether Karen and Max had fought, or whether he had stood her up, when she said, "Don't get excited. We didn't have a fight."

"I wish you would explain your interest in him. He's, what? Thirty years older than you?"

"But you have to admit,"—lopsided grin—"that he doesn't look more than fifteen." Her expression turned thoughtful. "It's his attitude, I think. I mean, he's good-looking, too—even *you* have to admit—wait a minute! That's it, isn't it? You're envious because he's in a lot better shape than you are."

"I've seen him, and that's not it. Some of us have better things to do with our time than to—"

"An hour a day. That's all. He gets up early, goes through his routine, hits the tanning bed a couple times a week. He says that all it takes is discipline, and everyone should develop it. Your body is all you've got."

She gulped the rest of the wine. "So, you see? It's like Michael Douglas nabbing Catherine Zeta Jones. If you click, age doesn't matter. Besides, Max appreciates that I stay in shape, and I appreciate that he's such a good cook. We're made for each other."

She sighed, then started up again. "You know, Jeff, I've been using Sheila's gym every morning. You could join me." She moved to the couch, then snuggled up beside him and patted his stomach.

He pushed her hand away, scooted over. "Damn it, Karen, don't change the subject. He's old enough to be your father."

She sat up. "And you're beginning to *sound* like my father. Since when did you become so high and mighty? You, who married my *younger* sister? You can't even look past dates on a calendar and see when two people are good together. Knock it off before I start thinking you're serious."

He *was* serious, but he kept his mouth shut.

She got up and poured another glass of wine, then sat beside him again and began rubbing his arm. "You're the one who hooked me up with him, you know. Maybe this isn't fatherly concern. Maybe it's jealousy."

"Jealousy." His voice was flat. "You *are* kidding, right?"

"Come on." She put her head on his shoulder, and the alcohol on her breath was overpowering. "Haven't you ever wondered what it would've been like if you had met me first?"

"Karen, don't go there. You've had way too much to drink, and you're going to wind up making a fool of yourself."

"Hardly." She nuzzled his neck.

He twisted away from her and went over to the fireplace, watching the flames and hoping desperately that she would just pass out. She was going to regret all of this tomorrow, *if* she remembered any of it.

She came up behind him then, and he braced himself as she wrapped her arms around his waist and leaned against his back. *Great,* he thought, *she's a clingy drunk, to boot.* He wondered what had prompted her to get so plastered. She didn't usually relinquish self-control.

"I never thanked you for suggesting I call Max, did I? I owe you a hug." She whipped around front of him—so fast that he couldn't believe it hadn't made her dizzy—and threw her arms around his neck. His heart pounded. She lingered, and he tried to unclasp her hands. He didn't know whether to be irritated or alarmed.

"Admit it, Jeff, we'd be good together. With Sheila, you're stuck in this dreary old house twenty-four-seven, locked in like prisoners—"

"Stop right there, Karen." He broke free, flushed with a mix of anger and embarrassment. "You know damned well it's not like that. There are a lot of things that make our marriage work, like love, and trust, and freedom—and something else you apparently haven't experienced: fidelity."

"Thanks a lot." Karen slumped onto the couch. "I watch how you are with my sister, so caring, so compassionate. I just needed a little of that TLC, you know? Max knows how to have a good time, but . . . okay, so there's a chink in his armor. Are you happy? He doesn't have those other qualities, like you do. I know you think I'm tough, always going for the shock value. But there are times when I'd like to be on the other side, see what it feels like. You're the only person I've ever met who is both those sides."

"You're wrong. Sheila is both those sides, too."

Karen tried to focus, but gave up. She laid her head back and closed her eyes. "Oh, I know that," she said sleepily. "Don't tell her I was a jerk tonight, okay?"

"No danger there. For one thing, our family's too small to be torn up by an alcohol-induced riff. More than that, though, I'm not into hurting her feelings."

"Neither am I, whether you believe me or not." She took a deep breath, and stretched out on her side.

Jeff shook his head. His sister-in-law had always been the adventurer, the unreliable one. Oddly, those traits in her had never bothered Sheila. But they had always bugged the hell out of him. Now, he wondered whether she was getting tired of the globe-trotting, the living out of suitcases, the "fun" relationships.

He debated talking to her, apologizing for whatever it was that had driven her to this place tonight. But, before he made up his mind, she had fallen asleep.

After covering her with a chenille throw, he cleared the barware from the coffee table. Greer would need the space the next morning for a large tray of hangover remedies.

He turned out the lights and headed upstairs. When he got to the bedroom, Sheila was awake and waiting for him. The flannel pajamas were in a heap on the floor.

Chapter Thirty-Four

IN THE END, it was the ladder that sold him.

Oh, he was a sucker for just about everything that the PT Cruiser offered: retro design, chrome car jewelry, honest-to-God fenders.

But when you're a picker, and the sales person says you can fit an eight-foot ladder inside and still close the rear hatch, then you've got yourself a tailor-made car.

Jeff drove the Patriot Blue PT Cruiser off the lot, and headed toward downtown Seattle. There were scant few shopping days left before Christmas—as the media frantically and continually reminded him—and he hadn't even started.

The house had been quiet that morning. Sheila wanted to sleep in, and he had no doubt that Karen's aching head would leave her no choice. He had called his insurance company about the wrecked car, then had called a specialty repair shop to make arrangements for the restoration of said car. During that time, Gadzinski had left a voice-mail message saying he'd spoken with Gordy.

Now, Jeff marked "throw money at new car" off his to-do list, and his chores for the day shrank considerably.

He pulled the little buggy into a hole-in-the-wall parking structure (surprised at how easy she was to maneuver) and darted around the corner toward Metsker Maps.

After purchasing an old, leather-bound atlas for Sheila, he debated whether to shop next at Elliott Bay Bookstore or at Seattle Mystery Bookshop. He blamed his Libra personality for trying to maintain balance: He could never buy anything in one of the stores without patronizing the other. Practicality ruled, and he went over to Elliott Bay on Main, so that he wouldn't have to haul his mystery purchases roundtrip.

After an hour among the maze, he paid for his selections, then walked toward the Cherry. He stopped into the Seattle's Best Coffeehouse located on the corner above the bookstore, and ordered a hazelnut latte. Typically, he wasn't one for frou-frou drinks—especially one that inspired the nickname *Latteland* for a city with more than its share of monikers and mottos—but the combination of book shopping and the holidays had put him in a rare, festive mood.

He drank the hot coffee while reading, ironically, a book on tea that he had bought for Blanche, then walked past the wrought-iron railing and switched back to the mystery shop's entrance a half-story down.

As always, the first thing he did was check to see whether the antique table was still there. It was. It stood just inside the door and to the left, a fabulous square of rich oak with huge ball and claw feet and a provenance that told like a fairy tale. The store's founder, Bill Farley, had previously shared the story with him of how his mother-in-law had paid only a few bucks for the table in 1913 and had carried it several miles to her home.

As Jeff ostensibly perused the books on the table, a friendly male voice asked if he needed any assistance. He turned. "Mister Farley? I heard that you had retired."

"Oh, I did. But I help out from time to time."

"You're the one who owns this table, aren't you? I wanted to see if it was still here."

"Still here, and not going anywhere."

"Well, you can't blame me for trying." He picked up a miniature book and inspected the tiny gold high heel dangling from a black satin ribbon that served as a bookmark. "You're that picker, aren't you? Used to be a G-man."

"Good memory."

The gent smiled and nodded his appreciation for the compliment.

"Just how much would you need to part with that table?"

Farley straightened a stack of red bookmarks by the cash register. "You'd have to go higher than the Smith Tower to meet my price."

Jeff was reaching for a novel whose jacket had caught his eye when the response registered. He stopped mid-air. "You know, that's only the second time I've heard that phrase, and I've lived here most of my life."

"Back when I was your age, that tower was the tallest thing in town. It lost some of its shine after they pricked the sky with the Space Needle."

Jeff turned that over in his mind. Farley said, "Are you sure I can't help you with a mystery today?"

Although he knew that the man meant mystery *novel,* he said, "Believe me, I think you already did."

He had planned to get his holiday shopping out of the way in the course of the afternoon, but, now, he didn't seem to have the energy for it. After promising to return later, he walked outside and hurried toward the parking structure. The information he had gotten from the man at the bookstore had given him an uneasy feeling, and he needed to find out why.

Chapter Thirty-Five

"WHAT'S THE CLIMATE like there, Greer?" Jeff asked when the butler answered the phone.

"The missus is lost in the dining room among toys and wrapping paper, sir, and Miss Karen is napping."

"I'm sure she wasn't easy to deal with this morning. No telling what she put you through, but thank you."

"Always a pleasure, sir."

"God, but you were taught well." He studied the car's interior, familiarizing himself with everything. "Do you think you can get Sheila to tear herself away long enough to come to the phone?"

"She's right here, sir."

"It's about time, Talbot," she said. "I'll assume you have wheels under you. Greer said that you wouldn't let him wait around at the dealership."

"I had already decided I wasn't going to leave there

without a vehicle. Besides, he has enough to do. That's why I'm leaving him the use of the Jimmy."

"He'll need it to haul my packages from the post office. I may have gotten too much Christmas spirit while shopping for the Rose children. I hope you don't mind."

"Nope. I'm actually looking forward to Tuesday." He tried to figure out how to use the complicated sound system. "Listen, I'm on my way home to change for Maura's wedding; thought I'd see if you need me to bring anything."

"I can't think of anything . . . wait a sec."

He heard a voice in the background, then Sheila came back on the line. "Karen just woke up. She asked if you would pick up some photos she had developed. They're at the same place as last time."

"Sure. How's she feeling today, by the way?"

"Not as bad as she would be, if Greer hadn't taken care of her all morning. She owes him."

"I've never seen her get that looped."

"She hasn't told me much yet, but I think Max canceled on her last night."

"I figured it had to be something like that."

"Things must be okay now. They have plans for later tonight."

"Good. I'll see you in a little while." He punched End, fought a mess of traffic getting to the photo processing store, then made up for it by scooting the car into a parking spot no bigger than a toolbox.

He checked his watch. Three-thirty. It hadn't rained all day, miraculously, and he hoped it would stay that way for Maura's wedding. He dashed in, picked up the photos, dashed back out—and got caught in a downpour before he located his car. It was almost like having a rental and forgetting to note what it looked like before walking away.

The drive home was interesting, as he reminded himself how to drive a manual shift. By the time he got home, he had it under control, for the most part.

Jeff stepped inside. No one was in the kitchen, but the mouthwatering aroma of roast beef filled the room. From somewhere inside the house came Mel Tormé's voice singing "The Christmas Song."

A light was on in the butler's pantry. There, Jeff found Greer seated at a small built-in desk, absorbed in the odd pairing of an old black leather ledger and a laptop computer, also black. Beyond him, through the door leading into the dining room, was Sheila, consumed with a volcano of color: toys, games, cylinders of festive paper, spools of ribbon.

He rapped his knuckles lightly on the door facing.

Greer sprang to his feet. "I'm sorry, sir. I was working out the details for Tuesday's dinner."

"Lord, man, don't apologize for that. How's it coming?"

"Very well, sir. The particulars of each guest have been gathered, the missus has planned the menu, and I've printed the menu cards and place cards." Greer moved the ledger toward his employer.

Jeff recognized it as the one that had been passed down to Greer by his grandfather, who had also been a butler. The page read:

CHRISTMAS DINNER
DECEMBER 25, 2001

HOSTS: Jeffrey and Sheila Talbot

HOUSEGUEST: Ms. Karen Gray

GUESTS:
Mrs. Blanche Appleby
Ms. Trudy Blessing
Mr. and Mrs. Sam Carver (Helen)
Mr. and Mrs. Nathan Rose (Melanie)
Masters Joshua and Logan Rose
Miss Margaret "Maggie" Rose

SPECIFICS:
Ms. Gray: Red wine (recent tendency to overdrink)
Mrs. Appleby: White wine, preferably German
Ms. Blessing: Chardonnay

Mr. Carver: Broken Rake Beer (Pyramid Brewery)
Mrs. Carver: Martini (gin) with lemon twist. *No mushrooms.*
Mr. Rose: Beer (not particular)
Mrs. Rose: Iced tea
Master Joshua: Grape juice before; whole milk with dinner.
Master Logan: Soft drinks. *Vegetarian.*
Miss Maggie: Soft drinks before; strawberry milk with dinner.

TABLE:
Flowers: Red roses and baby's breath, in honor of the Rose family
China: Spode Holiday pattern

MENU:
Assortment of appetizers; cheeses
Fruit Salads: Christmas (red); Pistachio (green)
Vegetable Salads: Cauliflower & Broccoli; Mixed Green Salad
Virginia Ham with Raisin Sauce
Roasted Cornish Game Hens with Dried Cranberry and Hazelnut Stuffing
Green Beans with Cashews
Mashed Potatoes with Cream Gravy
Candied Sweet Potatoes
Assortment of breads and butters
Sweet Breads: Cranberry; Zucchini; Apple Nut; Pumpkin Cream Cheese Roll
Desserts: Steamed Christmas Pudding with Orange Hard Sauce; Pumpkin Pie; Cranberry Cheesecake; assortment of cookies and candies
Coffee and tea, both hot and iced

Notes: Make it fun for the children. Make it memorable for the adults.

Jeff shook his head. "And to think, I came in here with hopes that someone remembered to buy a wedding gift for tonight. I should learn never to worry about anything."

"Yes, sir. The bride is registered at Bon Marche, and the missus sent me there for a set of crystal champagne flutes. I'll see to it that the gift is put in your car."

Immediately upon saying *car,* Greer's face lit up. "May I take a peek at her, sir?"

"Be my guest."

Jeff went to the dining room-slash-Santa's workshop to visit with a cute little blonde elf named Sheila. She was stationed at one side of the large table, wrapping toys.

He kissed her, then said, "Dinner smells great. Will we get to eat together?"

"Sure. Breakfast nook okay with you?"

"Sure." She surprised him with the suggestion, as she hadn't mentioned the alcove since it had been redecorated. "What do you think of the new look?"

"I like it. She did a good job."

That's it? Oh, well. She would probably go nuts over it after she tucked Christmas away for another year.

He let her get back to playing Santa's helper while he tended to account ledgers before dinner.

As he went upstairs to change for the wedding, he thought about the exquisite Russian marriage casket that would be Sheila's gift this Christmas.

It was sad that Verena had never had wedding memories to store in it. He wondered how long she had owned it, whether it had been handed down to her, or whether she had simply picked it up when someone else had cast it aside.

To him, it symbolized many things: beauty, sacrifice, survival, love. After all Sheila had been through, after all the two of them had experienced together, there really had been no question: The treasure belonged to her.

Perhaps thoughts of the casket influenced him, because he chose a vintage pair of Russian cuff links from his collection. These were late nineteenth century, gold with a red enamel ground, and Faberge's standard diamond-pattern weave, upon which small diamonds dotted each gold axis.

Only after he had finished dressing and looked in the

mirror to study the effect of the striking links with the black suit, the white shirt, and the claret silk tie, did he remember: The Russian cuff links had been a gift from Sheila for their own wedding.

Chapter Thirty-Six

THE WEDDING WAS like most others: twelve long months of preparation followed by twelve quick minutes of ceremony.

Jeff never looked forward to attending the things without his wife by his side. But he and Sam Carver had been friends since they were kids, and he had watched Maura grow up. Besides, Sheila had given him strict instructions to bring home a detailed account of the celebration.

He took it all in, committed to memory the fine points so that he might report them to his housebound wife.

Sam appeared uncomfortable in his tuxedo, but he beamed as father of the bride. Helen wore a stunning gold gown and was the epitome of poise and refinement—and she looked young enough to be the bride's sister. Speaking of sisters: Jeff remembered what Sam had said about all the complaints over gowns and shoes. But Maura's four female siblings were fashion plates in cranberry and gold brocade. Darius, the groom, looked nervous but proud. And happy, very happy.

Enter the bride: Maura Lavinia Carver soon-to-be Sinclair had miraculously erased all signs of stress and exhaustion that Jeff had seen on her face a few weeks earlier. Now, a bronze princess in winter white taffeta and fur, she was the most beautiful bride anyone had ever seen. Then again, aren't they all?

Jeff was swept along the receiving line with two hundred other guests. Afterward, he hung around just long enough for the cutting of the cake. A blues band kicked off the dancing, and Jeff considered whether a dance or two would work some of the soreness from his muscles. He'd been lucky: The accident could've killed him.

He opted to skip out. He got Sam's attention and gave him a salute, then left it all behind and made his way along the empty corridors to the exit.

He hurried through pelting rain to his car, threw his suitcoat in the backseat, then climbed inside.

It hadn't been easy to concentrate on wedding details and, now, he gave in to thoughts of parallel worlds, things past and present, people he had talked to recently, and what they had said. The most curious was the mention of the Smith Tower. Twice. Something about that rattled around in his brain, some shred of knowledge that he tried to assimilate. He almost had it . . . if only it would ring a bell.

His cell phone rang. Since the lights showed him that it was on the passenger floorboard, he pulled into a convenience store parking lot off Elliott and reached for the phone. He came up with the phone and a small plastic bag. Karen's photos. He had forgotten about them. He answered the phone.

Sheila said, "I almost hung up, Talbot. Are you ever coming home?"

"As a matter of fact, dear wife, I'm almost there." He pulled the photos from the pack. "What's up?"

"Oh, I'm just anxious to hear about the wedding. And, I thought you might want to watch a movie. Karen and Max are going to dinner—I forget where she said—followed by a horse-drawn carriage ride downtown. Apparently, he reserved a carriage for a couple of hours."

"That sounds serious." He glanced through images of landmarks while he talked. "Max had to have paid at least a couple hundred dollars, probably more since Christmas is only a few days away. Blanche told me that you have to pay extra for the rides that take in Fifth and Sixth avenues."

"Why?"

Although it had been years since he and Sheila had done all the Seattle holiday traditions—the Argosy cruises, the Nutcracker ballet, the carriage rides—her lapse in memory unsettled him. "Because that's where the best light displays are."

"That's right! It seems like a hundred years ago you took me on that ride. Remember how I wished they had blocked off the car traffic so we could transport ourselves to the past? How we took along hot chocolate and the antique fur lap throw that had belonged to your great-grandmother? How the horse's hooves *clop-clopped*, and the soft chime of the antique sleigh bells?"

"I sure do." His voice echoed relief more than warm memories, but both emotions sounded the same. He held up one of the photos for closer inspection. Something about it looked familiar. Probably reprints.

Sheila sighed. "You know, we could crawl under that fur throw in front of our bedroom's fireplace."

"Yeah. Hon? Has Karen left yet?"

"Talk about changing the subject. See if I try to seduce you again tonight."

"Sorry. Has she?"

"I think so. Why? What's wrong, Jeff?"

He didn't want to worry her, and it probably wouldn't hurt if he verified his suspicions once he got home. "I need to ask her a photography question. I'll be there in a few." He pressed End.

By the time he reached the top of Queen Anne Hill and was rounding the curve into the downtown segment of the neighborhood, the drizzle turned into a bonifide rain-shower. He reached for the knob to turn on the wipers, and instantly realized that there was no knob, and that this wasn't his car. Or, at least, not his woodie. *Damn it,* he thought, *I'll never get used to this thing.* Normally, he wouldn't have bothered with the wipers, but the accident had shaken him enough to prompt extra precaution.

He was messing with switches, levers, and pushbuttons while straining to see through the rain, when a truck whipped around the curve toward him. Its right headlight was out. He panicked, flashed back to the truck accident. His wipers shoved water off the windshield as another vehicle's headlights from a sidestreet illuminated the truck, spotlighting a wrecked fender.

"What's *he* doing up here?" Jeff said. Was Tinker prowling around looking for him? Or his house?

The neighborhood's downtown section was busy, with drivers trolling for parking spots and pedestrians laden with shopping bags darting across streets.

Jeff zigzagged the Cruiser amidst blasting horns and shot back down the hill. At the bottom, he saw a dark-colored truck turning left on Mercer. He couldn't be sure that it was Tinker's, but, for lack of a better plan, he took off after it.

The traffic was stacked. It was the last weekend before Christmas, so he guessed the crowds were headed to the Opera House to watch *The Nutcracker.* The pickup driver was as reckless as he had been two nights earlier, and Jeff had a challenge keeping him in his sights. He wondered whether the driver knew yet about the new Cruiser. If not, Jeff had an advantage.

He concentrated on the taillights, turned when the pickup turned, dodged in and out of traffic in order to keep up. Jeff wasn't familiar with the area and almost missed a tricky exchange when the pickup turned left from what looked like a right lane. Jeff squeezed into an opening where the woodie wouldn't have had a chance, and kept the truck in his sights.

The pickup parked, and the taillights went black. Jeff eased into a spot far enough away that he wouldn't be spotted. He turned off the ignition and waited.

Questions bombarded him: Why was Tinker parked

near a Lake Union houseboat community? Did he live here? How many of the subtle clues now shuffling through Jeff's mind pointed to Tinker as Verena's killer? Why was the Smith Tower important? And, what had he seen in Karen's photos that raised a red flag?

Wait a minute. It was coming together now. The pickup, the Tower. Tinker had been present, but that was all.

Slideshow images fluttered on a mental screen—two round headlights, like sinister eyes pursuing him. The run-in with Tinker. The old man's grandson pulling the truck away. Square headlights. The officer on the accident scene: "Chevy introduced square lamps in eighty." The loading docks at Blanche's antiques mall. Two pickups. Not one.

Then it hit him. The real answer was in the photos. One of the shots from Karen's roll was of her and Max—no doubt she had used a timer—in front of his seaplane. Each had an arm draped over the other's shoulder. They wore big cheesy grins.

Jeff had recently seen a similar pose in another photo. It was a black-and-white shot portraying two young men in front of a fighter plane. The snapshot had been sent to Verena Rose, and one of the young men looked *exactly* like Max Bolton.

He grabbed the phone, punched in Gadzinski's number, and hit Send.

While he waited, the stakes went up.

His sister-in-law got out of the passenger side of the truck.

The detective answered, as Max Bolton joined Karen on the floating boardwalk.

"Gadzinski, it's Talbot. I just found Andrew Rose."

Chapter Thirty-Seven

JEFF TOLD THE detective what he needed to know in two short sentences, then dropped the phone and got out of the car.

He ran across the lot, grateful that it had stopped raining.

At the end of the long boardwalk, the couple turned right. Jeff heard their voices but couldn't make out what they were saying. Bolton's tone indicated that he was irritated about something, though.

Jeff's dress shoes echoed on the boards, and he willed himself to walk slowly so that he wouldn't draw Bolton's attention. He prayed that they wouldn't turn around. His white shirt was like a beacon under the security lights.

They paid him no mind, walked to the last houseboat. Beyond it, bobbing on Lake Union, was the yellow and white floatplane Jeff had seen in Karen's photos.

Max fumbled with the key to the door. He got it open and stepped inside, leaving Karen on the stoop.

Gentlemanly.

Jeff hurried forward. "Karen! Don't go in!"

She turned toward him with her mouth slightly open. It was obvious that his command hadn't registered.

Max stepped back outside.

"Karen, go inside and start dinner. I'll take care of this."

"I've told you before, Max. I don't take orders."

She looked at Jeff. "Your *concern* is getting out of hand. What did you do? Follow us?"

"No," Jeff said. *Think fast.* "It's Sheila. She needs you to come home."

Karen made a little sound, started toward Jeff.

Bolton grabbed her arm.

Jeff stormed them, closing the gap and calculating his next move. He had to reach Bolton before the guy panicked and pulled Karen inside.

But Bolton fooled him. He slung Karen onto the boards.

She yelped, scrambling for purchase as she slid toward the water.

Jeff lunged.

With a guttural, Oriental cry, Max Bolton flew high into the air and hung, suspended, with limbs poised expertly. He drew up a knee and delivered a knife-like kick.

The last thing Jeff saw was a foot catapulting toward his chest.

The blow knocked the wind out of his lungs, and he struggled for air as his body, propelled by the impact, sailed off the walkway. He hit the icy water before he could get a breath, and his insides shuddered from the shock.

Do not panic. Do not panic. He repeated it like a mantra, in the deep, calming voice of his former partner, Gordy Easthope. The thought of the barrel-chested agent made him want to smile, and he questioned this sudden feeling of peace, wondering, in fact, if it was too late. If it all was too late.

His chest felt as if a sledgehammer had slammed into it. The pain snapped him to, and he found himself flailing in the depths. He opened his eyes to a blackness so dark that he couldn't tell which end was up. Fresh panic gripped him. Somewhere in the murky darkness he heard the muffled screams of a female voice.

Karen.

His head pounded. He couldn't think, didn't know how to find his way. Then he heard Sheila: *Relax. Float. Your body will take you there.*

How? How do you let go of your body *without* letting go of your mind?

He fought to maintain control, fought against giving in to the blackness, the pounding in his ears.

Do it! Gordy roared.

Jeff let go.

He floated, arms levitating, stretching toward the face of the water.

He surfaced, choking, and sucked in great volumes of air.

He was beside the floatplane.

Bolton had Karen in a choking armhold with the barrel of an automatic stuck behind her right ear. They were on the dock.

"Get in the plane, Talbot, or she's a goner."

Jeff fought against his violently shaking body. His teeth were clenched, and he exhaled, siphoning off adrenaline.

"Slow, now," Bolton said. "Don't upset the balance."

Jeff pulled himself onto the float, then climbed inside the plane.

Bolton said, "If either of you disobey me, I'll kill the other one. Got it?"

Both said they got it.

"Good. Talbot, get to the back."

Bolton stepped inside and used the weapon to motion Karen on board.

"Karen, don't," Jeff yelled.

Karen came through the door, and Bolton secured it shut.

Bolton tossed a roll of duct tape to Jeff. "Bind your ankles with it, and no tricks, you hear? The war taught me a lot of things, and I know what to do to people who don't follow orders."

When Jeff had finished, Bolton said to Karen, "Tape his wrists behind his back, then tape your ankles together."

"Why are you doing this?" Karen asked as she bound Jeff's wrists.

"I know why." Jeff locked eyes with Bolton. "Why did you kill your own mother?"

Behind him, Karen made a sound.

Bolton paused, and then a sinister grin filled the bottom half of his face. "Where'd I slip up?"

"Right at the beginning. Only an old-time Seattleite would use the phrase, 'higher than the Smith Tower.' After I found out Andrew was still alive, it made sense why you'd hide your familiarity with Seattle. Then you made the mistake of having your picture taken in a pose identical to one from your war years. You haven't changed that much. But I didn't put it all together until I saw you get out of your truck; the truck that ran me off the road when it looked like I was getting too close."

Karen moved to Jeff's side, began strapping her ankles.

Bolton shook his head impatiently. "I should've ditched the truck. But I didn't think you'd recover so quickly. Or at all. Now humor me. Tell me what you've got in the way of evidence."

Jeff looked at him evenly.

Bolton slapped Karen's face. Blood ran from the corner of her mouth.

Jeff stiffened, pulled against his shackles. He lost his balance and struggled to right himself. When he had, he looked up to speak, and Bolton's eyes were filled with an expression like a wild animal's.

"I *can* break you, boy. Do you think martial arts is the only thing I learned over there? When they put you in the foxholes fighting those heathens, you learn to do a lot of things in the name of survival." He dragged Karen toward him.

"It made you angry that I slapped a woman," he continued, "but I could tell that it didn't shock you. Maybe this will."

Slowly, expertly, he began unbuttoning Karen's blouse. When she protested, he poised his hand to strike her again.

She shut up.

"I've seen her naked, Talbot. Have you?"

"Andrew Rose's prints are on the murder weapon. Not Max Bolton's. There is no Max Bolton."

"Yeah, well, Nathan Rose's prints are there, too. If you had left things alone, you wouldn't be on your way out to sea."

"I read a letter your mother had written to you, just before you traded identities with Bolton."

"That's impossible. I destroyed all her letters."

"You never received this one. Apparently, she got word of your death before she mailed it. She loved you, but you were too damned cocky to realize it. She spent the rest of her *life* mourning your death."

"You're not telling me anything new. I came back after my wife died, tried to tell my mother that it was me. But she wouldn't even listen! Kept saying she had proof. Her son was a war hero. Isn't that a hoot? A war hero! She had built me up good in her mind, I'll give her that. But, when it came time to face reality, she wanted none of it."

"Why *did* you come back?"

"I told you, my wife had died. It's a woman's job to take care of the men in her life. My mother owed me that."

Jeff knew the man believed what he said. Bolton—Rose—was so dependent upon women that he became manipulative, abusive, when he couldn't control them. "That doesn't answer the question."

"I didn't go there to kill her. But she provoked me."

"How did she do that?"

"Enough with the stalling." Bolton bound Karen's hands, then taped Jeff's mouth. He smelled adhesive.

"It was fun, Karen, until you started acting like a women's libber." He tried to kiss her, but she bit his lip. Now he was bleeding. He slapped her again, then cut a piece of tape and pressed it over her mouth.

Jeff tried to lunge at Bolton. But the rocking of the seaplane threw him off balance again. He scooted to one side, leaned against it for support.

Bolton dragged Karen to the other side, balancing the load, then left them and went toward the cockpit. A moment later, the engine fired up and the seaplane started moving.

Chapter Thirty-Eight

THE DIN OF the engine made time immeasurable, and after a while, Jeff couldn't have said whether they were over Whidbey Island or Juneau, Alaska. He felt cold enough for it to be Alaska. His wet clothes clung to him like an icy shroud.

It was dark, except for a dim glow coming from the cockpit. He had already determined that there was nothing in his pockets to be used as a knife, and he assumed the same of Karen.

He got a sense that she was scooting across the floor, but he couldn't be sure what she was up to. She had been on board the craft several times; maybe she had remembered something that would help.

To maintain the craft's balance, he scooted in her direction until they bumped into each other.

She nudged him with her shoulder. He barely heard the guttural noises she was making.

She nodded once, and he understood that she was telling him to stay put. He acknowledged, and she worked her way around behind him. Had she found a sharp object? He remembered her kitchen skills. *Lack* of kitchen skills. Could he trust her not to cut off his hand? Strange, bizarre thoughts tumbled through his mind, and he realized that he could do without a hand if it meant overpowering Max Bolton and gaining control of the aircraft.

But then what? He couldn't fly the damn thing, and he was sure Karen couldn't, either. Trying was better than dying, he concluded. And the plane had to have a radio, right?

It seemed very movie-esque, but he was sure they could radio for help and someone could talk him down. Of all the situations he had been trained for as an agent, flying hadn't been one of them.

Karen *had* found something. She sawed at the tape around his wrists. He stretched his shaking hands apart to give her more room to work. His whole body was shuddering from cold.

The plane dipped, and they leaned against each other, forming a counterbalance until the wings leveled out.

After several tries, he finally broke free. Bracing himself, he yanked the tape from his mouth, then told Karen to brace herself. He ripped the tape from her face. He had to hand it to her. She didn't make a sound.

He leaned close to her ear. "You okay?"

"Been better, been worse."

"You'll have to tell me about the worse when we get out of this one."

"Don't know if you could handle it, bro."

Jeff looked at her. Would that be another of her exaggerations, like the drug cartel line she had fed him at the airport?

"There's a bread knife in my hand."

"I'll bet that's the first time you've used those words together in a sentence."

"Ha, ha. He keeps a picnic basket on board with supplies."

Gingerly, Jeff felt for the knife, and when he found it, he worked quickly to free her hands.

"Now what?" he said as they freed their ankles.

"Easy. You disarm him, and I'll turn this thing around."

"You're kidding? You know how to fly?"

"Oh, better than that. I know how to land."

"Good. Gives us more options." Jeff exhaled. "I'm the one with weapons training. I'll go in first."

Jeff crawled toward the cockpit so that Bolton wouldn't catch his reflection in the dark glass. The man had both hands on the controls.

Jeff calculated. Bolton was right-handed and had not been wearing a shoulder holster. He waited for his eyes to adjust, then located the revolver resting in a small impression surrounded by lighted dials between the two seats.

Jeff grabbed the gun.

Bolton pulled the throttle with one hand while he swung an arm toward Jeff. The plane tilted.

Jeff grabbed him around the throat, more to keep from falling than anything else.

Bolton pulled again. The plane swerved and rocked.

"Put him out," Karen said.

Jeff popped Bolton behind the ear with the butt of the gun, and the man went limp.

Karen moved in and took over the controls.

Jeff unbuckled the seat belt and dragged the man's dead weight to the back. He buckled Bolton into a passenger seat and taped him in.

"I radioed Sea-Tac, the Coast Guard, and everyone else I could think of," Karen said when Jeff returned. "There'll be a welcoming party at the dock." Karen took in the black void that surrounded the small craft.

Jeff strapped himself into the shotgun seat. "I'm sorry, Karen."

She moved a shoulder. "It happens. It's always a good day when you live to tell about it." She checked a gauge, then made a slight adjustment. "Do you think I can get some shots of him when we land? Maybe I can sell them somewhere."

"We don't have to open the door till we're ready to open the door."

She smiled. Her gold tooth caught the light. She brought the plane around and pointed it toward the distant, glittering skyline of downtown Seattle.

Gadzinski walked up to Jeff after the excitement died down. "Looks like you were right, Talbot. The nephew turned out okay."

Jeff was wrapped up like a mummy in some sort of heat blanket that looked like aluminum foil. He'd be lucky if he didn't get pneumonia.

Gadzinski waved a hand toward a knot of uniforms. "Your sister-in-law looks to be in a hell of a lot better shape than you are."

Jeff took in the scene. Karen was all pro now, having recovered from the ordeal faster than anything he had ever witnessed. She moved along beside the officers and paramedics, snapping photos of a piece of her past while a cop read him his rights.

"She's had more training than I've had," Jeff said.

"No kidding, she's an agent?"

"Something like that."

They were quiet for a moment. Jeff broke the silence. "Which one of you will be taking Bolton in?"

"You mean Rose, don't you?"

"No. Verena deserves better than that, don't you think?"

Chapter Thirty-Nine

IT WAS THE first time he remembered ever being excited about Christmas shopping.

He backed the PT Cruiser up the driveway of the Rose property to wait for Gadzinski, who had promised to meet him as soon as he was through reading the Sunday comics.

While Jeff waited, he cracked open a CD titled *In the Dust* and fed it into the slot. Sam had dropped it off the day before, claiming that it was a "toy for the PT." But Jeff knew it was an excuse to make sure he was really okay. The CD was the work of a friend of Sam's named Mike Blakely. *Texan, no doubt,* Jeff thought. He wasn't sure about country music being the first thing to come out of his new speakers, but for Sam, he would give it a whirl.

After the first run-through, he had to admit that Sam was right: This Blakely guy was good. And, according to some of his songs, he had had a lot better luck with pickup trucks than Jeff had recently.

Sam had seen firsthand that he was none the worse for wear. Jeff had Sheila to thank for it. She had fussed over him all day Saturday, feeding him homemade chicken soup and plenty of vitamin C. From what he'd been told, Greer had done the same things for Karen. This morning, both patients were pretty much back in top form.

He gave some credit to the fact that it wasn't raining. Even the sun had gotten the memo and occasionally cast a ray on the rain-glutted region. This, too, would pass. But for now he would enjoy it.

Next door, Erma Weldon looked out a window. Marty came out on the porch a minute later, picked up the newspaper, and went back inside. Business as usual.

When the detective pulled in, Jeff grabbed the two cups of coffee he had picked up at the café and headed for the porch.

"So, Detective. Are things back to normal in your world?"

"As normal as they can be, till the next psycho decides to off somebody." Gadzinski accepted the cup, and blew on the hot liquid. "You don't know what you're missing, Talbot. Are you sure you don't want to get back into the business?"

"Oh, I do, and that's why I don't."

"I'll bet you think about it, though."

"No, but do you know what's strange? I've seen more crime in this cutthroat antiques world than I did in all my years with the Bureau."

"I don't doubt it."

"Do you think he killed Bolton? The real Bolton?"

"He says he didn't. Claims that when his buddy was killed in action, he made a snap decision: trade identities, go on the lam for awhile, get his mother's attention. He got her attention, all right. Imagine it: faking your own death just to punish your mother."

"The sad thing is," Jeff said, "Verena probably would've gone through with her marriage if she had known that her son was still alive."

"Meaning, his plan worked—on some bizarre level, anyway."

"How old was he, when he joined up? Sixteen, seventeen?"

"Fifteen. Can you believe that? I've got a fifteen-year-old boy who still sleeps with a nightlight."

"Maybe you should be thankful."

The detective's expression said that he hadn't considered that.

"Punishing her is one thing. Why did he kill her?"

"He says she provoked him. He offered all kinds of proof that he was her son, and she wouldn't buy it."

"So, he went into a rage and killed his own mother because she upheld his war hero status after his death. And he's the one who instigated it."

"Yeah. Ironic, isn't it?" The detective dug a key out of his pocket and handed it to Jeff. "Since the old lady's will was indisputable, the goods are yours."

Jeff took the key and thanked him.

"So, Talbot. You got big plans for the holidays?"

Jeff considered the list of those who would be a part of the Talbot Christmas. Greer, helping Sheila in the kitchen; Karen, of course; Nathan and Melanie and their three children; Blanche Appleby and Trudy Blessing. Also, Sam and Helen Carver (they had thrown enough weddings to know that they wouldn't have the energy for holiday cooking); most of the Carvers' extended family would drop by later (Maura and Darius might be considered the smartest of the lot for having chosen a warm, sunny Caribbean beach honeymoon).

Why tempt fate, though? He looked at the detective and shrugged. "Not really. Just a few friends dropping by."

Gadzinski nodded, then retrieved a gadget from his pocket and checked something. "Well, I've got a lot of time scheduled to do nothing today, so I'd better get going." He extended his hand. "I hope I don't see you again, Talbot."

Jeff smiled, took the man's hand in a firm grip. "Two-way street, Detective."

Jeff rubbed the key, anxious to gain access once again to the Rose property. He had two days until Christmas, and he planned to finish up his gift shopping among Verena's stuff.

He let himself in, started flipping light switches, and realized that he hadn't remembered how dim the place was. Although he had left the blackout coverings in place on the windows as a means of deflecting the curiosity of vandals and vagrants, he decided that he could at least remove the thumbtacks from the bottom and up one side of each, then tack back the cloths in order to allow a little light into the dungeon. It would be easy enough to let them back down before he left.

He went upstairs to what had been her bedroom. As he started prying the stubborn tacks loose with the blade of his pocketknife, he thought about the protection that the heavy fabric had given to all of the house's contents: books, art, rugs that hadn't seen a fading ray of sun since they had been incorporated into Verena's world. And, he thought about the woman who had secluded herself among these rooms for more than five decades. In that respect, she wasn't all that different from his wife. True, Verena had ventured out of her home, but she had experienced virtually no interaction with others. He had learned that she pushed a wheeled, wire basket to yard sales, where she filled it with the castoffs of others, and to the corner market, where she filled it with off-brand staples and day-old bread. Other than those outings, and the occasional doctor's visit, no one—other than her nephew—saw her. Or called on her. Or befriended her.

How different this house would've been, how different that woman's life would have been, if she hadn't put so much store in her son.

Convinced as a boy that she didn't love him, Andrew Rose had staged an emotional blow from which his mother had never recovered. Then, years later, when her loyalty to his memory proved that she had loved him beyond all reason, he had brutally taken her life.

Sometimes, love isn't enough.

He popped the last tack and started to pull the corner

back when he noticed that what he thought was heavy upholstery fabric was actually two layers of tightly woven cloth. Even at that, they shouldn't have equaled the heft he now felt.

Carefully, he peeled apart the layers of fabric until he was able to get a hint of what was inside.

Some sort of paper. Rather than risk damage, he removed the tacks from the other side and then the top, working carefully, so as not to crease the paper.

He laid the large packet on the bed, peeled away the black cloth, and found himself gazing into the hazel eyes of Veronica Lake . . .

It's 1942. The world is at war, and on the homefront a teenager with a limp is walking a dame home after his night shift at the bijou.

The woman has put in a long night herself, waiting tables at the diner and hoping the cook will send her away with some food for her son. He's twelve now, and eating enough to feed three soldiers.

The teenager says, "Old man Taylor gave me a swell one-sheet tonight." He unfolds it, careful-like, holds it up so she can see it. "You want it?"

She studies the poster. "*This Gun for Hire.* Lots of customers at the diner said it was a good movie. Marty, honey, are you *sure* you want to part with it, though? Veronica's your favorite, and I'll understand if you want to keep it."

"I want you to have it, Verena." She recently said he could call her by her first name, and he likes hearing himself say it. "There'll always be another Veronica Lake poster." He folds it, real careful-like, and hands it to her.

She takes it, then leans over and kisses his cheek. "You're the best, Marty. You're the best."

Marty goes home and thinks about the nice lady next door and how she works *so* hard and how her kid should treat her better.

Chapter Forty

"How many posters again?"

Jeff washed stalks of celery as he repeated the information to Sheila. "Ninety-three. All copyrighted between nineteen forty and forty-five."

He exhaled. The sheer number of posters he had discovered was astounding enough. The fact that they were originals in excellent condition staggered the mind.

Sheila finished stuffing the game hens and set about trussing them. "Have you told Nathan what you're going to do?"

"Not yet. I want to give him the news in person."

"But you reached your friend from the Bureau?"

"Heather? Yeah. She's going to take care of everything." Heather Neal, an FBI historian and collector of movie memorabilia pertaining to films about the FBI, had agreed to oversee arrangements for an auction of the posters.

Those who had judged Verena Rose for her lack of patriotism were, at the very least, ignorant and insensitive. Had they bothered to learn about *her,* the person, they would have seen that she had not only participated but had done so with complete dedication.

She had taken to heart the order to black out the windows. Whether she had added the posters to insure total blackout, or whether they had been included for extra insulation in order to reserve energy, he didn't know. Either way, though, she had done it in the name of sacrifice. And, Jeff knew just what to do so that that sacrifice would benefit one of her own. The profits from the auction would be used to pay Josh Rose's medical bills that the insurance wouldn't cover.

"Okay," Sheila said. "Do you think we're ready?"

Greer appeared with a notebook and gave a summarized report. "Poinsettias and roses are in place, one small gift has been put at each guest's place setting, and all other presents are under the tree in the parlor. The tree lights are on in every room. Activities to keep the children busy are in place." He looked up.

"Add people, and stir well," Sheila said. "Thank you, Greer."

"My pleasure as always, madam."

Sheila tapped a long wooden spoon on the edge of a yellow-ware bowl, then raised her arms and faced Jeff as if he were the Mormon Tabernacle Choir. It was her annual cue to him to complete two more tasks.

"Yes, maestro," he said with a bow.

He went first to the parlor, where the track of his prewar Lionel encircled a Victorian village. He flipped the switch on the transformer, and the engine jolted and chugged its way past the depot, pulling cars and building momentum until it seemed as if the entire village came alive. Trains made you want to *move.* The whistle sounded, and the red caboose rolled by.

He crossed the wide foyer to the library and put the American Flyer in motion around the tree. The post-war model was the last gift he had received from his parents before their deaths. He spent an extra moment reminiscing about his childhood Christmases before moving on.

In the den, he put power to the Marklin train set, then programmed the hundred-disk CD unit to play a continuous loop of six different holiday collections. The speaker system would pipe the music into the dining room and kitchen as well. Gadzinski wasn't the only one with gadgets.

Bing Crosby crooned "I'll Be Home for Christmas," while Jeff returned to the kitchen and went over to the window to look outside.

Soon, their home would fill with family and friends, and this brief, quiet moment between preparation and festivity would be gone.

The forecasters had predicted that Christmas would be the city's coldest day of the month, and Jeff didn't doubt it. It even *looked* cold.

He studied the profile of his new Cruiser, which was parked on the driveway. As he did so, he saw against the backdrop of the dark blue car a snowflake drift past.

Should he tell Sheila? She lived for snowflakes on Christmas but he hadn't seen her go near a window in months. Another flake fell, then another. As he contemplated how to help her enjoy this, two arms wrapped around his waist. He smiled. He knew her touch, knew it was her. He covered her arms with his own.

"Snow." He said it softly, just the one word. Let her decide for herself.

She clung to him, slid around just enough to see, then gave him a squeeze. "It's perfect now."

After a second, her arms went slack. She peered out the glass. "Whose car is that?"

Jeff chuckled. "It's mine, remember?"

"You almost got yourself killed twice this week, and you expect me to think about a new car? That was the last thing on my mind."

He should have guessed that, since cars were no longer a part of her daily life. "She's got lots of chrome and a retro personality like the woodie, and she handles like a dream."

Sheila didn't say anything.

"So?" He prompted, looking at her. "What do you think?"

She gripped his waist again, as if anchoring herself to safe ground.

"Why didn't you get the red one?"

Please turn the page for recommendations from Jeff Talbot, and a webliography from his wife, Sheila

RECOMMENDATIONS FROM JEFF TALBOT

Resources. Never before have there been so many sources available to the collector. Books, magazines, and newsletters. The Internet. Museums. A variety of antiques venues. Clubs, organizations, and societies. All can be valuable, whether you're looking for information about what you currently collect, or are just interested in learning more about the things highlighted in my recent adventure.

Older books still serve as wonderful sources for information and identification. They're easier to track down now by searching Internet sites that offer used books and even by checking on-line auctions. Also, remember to check libraries, used bookstores, museum gift shops, and flea markets when searching out resource materials about any given collectible or subject.

There are many crossovers in the following segments, so be sure to check the listings in Sheila's webliography (following my print recommendations) for additional leads.

That prompts me to point out something: If you

haven't already realized it, collecting involves quite a bit of detecting. You must follow leads, solve mysteries, investigate, determine what's fake and what isn't, and pinpoint an item's worth, or—more important—what it's worth to you. *It's an ongoing quest for the collector and is a large part of the appeal of collecting.*

The following recommendations are but a scratch on the surface, a few of the volumes I consulted while determining value, authenticity, and history of the items I acquired, not only at the Rose property but also while picking.

At least I have all that stuff to keep me busy while I patiently wait for my '48 Chevy woodie to be returned to her full glory. She's in the shop now, and the restorers claim it's going to take months *to put her back together. I'll let you know when it's time to pick her up.*

Until then . . .
Jeff Talbot

Although it can be a challenge to find information about marriage caskets, here are a few sources to get you started. An old but helpful book (which you might find at a flea market, as I did, or in the reference section of a library) is *The Complete Encyclopedia of Antiques*, L.G.G. Ramsey, editor (Hawthorn Books, Inc., 1962). Plate 195 on page 547 shows some designs similar to the marriage casket I found in Verena's belongings; consult the book's index for more information. Finally, for some striking photos of Tula steel items, check out the Web site Sheila listed for the St. Petersburg's Hermitage Museum.

Another book that will call to your aesthetic senses if you appreciate the workmanship of boxes and containers is *Treasure Chests: The Legacy of Extraordinary Boxes*, by Lon Schleining (The Taunton Press, 2001). This work has many color photos, but the one I found phenomenal (and the reason I gave a copy of this book to my buddy Sam for Christmas) is the tool chest showcased on pages 66 and 67.

It's a true work of art, constructed in the nineteenth century by a Massachusetts piano maker.

A fascinating aside: *Treasure Chests* also has information and photos about Jean Clemens, daughter of Mark Twain, who did woodcarving while isolated for the treatment of epilepsy. She died at the age of 29 on Christmas Eve in 1909. Some of her work is showcased in the Mark Twain House, a museum in Hartford, Connecticut.

Remember the jewelry I sold to Blanche? You'll find the backgrounds of all those designers she identified, as well as many wonderful color photos of similar pieces, in *Signed Beauties of Costume Jewelry*, by Marcia "Sparkles" Brown (Collector Books, 2002). This visually appealing publication includes a glossary and a bibliography. Brown is also the author of *Unsigned Beauties of Costume Jewelry*.

If you're looking for more specifics on the identifying marks of jewelry, consult *How to be a Jewelry Detective*, by C. Jeanenne Bell, G.G. (A.D. Publishing, 2001; 5th edition). Known as "The Jewelry Detective," Bell is touted as one of the nation's leading authorities on jewelry. (Don't forget Sheila's webliography. She found a site that shows hundreds of the marks to be found on signed jewelry.)

Prices for jadite (jad-ite, jade-ite, jadeite) are back to a semblance of "normal" after that collectible's Millennium surge, and the milky green glassware is still very popular. If you're new to the general glassware craze, I recommend beginning with *Anchor Hocking's Fire-King & More*, by Gene Florence (Collector Books, 2000; with updated values). Florence is said to be the most prolific author of glassware reference books, and this particular title will introduce you to several collectibles in addition to Jade-ite (Anchor Hocking's spelling, which makes me wonder if it was meant to echo the hyphenated "Fire-King").

A publication that deals with jadite specifically is *Jadite: An Identification and Price Guide*, by Joe Keller and David Ross (Schiffer Publishing, 2000). The authors focus on the three major glass companies that produced jadite—McKee, Jeannette, and Anchor Hocking—and the book identifies over a thousand of the sought-after green treasures.

Learn more about the Autumn Leaf china that Sheila traditionally uses for Thanksgiving dinner in *Collectors Encyclopedia of Hall China*, by Margaret and Kenn Whitmyer (Collector Books, 2001; 3rd edition). The Whitmyers are also the authors of the popular *Christmas Collectibles* (Collector Books, 1994; 2nd edition).

World War II continues to fascinate, and there are thousands of books on the subject. Here are but a few:

Design for Victory: World War II Posters on the American Home Front, by William L. Bird, Jr. and Harry R. Rubenstein (Princeton Architectural Press, 1998). This publication showcases production-incentive posters culled from the collections of the National Museum of American History, Smithsonian Institution. An enlightening book.

The Good War: An Oral History of World War Two, by Studs Terkel (Pantheon Books, 1984). The gold standard by which others are evaluated.

The Greatest Generation, by Tom Brokaw, the most current sensation in books about the people of the Big One. Brokaw spent a decade researching and compiling this poignant study after an assignment in Europe sparked his interest in WWII.

Hiroshima, by Pulitzer prize-winning author John Hersey, was first published in 1946. Nearly four decades later, Hersey returned to Hiroshima in search of the people whose stories he had told. His account of what he discovered is the final chapter of the reprint edition (Vintage Books, 1989).

The Rising Sun: The Decline and Fall of the Japanese Empire, 1936–1945, by John Toland (Random House, 1970), is a Pulitzer Prize-winning history of World War II that chronicles the last days of imperial Japan.

While studying photos of the liberation of Santo Tomas in a 1945 edition of *Life* magazine, Sinclair Browning looked at a blonde, curly-headed boy in the second story window of one of the buildings held by the Japanese. "The boy," she relates in the Afterword of *America's Best*, "who looked so much like my own son, was my husband."

Browning (who's also a mystery author), wrote a fictionalized version of what happened to her husband's family after the boy's father was asked to go to Corregidor by General MacArthur, was interned at Cabanatuan, and was killed on board the *Arisan Maru*. Although the hardcover publication (AMC Publishing, 1995) is out of print, it can be tracked down online; the book has also been released by iUniverse.com.

I've found several trunks full of Verena's clothing, shoes, and accessories from the thirties and forties. Trudy Blessing (Blanche's assistant) is categorizing them, and has suggested that anyone searching for a good book about these much desired vintage items will want to peruse *Ladies' Vintage Accessories: Identification & Value Guide*, by LaRee Johnson Bruton (Collector Books, 2001). Trudy adds that some important features of this book are the inclusion of advertising from those decades (which can quickly help nail down the age of an object), the generous number of color photos, and the chronological layout that makes it easy to find a particular decade.

One of Greer's favorite books for inspiration when "dressing the dining room," as he puts it, is *Antiques for the Table*, by Sheila Chefetz (Penguin Studio, 1993). He also recommends *Miller's Collecting Silver: The Facts at Your Fingertips*, by Jill Bace (Mitchell Beazley, 1999), for its essential information and hundreds of color photos.

I received two coffee books as Christmas gifts: *Coffee & Bites*, by Susie Theodorou (Murdoch Books, 2001), and *Uncommon Grounds: The History of Coffee and How It Transformed Our World*, by Mark Pendergrast (Basic Books, 2000). The first offers many recipes to complement coffee, and assures the reader that "there's a coffee out there for everybody, and *Coffee & Bites* aims to help you find it." Sounds like a plan to me. The title of the second says it all, and *Uncommon Grounds* reveals meticulous research on the author's part. I'm finding the history fascinating.

If you're looking for pricing on vintage toy trains, check out Greenberg's Pocket Price Guides, published annually by Kalmbach Publishing Co. For more than pricing, though, consult *O'Brien's Collecting Toy Trains: Identification and Value Guide*, Elizabeth A. Stephan, editor (Krause Publications, 1999). This fifth edition has a new alphabetized format to aid you in your quest, and expanded sections listing clubs, collectors, and dealers.

Christmas: Antiques, Decorations and Traditions, by Constance King (Antique Collectors' Club, 1999), provides a lot of history about the celebration of Christmas, as well as many color plates.

The old letters I found in the marriage casket prompt me to share with you some volumes on letters. Since Sheila collects letters and stationery, she has a wealth of books on the subject.

Letter-writing isn't what it used to be; perhaps that fact has contributed to the collectibility not only of ephemera such as letters, postcards, and stationery, but also of the accoutrements (inkwells, pens, etc.) related to correspondence. Whether you wish to read excerpts from letters penned by writers long passed, or seek guidance for writing your own for any occasion, *The Pleasures of Staying in Touch*, by Jennifer Williams (Hearst Books, 1998), offers both glimpses and guidance. At the back of this slim volume, you'll find that the "Permissions" page offers a bibliography of several collections of letters that were consulted by author Williams.

I highly recommend *Famous Letters: Messages & Thoughts That Shaped Our World*, edited by Frank McLynn (The Reader's Digest Association, Inc., 1993). This historical and visual feast is arranged by category ("Encounters & Discoveries" and "Love, Death & Friendship," for example), has a detailed index, and suggests several other volumes in which to find letters ("Further Reading," page 157). The appealing design provides, in addition to letters, engaging history, museum-quality photos of antiques that belonged to the correspondents, and biographies of some of our history's most fascinating individuals.

Even though Karen won't admit to collecting cameras and photographs, she nonetheless provided the following suggestions: *Collecting and Using Classic Cameras*, by

Ivor Matanle (Thames & Hudson, 1992); *A Century of photographs, 1846–1946: selected from the collections of the Library of Congress*, by Renata V. Shaw (Library of Congress, 1980); *Collectors' Guide to Nineteenth-century Photographs*, by William Welling (Macmillan, 1976); and *Collector's Guide to Early Photographs*, by O. Henry Mace (Krause Publications, March 1999; 2nd edition).

Here's a crossover for you: Two subjects found in *The Marriage Casket* are touched on in *Armed With Cameras: The American Military Photographers of World War II*, by Peter Maslowski (Free Press, 1993). It's a chronicle of the frontline photographers of World War II, the men armed only with cameras who accompanied the soldiers into battle. Note: The author's father was an Air Force combat photographer in 1944.

If Verena's letter sparked your interest in reading more, look up *Since You Went Away: World War II Letters from American Women on the Home Front*, edited by Judy Barrett Litoff and David C. Smith (University of Kansas Press, 1995).

I'll Be Home for Christmas: The Library of Congress Revisits the Spirit of Christmas During World War II, from the Library of Congress (Delacorte Press, 1999). Contains journal entries, correspondence, magazine articles, and over one hundred photographs.

Imperial Russia has always held a certain fascination for me, and there are many fine volumes about Nicholas and Alexandra. If the artistic design of this period intrigues you, you'll enjoy *Nicholas & Alexandra: The Last Imperial Family of Tsarist Russia*, from the State Hermitage Museum and the State Archive of the Russian Federation (published in North America by Harry N. Abrams, Inc., 1998). Many well-documented antiques, and a detailed look at treasures created by Faberge, who was jeweler to the Tsars. The photos provide a remarkable glimpse behind the scenes of Russian royalty.

Books on Japanese inro can be pricey, so my advice is to begin with *The Bulfinch Illustrated Encyclopedia of Antiques*, Paul Atterbury and Lars Tharp, consulting editors (Bulfinch Press, First North American Paperback Edition,

1998). If this sounds familiar, it's probably because I recommended it in *Death is a Cabaret.* Bulfinch's is a wonderful source for a wide variety of antiques.

The book from which Blanche enjoys trying recipes is the *Celestial Seasonings Cookbook: Cooking With Tea*, by Jennifer Cook Siegel (Park Lane Press, 1996). Siegel's husband is one of the founders of Celestial Seasonings, and this collection provides over 100 recipes made with the company's tea blends.

Naval china belongs to the group called restaurant ware—the heavy, commercial stuff that's made to last. In *Restaurant China, Volume I* (Collector Books, 1998; values updated, 2000), Barbara J. Conroy showcases many categories—railroad, military, and western, to name a few—and provides much history. This volume concentrates on the topmarks (logos), and provides a wealth of photos and charts. For information on backstamps (manufacturer's marks, date codes, etc.), consult Conroy's *Restaurant China, Volume II*.

The first movie poster I uncovered in Verena's home can be seen on page fifteen of the stunning coffee table book, *The Art of Noir: The Posters and Graphics From the Classic Era of Film Noir*, by Eddie Muller (The Overlook Press, 2002). Muller, who is a recognized authority on film *noir* and a collector of vintage posters, has put together a fascinating duo of film history and eye candy.

Miller's Movie Collectibles, by Rudy and Barbara Franchi (Mitchell Beazley, 2002), is a comprehensive guide to collecting movie memorabilia. The focus is on posters, but a segment on other memorabilia offers a wealth of history, information, and color photos about such subjects as autographs, props, slides, and lobby art. There is also an enlightening chapter about the care and restoration of movie posters. The Franchis know their stuff! They've been dealing in original movie memorabilia for over 30 years (www.nostalgia.com). If their names seem familiar, it might be that you've seen them on PBS—they're appraisers for the *Antiques Roadshow*.

The Shaker Legacy: Perspectives on an Enduring Furniture Style, by Christian Becksvoort (Taunton Press, August 2000). Becksvoort, an experienced custom furniture maker and restorer who's worked for the last remaining Shaker community at Sabbathday Lake, Maine, examines the Shakers' faith in relation to their furniture. This book offers insight into the Shaker culture, how that culture influenced the design, and how it influenced other styles.

American craftsmanship continues to be prized. One book that provides information on a variety of American antiques is the *Catalog of American Antiques*, by Susan Ward (first published in the United States by the Mallard Press, 1990). Whether you're researching furniture or firearms, textiles or toys, this is a good place to start. Color photos throughout.

The fun—and authenticity—of *The Victorian Bathroom Catalogue* is due to its origins. Studio Editions (1996) compiled illustrated pages from six manufacturers' catalogues published in Britain, France and the United States between 1885 and 1900. Introduction by Kit Wedd.

Sheila Talbot's Webliography

CHRISTMAS:

Bill's Antique Christmas Light Site

www.oldchristmaslights.com
Lots of history and information, as well as photos of vintage advertising, and just about anything you might want to know regarding antique Christmas lights.

Christmas Cookies

www.christmas-cookies.com
Hundreds of recipes, extensive list of categories, cookbooks, tools for cooks, and much more!

Golden Glow of Christmas Past

http://my.execpc.com/~gmoe/gg-web2
If you're a collector of anything Christmas, you're likely aware of this organization. Check the site for information about the annual convention, which is usually a "Christmas in July" event. Members receive a bimonthly newsletter, "The Glow."

TOY TRAINS:

www.lionelcollectors.org
The Lionel Collectors Club of America creates five publications (two print, three on-line). The Club was founded in 1970, and holds an annual convention. Check out the FAQ page for answers to collecting questions, and a concise date chart for pre-war, post-war, and modern classifications.

www.marklin.com
Here, you'll find history as well as a technical resource center. Marklin produces more than just trains, and states that their reproductions have detail changes to exclude the possibility of mistaking the reproductions for historic, original models. The site also has a great page for determining differences in the various scales, or gauges, offered.

www.modeltrainsmuseum.bc.ca/
Although the Granville Islands Train Museum is only about three hours north of Seattle in Vancouver, BC, Canada, we've never been. But the Web site is loaded with information, offers an extensive links page for all things *train*, and has the world's largest collection of model and toy trains on public display. There's even a rare pink Lionel train set, circa 1958, that was designed for girls!

www.traincollectors.org
The Train Collectors Association was organized in 1954; that means its 50th birthday is coming up! Headquartered at the National Toy Train Museum in Strasburg, Pennsylvania.

www.ttos.org
Web site of the Toy Train Operating Society, Inc., which was founded in 1966. The organization offers two publications for its members. Check out their links page.

OTHER SITES:

www.alphabetilately.com
The name of this site was made from the words "alphabet" and "philately." (Philately is stamp collecting.) Both the concept and the art here are fabulous. There are twenty-six stamps, created by as many artists, laid out alphabetically. Click the top banner for the index, then check out the "V is for V-Mail" stamp (which got Jeff's attention). Vintage letters and envelopes are why I fell in love with this site, and perusing any number of the alphabetized stamps will give you a look at vintage ephemera.

www.countryliving.com
Country Living magazine offers American antiques and collectibles information in every issue. In addition, the editors provide loads of information on their Web site. Go to the segment on antiques and collectibles, and allow plenty of time!

www.deborahmorgan.com
The author's Web site now offers an extensive list of periodicals that focus on antiques and collectibles. You'll also discover that many holiday recipes have been added to my recipe box.

www.eastman.org
The technology collection at the George Eastman House is made up of more than 15,000 separate items. An eighteenth-century camera obscura is the oldest item in the collection, and the Speed Graphic camera used by Joe Rosenthal for the 1945 photograph of the flag raising on Iwo Jima is housed there.

www.goldstarmoms.com
If you would like to learn more about the flag that Jeff found in the marriage casket, The American Gold Star Mothers site is the place. The Gold Star gained special significance at the end of World War I, and its symbolism became more prominent during World War II.

www.hermitagemuseum.org
St. Petersburg's (Russia) Hermitage Museum offers interesting information and photos of the diamond-cut steel like that of Verena's marriage casket. Conduct a search of the word *Tula* for a list of pages.

www.Krphoto.com
Go to Ken Riley's camera site links page and click the Antique and Classic Camera Collectors' link for an extensive listing of Web sites. This site is dedicated to providing the camera collector with useful information about camera repair, films and darkroom supplies for the classics, and other photographic resources. (This is one of Karen's sources.)

www.monopoly.com
Here's some interesting information about Monopoly during WWII, which I discovered at the site: Escape maps, compasses, and files were inserted into Monopoly game boards and smuggled into POW camps inside Germany during World War II. Also, real money for escapees was slipped into the packs of Monopoly money.

www.morninggloryantiques.com
Morning Glory Antiques and Jewelry offers a free online magazine called "Jewel Chat," in addition to hundreds of photos of jewelry marks and the dates those marks were used, and photos of vintage jewelry advertising (which help in identification).

www.nalcc.org
Here, you'll find the official Web site of the National Autumn Leaf Collectors Club. I'm fortunate to have inherited my set of the Hall China/Jewel Tea dishes from my Pennsylvania grandmother. The stuff's a lot harder to come by here in Washington!

www.pastaco.com
One of my favorite items from this neighborhood store is the black pasta (the color is achieved with squid ink, which does *not* alter the taste); it makes a wonderful presentation with some of my sauces. If you're in our neighborhood north of Seattle, drop by Pasta and Co. and tell them we sent you. They're at 2109 Queen Anne Avenue North.

www.sparklz.com
The Information and Reference button takes you to hundreds of jewelry links, as well as tips and guides for cleaning and repairing jewelry.

www.vaselineglass.org
This official site of the Vaseline Glass Collectors, Inc., contains a wealth of information about the "glowing" collectible. Lots of history, many links, and information on joining the group. You'll also find news of the organization's annual convention, and a list of recommended books.

www.monopoly.com
Here's some interesting information about Monopoly during WWII, which I discovered at this site: Escape maps, compasses, and files were inserted into Monopoly game boards and smuggled into POW camps inside Germany during World War II. Also, real money for escapees was slipped into the stacks of Monopoly money.

www.morninggloryantiques.com
Morning Glory Antiques and Jewelry offers a free online magazine called "Jewel Chat," in addition to hundreds of photos of jewelry marks and the dates those marks were used, and photos of vintage jewelry advertising (which help in identification).

www.nalcc.org
Here you'll find the official Web site of the National Autumn Leaf Collectors Club. I'm fortunate to have inherited my set of the Hall China Jewel Tea dishes from my Pennsylvania grandmother. The stuff's a lot harder to come by here in Washington!

www.pastaco.com
One of my favorite items from this neighborhood store is the black pasta (the color is achieved with squid ink, which does not alter the taste); it makes a wonderful presentation with some of my sauces. If you're in our neighborhood north of Seattle, stop by Pasta and Co. and tell them we sent you. They're at 2109 Queen Anne Avenue North.

[illegible].com
The Information and Reference button takes you to hundreds of jewelry links, as well as tips and guides for cleaning and repairing jewelry.

www.vaselineglass.org
This official site of the Vaseline Glass Collectors, Inc., contains a wealth of information about the "glowing" collectible. Lots of history, many links, and information on joining the group. You'll also find news of the organization's annual convention, and a list of recommended books.

About the Author

Deborah Morgan fights the urge to track down and purchase *all* the antiques and collectibles mentioned in her antique lover's mystery series. *The Marriage Casket* is the third novel featuring antiques picker Jeff Talbot. Morgan and her husband, author Loren D. Estleman, live in Michigan. For more information, visit her Web site at www.deborahmorgan.com.